THE SECRET OF SKYE ISLE

Book III of The Ladies Of Lore Series

MARISA DILLON

Believe in Love!
Marisa

SOUL MATE PUBLISHING

New York

THE SECRET OF SKYE ISLE

MARISA DILLON

Cover Design by Anna Lena-Spies

Published in the United States of America by
Soul Mate Publishing
P.O. Box 24
Macedon, New York, 14502

ISBN: 978-1-64716-017-3

email ISBN: 978-1-68291-983-5

www.SoulMatePublishing.com

To my family

for their never-ending support.

Acknowledgments

The author thanks:

The best modern day Highlander ever, Steve Cairns, whose knowledge of the Highlands and the Isle of Skye was invaluable to writing this story.

The professionals: Publisher Debby Gilbert; Editor Tamara Hughes; authors Terri Valentine, Violetta Rand and Karin Shah, who lighted the path to publication.

My family: sons Jamie and Zach, who are my best creations and who support me in so many ways; my parents Alf and Celia Hansen, who took me all over the world as a young girl, influencing my storytelling today; my brother Eric, writer and author; my supportive sister Carina; my aunt Linda, the ultimate beta reader; and my husband, Jim, the best surrogate critique partner ever.

My friends and neighbors, particularly Rich and Robbie Schultze, who endured a seven-hour drive across Scotland to the Isle of Skye on a tight itinerary, and over the course of four days, stops at twelve castles. Robin Michaels, who provides the best promotional support; Melissa Johnson, whose counsel is invaluable; Cairo Mama, who is the best dance sister ever; and my advisor Jeff Bruce, whose guidance is essential.

Without all of their support, this book would not exist.

Chapter 1

Aberdeenshire, Scotland
1487

The great hall at Fyvie Castle had been cleared of the cursory royal courtesans, and those who remained were bound by blood or oath. Tossing a handful of gold coins in the middle of the rough trestle table reminded Ethan his good luck was never random and the quest for power ever present.

Surrounded by Luttrells and with high stakes on the line, he reached into the deerskin pouch next to his dagger and found the cool, smooth square stones that had secured his fate the last time he'd rolled them.

"We should have booted your arse out, but gaming is better sport," Ethan's twin brother Lachlan claimed, shoving his coins to the table's center.

Eyeing the group, their half-brother James reached for a pair of dice. When he rolled, the white squares bounced and clattered on the naked table.

"A pair of fives. Now I'm at thirty," James shouted, slapping his knee hard and laughing like a thief. "Beat that," James challenged Ethan with a sharp nod of his chin.

When the bowl was passed his way, Ethan reached in just as eagerly for a pair of dice, but instead of letting them fly, he elbowed his tankard. As it crashed to the wooden planks, Ethan's dice went with it.

"Cut him off," Lachlan shouted. "Drunken gambling will not be tolerated by the chieftain of this clan."

The others laughed with Lachlan, and that was when Ethan made his move and swapped the dice.

Rising up from retrieving his tankard, Ethan stared back at his well-groomed twin, his brother Lachlan's chiseled features resembling his own. He grinned before he claimed, "'Tis not the ale that got the best of me." Then his gaze met the player sitting across from him.

The fourth player stayed silent. Ursula's dark, brooding eyes studied Ethan as if his game was already up. He didn't blink but stared right back at the raven-haired beauty as he held the dice high over the table's midsection until he let them spill from the tips of his fingers. Bouncing between the gold coins, the dice tumbled toward Ethan.

"A pair of sixes," James called out. "You have thirty-one!"

"Aye, thirty-one, beating James by a point," Lachlan said stoically.

James appeared to accept the loss, even though it was the third time Ethan had taken the winnings that evening, but the first time he'd resorted to using his personal dice.

The amount of gold coins shoved into Ethan's corner by the other players amounted to a reasonable fortune, and the stakes on this last round had doubled from the previous one.

Satisfied with his winnings, Ethan eased his chair from the trestle table. But when Lachlan clasped a strong hand on his wrist, the gold coins he held tumbled back onto the table.

"One more round, brother. All or nothing," Lachlan urged.

"I have all I need," Ethan said calmly, turning to meet his twin's steady scrutiny. Lachlan hated losing.

"You have all I need," Lachlan replied back.

"Then let's raise the stakes," Ethan challenged his twin. "Gold satisfies greed, but land guarantees power."

"Too rich for my blood," James responded, folding his thick warrior arms over his chest in resignation. "England's

King Henry pays the Garter knights a fair wage," James added, "but not enough for me to gamble this much."

When Ethan glanced to Ursula, she pushed away the dice and shook her head.

"Let it be known Eilean Donan Castle is on the table," Lachlan said, taking a dragon tail ring from his right hand and placing it in the center of the trestle table.

Ethan scoffed. "Eilean Donan is property of Clan MacKenzie, not the Luttrells of England." At this point Ethan began to rise from the table, prepared to walk away with his winnings.

"Do not forget, brother, our mother was Colleen MacKenzie," Lachlan stated plainly.

Ethan sat back in his chair at the mention of their mother.

"When you poisoned her, did you kill your memories, too?"

Lachlan made the dig as he always did. It was true Ethan had poisoned their mother, but it had been an accident. And no matter how many times he argued the circumstances of her death, Lachlan never relented.

"You suggest if I accept your bid, I wager my only land holding?" Ethan asked, ignoring Lachlan's insinuation and finally rising to his feet.

"Nay, Lachlan," James chimed in, "Dunster Castle in Somerset is Ethan's only property. 'Tis a lopsided contest," defended James, who on all accounts was the noblest knight he'd ever met. Whenever there were disagreements between Ethan and his identical twin brother, his Garter knight half-brother would demand fairness.

"If it is justice we seek, Ethan should return all of our gold," Lachlan charged.

"He switched the dice when he knocked his chalice to the floor," Ursula said, breaking her long silence.

Now it was Ethan's turn to glare. "Witch," he said under his breath.

Lachlan snatched Ethan's dice from the table and examined them. When James grunted, Lachlan handed them to the Garter knight who turned them over in his hands, scrutinizing them more closely. The dice were dwarfed by James's enormous palms.

"God's teeth, Ethan, why would you cheat?" James asked, weighing the ivory nuggets individually in each hand.

Ethan wasn't sure either of them could find anything wrong with the dice by studying them.

"Roll them," Ursula ordered as if she was waiting to be vindicated.

"Witch," Ethan said again, louder. This time both brothers' heads swung his direction. Shrugging his shoulders was his only defense. Ethan wasn't going to deny the dice had been switched. He just wasn't going to admit they were modified.

James appeared perturbed by the order, but they'd all been in Ursula's company over the last few months and had learned the woman had unusual powers.

As the knight pondered the square ivory pieces, a smile finally softened his stern frown. Instead of dropping them on the table as Ethan expected, he tossed them in his goblet of wine.

James turned his attention to Ethan. "You must know at King Henry's court the punishment for cheating in gaming is a nail through the palm."

Ursula gasped. When Ethan shot her a glance, her eyes lowered. He hoped she felt remorse for speaking against him, but she refused to meet his probing glare.

James chuckled. "'Tis lucky, Lord Ethan, you are not in King Henry's court. As his loyal agent, however, I cannot ignore the offense, but I may forget this friendly game if you return the gold to the rightful owners and thus free me of any guilt."

Ethan studied his elder half-brother, who neither resembled any of the Luttrells nor acted like them. His enviable mane of golden hair did not minimize his might. Punctuated by well-defined muscles, James was formidable even as an ally. His steel-blue gaze could all but slice through skin.

Relieved the Garter knight had stopped the inquisition, Ethan lowered his head, and instead of defending himself as was his style, he began to count the gold back to James first, then Ursula, who still refused to meet his gaze.

After he'd given his brother Lachlan the remaining coins, his twin rested a hand on Ethan's shoulder and said, "Now that we've agreed this evening was just for entertainment, and James has spared hauling your arse to a royal court, there's still the matter of the final bet."

Ethan considered what was at stake. Although his luck would not be guaranteed, he could never resist a bet when his twin offered. It had been that way as long as he could remember.

"Fyvie for you, and Dunster for me?" Ethan hoped.

"Nay, Fyvie belongs to my wife, Rosalyn. I cannot barter what's not mine," Lachlan replied.

Ethan burst out laughing. "You are the clan leader, but you give your wife the land rights?"

"That was our deal," Lachlan defended. "I took her name and her heart, and we rule together. Fyvie belongs to her, and we'd settled that months ago."

"You cannot be a leader and a follower at the same time, Lachlan," he said, egging him on.

His twin refused to be baited, and he shoved Ethan's shoulder, thrusting him back into his chair. As soon as Lachlan started around the table, Ursula vacated her seat and stood next to James as if she needed protection from what could come.

Once Lachlan was settled across from Ethan, he reached into the bowl for a fresh pair of dice, then handed the bowl to James. Instead of passing the bowl to Ethan, James selected two dice and gave them to Ethan.

His cheeks heated, but Ethan said nothing.

Lachlan picked up the ring again and set it back on the table. “Eilean Donan Castle.”

Ethan had a matching dragon tail ring. He tugged on it until it slid over his rough knuckle. “Dunster Castle,” he stated evenly, then he placed the gift from his father next to his twin’s ring. When James began to object, Ethan held his hand up and stood his ground.

Ethan rolled first and scored a twelve.

Lachlan did the same.

On the next turn, Ethan rolled two fives.

His twin scored on snake eyes.

The tally was now Ethan twenty-two, Lachlan fourteen.

With only two in rotation, this game for thrones would be over quickly and their fates settled without bloodshed. Rarely were castles exchanged without lifting lance or sword, even within families.

Although Lachlan had forsaken the name, they were still the notorious Luttrells of England. The most flagrant had been his father Nicholas, who had pitted the boys against each other as lads. Even though he was gone, his father’s antics had been the catalyst for their competitive spirits today.

No doubt his father was watching over the competition. It wouldn’t matter if his seat was in heaven or hell, Ethan was certain Nicholas would approve.

Ethan eyed his twin.

Lachlan glared back.

Ethan kept his game face on when his next roll delivered eight points and his score totaled thirty. He hadn’t won yet but would have to hold at thirty until Lachlan caught up, beat him at thirty-one, or went over.

Ethan gave a sideways glance to the spectators, finding both Ursula and James leaning over the table for a better look at the dice as Lachlan took two more turns. On the last, when the dice fell, Ethan squeezed his eyes shut.

"He's at twenty-six," James shouted.

"Ethan, let's sweeten the deal." Lachlan offered, clipping James's enthusiasm.

Ethan waited with his eyes still shut, letting Lachlan know he was at least willing to hear his proposition.

Lachlan cleared his throat. "Because we are family, and forfeiting a castle is a bigger loss than most, I propose the loser receives an order of favor from the other."

Ethan choked on a laugh when he finally opened his eyes. "You did not learn from the challenge at Berwick Castle?" Months ago, Ethan had accepted a wager where each pledged to do the other's bidding. Ethan had lost, and in a way, so had Lachlan, for Ethan never honored the promise.

He glanced at Ursula. Their history was filled with lost opportunity and broken vows. She no doubt remembered the failed promise as well, for it had unraveled after Ethan had pretended to be Lachlan. Posing as his brother had been a brilliant form of deception, allowing Ethan access to people and property he'd normally been denied.

Ursula was either avoiding his probing glance or fixated on the outcome. He'd bet on the former as his attention went back to the game.

When Lachlan took his final turn, his dice bounced on the table, the sound resonating throughout the great hall as if all activity in the castle had ceased, waiting for that final roll.

James spoke first. "Well, I wouldn't have expected that."

Chapter 2

"Castle Fyvie is still in your possession," Ursula declared as she swept into the bedchamber to visit her charge later that afternoon.

"Why would it nae be?" Rosalyn blinked rapidly.

"Your husband gambled away one of his family holdings—Eilean Donan Castle in Kyle of Lochalsh."

Rosalyn hooted. "That old place?" the lady of Castle Fyvie asked as she attempted to get up from her seat by the fire. "Clan MacKenzie's castle? Near the Isle of Skye?"

By the time her sister of the heart had asked the second question, Ursula was by her side. "Now, donnae be attempting to rise from your chair like you did before you were carrying twins," Ursula scolded, taking up a sturdy stool next to her friend.

Rosalyn absentmindedly put both hands on her bulging belly and rubbed it lovingly. "Aye,"—she nodded—"but my mind and my mouth still work without your help."

That made Ursula grin. She reached over and rubbed Rosalyn's belly, too. "And I'm sure you will want to save that piece of your mind for Lachlan and not waste it on your midwife."

Rosalyn chuckled. "I shall save the tongue-lashing for Lachlan, because he enjoys it," she said as she turned her head and stared into the flames. "Yet this castle that he's gambled away"—she paused, ruminating on the news, then began again—"'tis odd he even considers the ownership. 'Twas in his mother's family. She was a MacKenzie."

Ursula was not surprised. Lachlan was a Luttrell, and even though he was not undermining like his brother and father, he had a thirst for land that was hard to quench. When they first met, Rosalyn and Lachlan had fought for Fyvie like bitter enemies.

Rosalyn sat upright. As upright as a woman could with twins in her belly. Liked she'd been pinched. "Who's the new lord at Kyle of Lochalsh?"

"Your brother-in-law, Ethan," she said plainly.

"The competition between them never ceases. It's a fool's prize Lachlan has given to his brother. The castle has a storied past. More Viking than Highlander at its inception. There's been many a bloody battle over its gates." Her gaze narrowed on Ursula. "Why were you an observer?"

"I was pulled in as the fourth."

"You, gambling with men?"

"Would it have been better if I'd gambled with ladies?"

Rosalyn huffed.

"I had no choice in the matter. You know what happens when 'tis just the two of them," Ursula said. They'd both seen this firsthand. "James came to their rescue, and then I came to James's."

Rosalyn balked. "When does a Knight of the Garter need rescuing?"

"You know better than anyone that Ethan and Lachlan could end up in a duel to the death if a competition between them goes unchecked," Ursula said. "Luckily, James was the referee even up to the last when the game was tied and the final win was decided in a roll off."

Rosalyn acquiesced with a shrug. "Wasnae Lachlan upset about losing?"

"Nay, for there was a caveat for the loser."

"Let me guess," Rosalyn said, grinning. "Ethan promised to do Lachlan's bidding when he needed to call on him."

Ursula nodded rapidly and patted Rosalyn on the hand. "We both know how that worked out last time," she said, rising, then walking to a storage cupboard in the far corner of the bedchamber.

"Ethan has made some amends," Rosalyn defended. "It's been six months since Christmastide."

Ursula nodded half-heartedly as she made her way to the expansive worktable that had been set up in Rosalyn's chamber for her midwifery. The babes were nae due for about five more weeks, but with twins, you never could be assured of anything.

Ursula caught herself in the mirror that hung over the workstation. Designed for light reflection, not vanity, she used the mirror to heat some of her herbal concoctions with the sun's rays. Although she'd never been one to fuss over her appearance, she noted her skin looked much too pale next to her inky black hair. No doubt she was pasty from worry over her good friend Rosalyn.

As Ursula took the elderberries and crushed them in the mortar with the pestle, she thought about how to approach Rosalyn on the idea of her leaving for a short while before the babes were born.

"Absolutely not. You are nae to set a foot outside this castle until these bairns are born," Rosalyn commanded.

Ursula spun around, almost knocking her mortar over in her haste. She scoffed. "What?" *Had she been daydreaming?*

"You clearly heard what I said."

"Aye, but how did you know what I said in my head?"

"You donnae think I've learned anything from you in a year studying by your side?" Rosalyn asked.

"Well, *sight* is not normally learned. I've told you it's inborn," Ursula said. It had been for Ursula and all the women in her family over many generations of Frasers.

"Do nae start getting haughty with me now," Rosalyn said, sounding wounded.

Ursula snapped her fingers. "It must be triggered by the pregnancy. You have always had good healing instincts, and your mastery of herbs is extraordinary, but admit it, Rosalyn, this is the first time you've *seen* my thoughts."

Her friend raised one brow. "I thank you for the compliments," Rosalyn said, "but how certain are you about this being the first time?"

Ursula turned her back on Rosalyn. "I should have said during your pregnancy." She tossed more berries in the mortar and began beating at them in a fury.

Ursula turned around again to face her friend but took the mortar with her this time. Crushing the berries at a fervent pace, she said, "Well, reading my thoughts, you know I must leave this place in search of a rare variety of the guelder rose that only grows on the Isle of Skye."

"Nay!" Rosalyn all but jumped up from her seat, which wasnae possible for her.

"Nay? Nay what?" Ursula asked cocking her head to one side.

"Nay, you may not leave this place. The birthing is too close," Rosalyn said. "There's no one I trust to travel with you. With . . ."

"With Joshua gone?"

"I did nae want to say that."

"To bring up his name?"

"To bring up his memory," Rosalyn said with a palpable hollowness in her voice.

Joshua. Ursula spun away from Rosalyn, knowing the tears welling in her eyes would not stay there long. She couldn't let her friend know how much her heart was aching. With Rosalyn's frequent weepy outbursts, the last thing Ursula wanted was to trigger another.

"You know I've traveled alone many times. And I like it that way." Ursula discreetly wiped her tears before she looked over her shoulder, surprised to find Rosalyn waddling across the ornate tapestry rug to her table.

"Nay, you shouldnae be walking by yourself." Ursula rushed over and wrapped an arm around her waist.

"How can you propose one rule for me, but ignore your own advice?" Rosalyn asked as she draped an arm over Ursula's shoulder.

Ursula started to say something but sputtered instead. Rosalyn was right, she admitted begrudgingly to herself as she guided Rosalyn back to her chair and took the stool across from her again. The afternoon herbal mixture could wait a few minutes while she figured out how to negotiate her way to the isle.

"Lachlan will go with you," Rosalyn blurted out.

"Nay, he must be here by your side and manage the clan. Your husband should not be away at this time. I cannot allow it."

Rosalyn raised a brow again.

Ursula amended her response, "My lady, it would not be advisable for you to send your husband on a mission at this time."

"James?"

"Committed to returning to King Henry's Court to be with his new wife and son."

"There are more knights to be had as escort. Do not believe you can sashay out the Fyvie gates on your own."

Ursula sighed. She'd already learned that when Rosalyn set her mind to something, it was difficult to change it. She shrugged her shoulders and pinched her lips shut, not wanting to lie, but she wasn't beyond sneaking out if she had to. Ursula patted her friend's hands and walked back to her table.

"Let me finish the afternoon herbs," she told Rosalyn and returned to stirring the berries in the mortar, glancing over her shoulder occasionally. It wasn't long before Rosalyn was napping.

An da shealladh–the second sight. Ursula had believed it was inherited. The shock was beginning to wear off though as she was left to her conflicted assumptions and questioning her mother's claims.

Could Rosalyn have learned some of the necessary skills, power of observation, keen listening?

But not intuition. That was God given.

The idea of Rosalyn's senses being heightened by her pregnancy seemed reasonable. The girl had picked out every spice in the roasted vegetable stew last night, or at least she'd appeared to have the skill. She'd sent the server back to the kitchen three different times to confirm the cook had used coriander, then turmeric, and finally, saffron.

"I know my spices," Rosalyn bragged and raised a groggy head just as her husband burst through the door without knocking.

Chapter 3

"My Lord, you rule Fyvie castle, but I rule this bedchamber," Ursula chided Rosalyn's dashing English husband before she shut the door behind him.

The impeccably manicured clan leader swept into a low bow, not a hair on his head out of place, and with a mischievous glint in his eyes.

"Good woman, I do not want your wrath or oaths upon me. Forgive my eagerness to visit my lovely bride when I can, but I've been at Ma Cameron's Tavern for hours meeting with rival clans and I wanted a moment with my love."

When he bent even farther into his bow, Lachlan's richly embroidered cape came about his ears. Before he rose, he turned his face up and tossed a wicked grin toward his wife.

Rosalyn struggled to get up from the chair to greet him.

"Wife, we've talked about this," Lachlan said in a clipped-tone, rushing to her side. "Do not attempt to greet me as you did before your belly was full of two babes."

Rosalyn shrieked and held her side gingerly. After her initial grimace faded, she flashed him a dazzling smile.

"Husband, they are kicking again."

He gazed lovingly at Rosalyn before he brushed a stray, flaming-red lock from her brow, then laid a hand on her bulging belly.

Ursula had met them both when she was in service at Berwick Castle. Rosalyn was still as feisty now as she'd been when she'd met Lachlan, both tied to a hitching post, in Berwick's dungeon. They'd been at odds then, but it was hard to imagine she'd tried to poison him to get what she wanted.

Fortunately, they'd both gotten what they desired—Fyvie Castle and a lifetime commitment to each other.

"Whoa," Lachlan exclaimed when it appeared the bairns were kicking under his hand. After the kicks came again, Lachlan took his hand away.

Rosalyn giggled. "The lads are asserting their independence already, husband. Clearly they prefer my hand to yours."

His chuckle mingled with her amusement. Then he leaned over, apparently ready to give Rosalyn a kiss, but stopped within inches of her lips. "Lads?"

"Call it mother's instinct," Ursula said, taking up a stool next to Rosalyn, interrupting Lachlan's intention as she began to administer the afternoon herbs to her friend.

Ursula couldn't help but feel she was intruding on their privacy. During Rosalyn's pregnancy, the three of them were almost inseparable. But when the intimacy between husband and wife got too intense, she'd excuse herself. Their love was an envious one. Although she never wanted to pry, she couldn't help but read their thoughts when they popped into her head.

The potion went to work instantly, and in a few short moments, while Lachlan attended to his wife's comfort, Rosalyn fell into a deep sleep. That's why she was surprised to find Lachlan's thoughts turning dark.

"I would take a blade or arrow before I'd let anything or anyone harm your beautiful wife," she said in response to what Lachlan was thinking.

His gaze shot up to meet hers and his features clouded over in concern. "How? Did I? He stammered in response.

She shrugged her shoulders when he shook his head, apparently believing her words of support were just a coincidence.

Even though he wasn't accustomed to her talents, Ursula couldn't help blurting out what he'd been contemplating. On the other hand, she couldn't read everyone, particularly not his brother Ethan. Ursula had the best results with those who were pure of heart. It was a compliment and a curse, filled with banes and blessings.

Rosalyn was one of her blessings, and although she had resisted Ursula leaving, it would be her husband's permission Ursula would need

Even though Lachlan's devoted gaze had returned to his wife, now was the time to make her appeal, but not within earshot of Rosalyn.

Ursula took the laird's hand and led him toward a storage cupboard, knowing the familiarity would not rattle him. It had been made clear before he'd married, Rosalyn and Ursula had formed a sisterhood beyond blood.

"Listen," Ursula said in a harsh whisper, "your wife is doing well under the circumstances, but her chances of delivering two babes without dying are nae good."

When Lachlan made a "tsk" sound, Ursula's hands fisted at her side. She was certain her pale skin was turning pink as her anger rose.

"Lachlan, do nae be an irresponsible man. Your own birth was one of the rare occasions when the mother lived after delivery of twins." She studied him before going on, then shook her head. "'Tis nae likely you know much of these things."

"I do not understand much of child birthing, but you must understand I love my wife and I'll do anything for her," Lachlan growled.

"Then you will support me when I say I need to leave on the morrow . . . the next day at the latest." Ursula was a terrible liar. Truth would be her ally. "I must go to the Isle of Skye for a rare flower. I must have it for the birthing."

"You're her midwife. Twin babes come early. Now *who* is being reckless?" he said, his voice rising.

When Rosalyn groaned from her chair by the fire, both their heads turned in her direction.

After Rosalyn settled back into even, heavy breathing, Lachlan's and Ursula's eyes met again. He tossed her an apologetic-looking grin after almost waking Rosalyn.

"Let me send someone else from my arsenal to bring the flower here," Lachlan offered. "The journey is at least five days each way, and there are many riotous clans to contend with throughout the Highlands. Although we have only one Garter knight in residence, I retain a loyal group of guards and soldiers. Any one of them is willing to do my bidding," he said.

Ursula wrinkled her nose. "Thank you, but I willnae need the escort. I've travelled the path before alone. I will do it again," she said with determination.

Lachlan snorted. "That was afore you were a member of this household." He glanced over at the serene, peaceful face of his sleeping wife before he asked, "Are you not putting Rosalyn in more danger by leaving her?"

When Ursula hesitated, he nodded in his wife's direction. "You discussed it with Rosalyn, I suspect?"

She cast her eyes to the floor, giving Lachlan his answer. After a long pause, Ursula grabbed his sleeve with a desperate grip.

"Lachlan, you do nae understand. I am the only one who will recognize this rare form of the guelder rose. It grows only in the faerie grove at Glenbrittle, before the Cuillin Mountains." She paused and stared deep into his eyes without blinking. "No mortal may walk there without consequence."

Lachlan flinched. Shrinking back from her, he said, "Many call you witch, but Rosalyn calls you sister, and I consider you an ally." He ran his hand through his well-groomed beard, no doubt contemplating the urgency of her request. "Your talents are many, and I will not dictate what you do, but consider taking the proper precautions." He weighed his words. "In the event you do not return."

Chapter 4

Walking into the keep's kitchen early the next morning, Ursula was still unsettled from her conversation with Lachlan. Although he'd agreed he would not stop her from her quest to bring back the guelder rose, he did not give her the satisfaction of his blessing either.

She hoped now to lighten her mood and shake off the seriousness of last night's debate. Of all the places at Fyvie, the kitchen was her favorite. Except for an occasional servant sleeping near the fire or a castle dog looking for scraps, she could count on having the space to herself this time of day. Here was where she could plan her herbal remedies and experiment with potions using the castle's caldrons.

Humming her favorite Scottish ballad, Ursula began unpacking her herbs, but when something touched her shoulder, she shrieked, bringing the dogs to barking.

Whirling around, Ursula found a grinning twin.

Lachlan? Ethan? She was not sure which. The two looked so alike it was frightening and frustrating at the same time.

"You scared me," she said, holding her hand against her heart, hoping the steady pressure would slow its beat.

A laugh followed her admission. It was Ethan. That was the only way she could tell them apart. She backed up from him.

"Do not look like a cornered kitten ready to scurry under the butcher's table," Ethan said, closing the gap between them. "Like you, I made my way here hoping it would be vacant."

Ursula let out the breath she was holding and relaxed a little. He had been frightening before Lachlan's wedding, but he had changed since then. She found him to be much different after he'd come to visit at Easter and decided to stay. Ethan had explained it as a change of heart, but she suspected there was something more. He still had called her a witch yesterday in the great hall. Although she did not take offense, he most likely had meant it as one.

"No matter how long you stare at me, it will not help you unravel my secrets," Ethan said, following the flirty challenge with a grin.

Her heart fluttered. Her emotions declared freedom from her resistance. Her hardened will almost melted as his warm gaze swept over her like a gentle embrace.

"Come," he said as he took her elbow. "I suspect you had similar goals here this morning," Ethan said as he walked her to the hearth toward the servants' stools. He sat easily and waited.

"Sit," he said without force or malice after a few moments of watching her stare at the wooden seat.

She blinked, gaining her composure, and glared at the stool as if it were something to fear.

"I won't bite," he promised, extending a sweeping arm toward the seat.

When she hesitated, he let out a frustrated huff. "Well, you may stand while I work," he said, then swung the caldron out from under the flames and peered inside. "I just assumed you'd be more comfortable sitting."

Ethan ignored her as he reached into a satchel he carried and withdrew many items that were familiar to her. He set them all on the cook's workstation by the hearth.

After he gazed up from his work to look at her, Ursula's mouth moved, but she said nothing.

"I'm making an antidote for poison," Ethan explained.

"Aye, you are," Ursula concurred, finally finding her voice. "But what is that?" she asked, pointing to the bunch of dried flowers he held. Fragile blooms that once must have been a soft yellow.

"Petals of the yellow flag iris, from the Isle of Skye."

"Really?" She paused, dumbfounded. "When were you last on the isle?"

"Just after Christmastide. I needed to sulk." Then his eyes clouded, and he stopped.

"I know you lost your mother. She was from the Highlands?"

"Killed her, you mean."

"You once said it was an accident? Was it?"

"Not according to my brother, Lachlan. He blames me. And yes, I was responsible, but . . ."

He stood and paced in the restrictive space. "Once I found out how rowen berries become poisonous when heated, I vowed I'd develop an antidote. I buried my pain by studying how to make poisons and how to reverse the outcome." He stopped and gave her an odd look. "The skill has come in handy," he admitted, "but I realize I have a condition beyond my control. I am trying to correct it."

Ursula detected the pain in his voice. It was palpable. He gazed at her with a haunting woundedness. Looking into his eyes was like staring into a dangerous, dark potion mixed with arrogance, lust, and angst. It was intoxicating and frightening.

She swooned a little and then righted herself as if she'd had a whiff of smelling salts. Even if she was attracted to him at times, Ethan displayed signs of unpredictable madness. The brutish behavior, groping and taking unwelcomed liberties when they were alone at Christmastide, still haunted her. She was never sure which Ethan would greet her each time they met.

But she needed to confide in him. Perhaps even convince him to confirm what she believed true. "Do you know of the guelder rose? To my knowledge, it only grows on the isle."

His eyes narrowed as if he was calculating what helping her would be worth to him and how he'd barter for it. Or perhaps, how he'd take his payment.

But before he had a chance to respond, Lachlan called from the doorway to the great hall.

"Ethan. Your presence is required."

Instead of answering his twin, Ethan mocked him, mouthing words without sound, his back to the opening that connected the two rooms.

"Ethan!"

Ursula couldn't help but laugh when Ethan's expression reflected his annoyance as the tall, dark, and dangerous Luttrell twin raced out of the room.

~ ~ ~

James paced in front of the blazing fire in the great hall's hearth, arms crossed and brows knotted, preparing for a battle of wills.

Even though this urgent family meeting interrupted his time with Ursula in the kitchen, Ethan would not let it undermine his pleasure. As he quickened his steps to join Lachlan and James, he was still grinning from ear to ear, pleased he'd found a way to manipulate her affections. He refused to let his twin intimidate him.

"Come, James, delay your return to Windsor. Do it for my heirs," Lachlan blurted out. "Ursula brought your son into the world. You owe her a noble deed in return."

The Garter knight stopped pacing and swung a huge arm at Lachlan. But when James's massive hand came to rest on Lachlan's shoulder instead of jabbing him in the face, Lachlan burst out laughing. Apparently undaunted,

Lachlan continued his plea, "Less than a sennight, James. And Ursula is well traveled. She's as cooperative as a well-trained palfrey."

"You're comparing a woman to a horse? Be careful, Lachlan," Ethan said. "That could get back to the witch."

"Mind what you call her, Ethan," Lachlan said.

"I'm certain Ursula would prefer to be called a witch over a horse," Ethan bit back.

James took his hand off Lachlan's shoulder and moved toward a group of formal chairs near the kitchen entrance where Ethan had entered the room. "'Tis time for a family meeting," James said, changing the tone of the conversation.

Lachlan glared at Ethan, and he returned the sentiment as they joined James at the table. The more he thought on it, the more Ethan was grateful for his half-brother's refereeing. He'd been in residence for a mere two months and was certain if it were not for James, Ethan would be locked in Fyvie's dungeon by now.

"'Twas not long ago," James began, "shortly after Nicholas Luttrell died, our lands were divided."

"You still cannot call him Father?" Ethan asked James.

"He provided a seed, nothing more," James replied stoically.

Lachlan had no love for their deceased father either, but Ethan had idolized him.

As they took up their seats, James positioned himself in the middle and continued with the mediation, "With the wager won at the gaming table, Ethan becomes the new landholder of Eilean Donan Castle. But it has come to my attention that this ownership must be explored further."

After a few moments of silence, Lachlan spoke. "'Twas mine to give."

"A MacKenzie was laird when last I visited," Ethan said.

"If there is no Luttrell in residence, then any Highlander with enough fighting men behind him can claim lairdship,"

James explained. "Consider yourself fortunate that you both have a Scottish home here at Fyvie and an English one in Dunster."

"The Highlands were once home to us both, but Eilean Donan Castle requires a respected Luttrell to reestablish the name," Ethan said, looking at James.

The Garter knight sat with arms folded over his massive chest and his eyes closed.

"This one time, Brother Lachlan, I will allow you to make my assignment," James said, opening his steely blue eyes, their piercing focus aimed at Ethan. "Although I miss my wife and son at court, King Henry has yet to order my return to Windsor Castle, and clearly there is much at stake."

"'Tis much at stake," chimed in a feminine voice from just inside the kitchen entrance.

Lachlan stood abruptly, almost knocking his chair back. "Show yourself," he demanded.

"I be neither witch nor horse. Perhaps I'm both," Ursula said while striding into the room. "'Tis my fate you discuss." She took a chair in the group across from James without invitation.

Ethan looked at her and asked, "Which do you prefer?"

Ursula embraced the taunt. "A magical unicorn if you please. Fittingly, 'tis the symbol of Scotland," she said smugly.

Ethan had no counter, and Ursula smiled. A rare occurrence that.

When silence ensued, James stood and paced again, this time behind his chair.

"Let me make sure I understand the assignment. I shall be taking a wary laird and a unicorn with me to Skye Isle," James said. "My charge is to oust the current Highland leader and place my half-brother on the throne as rightful owner of Eilean Donan Castle." He turned his focus to Ursula.

"At the same time, I'm to make sure Ursula is safely transported to the pools of the faerie glen, where no mortals may walk, to steal a rare and most likely heavily guarded flower, and bring her back without incident," James said.

They all looked at James and nodded.

"I've already offered to go alone," Ursula said softly. "I do nae need an escort." She stood, clearly agitated. "Mortal men do nae know how to move through the faerielands, and I do nae want to have your deaths on my conscious."

James chuckled at Ursula's warning and settled himself back at the table, but Ethan stood to defend her. "She speaks the truth. We should not travel anywhere near the faerie glen."

James was about to object, but Ethan cut him off. "We can escort her to the border, but from there she should travel alone." He paused, then added, "Unicorns and faeries get along."

Ursula perked up at Ethan's words and appeared content with this resolution, but Lachlan's face was grim and clouded with doubt.

It was Lachlan's turn to stand. "James, your presence here is invaluable, and Ursula"—he turned to face her—"I can barely fathom your absence when Rosalyn needs you most."

Ethan's twin began to pace in front of the hearth with his hands clasped tightly behind his back. "You know the clans had been peaceful until a sennight ago," Lachlan volunteered. "A number of suspicious fires destroyed homes and fields impacting clans Hays, Keith, and Innes. So far no loss of life, but the loss of income has been nearly as devastating for them. Now they challenge my new lairdship. I cannot fathom losing the home my wife loves so dearly, and I can't risk losing my wife if Ursula lingers too long."

Then Lachlan turned to James. "I could have a full-fledged war underway when you return."

They were all standing except James. He glanced from face to face, then he rose slowly as if he carried a burden on his shoulders. "A Garter knight does not take his oath lightly. When we are called, by king or queen, laird or lady, we must answer. I'm at your service until my sovereign requires my return," he pledged.

Lachlan took his two hands to grasp James's right, "My future rests with you." Then he pulled the knight aside and began to talk in hushed tones, while Ursula disappeared through the servant's entrance without any further remarks.

The sentiments of Lachlan were not lost on Ethan, and it was clear his twin found him of little value. As the journey was about to get under way, Ethan crafted his own plot, one that would cast Ursula in a new role. Although she was not from noble lineage, he was certain she'd make a splendid Lady of Eilean Donan.

Chapter 5

Alasdair was the eighth laird of Clan MacLeod, son of William Long Sword. The western edge of Skye Isle was where his Castle Dunvegan stood, the last of the Scottish outposts of protection for King James III.

It had been at least three years since he'd ventured this far from his Highland stronghold, but it was at the invitation of his sovereign to meet in Aberdeenshire at Ravenscraig Castle, the fortress of the Sinclair clan, for a leadership summit.

A summons from was a king was a rare occasion, and Alasdair was honored when he'd received the written request by royal messenger. The missive had explained, in the king's words, how he considered Alasdair an important ally and critical to Scotland's independence.

Shortly after Alasdair arrived at Ravenscraig, the castle steward led him through a series of grand gathering rooms until he finally ushered him in the king's private chamber.

King James smiled at Alasdair graciously, then welcomed him to Aberdeen and invited him to sit at a grand table filled with deerskin maps, writing instruments, and a unique collection of weapons.

The king eased himself back into a gilded chair before he spoke. "Alasdair, I need not recount the tumultuous history of Scotland to you as a respected leader of the Highlands. I am pleased your clan's loyalty never falters. While the MacDonalds have tried to usurp my power, you and your father have always supported my efforts."

"Your Grace, it is an honor to serve you," Alasdair said with reverence.

"What clan alliances or treaties have you formed? Please share with me what has been accomplished in the name of unity for Scotland."

"The important ones are in the Hebrides, Shetland, Orkney Isles," Alasdair said. "I have made treaties with the clans MacLean, MacNeil, and the MacLeods of Lewis. Before that tour, I also secured allegiances with the more powerful clans of Douglas, Leslie, and Ferguson."

The king steepled his fingers and nodded over them, apparently pleased with what Alasdair had said.

"Your family has suffered greatly defending our homeland, first from the marauding Vikings, and then from their heirs in the Orkney and Hebrides Isles."

"It is our honor to serve you, King James, as my father William did afore."

The king leaned an elbow on the table, as if to provide a special consult before he said, "There is new leadership in Aberdeenshire. A husband and wife share the title at Fyvie Castle. He is half-Scot, and she is from Clan MacPherson.

"Yet, they are dealing with revolts from nearby clans. The Hays, Keith, and Innes. Some homes have been destroyed by fire, and my worry is they may have to forfeit the lairdship of Fyvie." The king waved a royal hand. "I cannot afford to have it under siege. You understand. Peace is my first priority."

Alasdair nodded reverently, surprised to have such an intimate, strategic talk with the ruler of Scotland.

"After our meetings here, I entrust you to deliver this message from me to Lachlan MacPherson before you return to Dunvegan," the king said, selecting a rolled scroll from the desk behind him. It was secured with a red wax stamp.

"'Twill be my honor, Your Majesty," Alasdair said, accepting the missive.

"If you can prove your worthiness, I will bestow upon you the title Lord of the Isles."

"You can trust my worthiness, Your Grace," Alasdair promised as he bowed and left the king's private chamber, anxious to be done with the perfunctory meetings and on his way to Fyvie Castle and his new title.

~ ~ ~

Ursula stood on the parapet that evening, facing the setting sun and watching the sky splinter into shades of russet-orange and burnished gold, like the flames of a well-stoked fire. She imagined the orb hissing like a burning log on the hearth as it began its descent.

She was enjoying some solitude as she made a mental list of what she'd need for the journey to Skye Isle.

First, she'd make a combined protection and cooperation potion for Ethan. Because he was a dangerous deviant, she had to find a way to shield herself when his intentions became erratic.

Thankfully, she'd been whipping up batches of protection potions since the age of ten and two, ever since her mother's brother tried to get under her skirts. That was also the first time she realized kicking a man in the groin was effective.

Protection potions were also simple to administer. Because they were tasteless, the ingredients could be added to a stew or soup if necessary, but they were most potent when mixed with wine.

Wine was the mainstay of Ethan's diet, and she expected it would be easy to keep him under her influence as she kept his goblet full. This gave her hope that the quest for the rare flower was achievable, even if Ethan was more determined than most men in pursuing her, for she took pride in her standoffishness to unwanted affection. His attempts, however, were aggressive, the most disastrous when they first met in Berwickshire over a year ago and he'd showed up naked in her bed uninvited.

Although Ursula still preferred to make the journey alone, at least with Ethan under her spell, he'd be less dangerous.

She rubbed her hands together in satisfaction, but the next moment she was thrusting them forward to catch herself from tumbling over the parapet.

An ugly laugh followed her shriek, and by the time she caught herself, unwelcomed hands were around her waist.

"Och! Nay! Off of me, you brute." Ursula attempted to break free of the uninvited embrace. No man dared place a finger on her unless she gave him permission.

The laughter surfaced again.

"Ethan!" Struggling to free herself, Ursula finally stomped hard on his foot with the heel of her boot.

A curse followed, and finally, freedom.

"Attacking your protector is not prudent."

"Attacking your protectee is not prudent," she huffed, smoothing down her bodice and taking a measured step away from him and the parapet.

Ursula pursed her lips, ready to persuade Ethan to stay at Fyvie, where harassing his twin would suit him far better than traipsing across Scotland with her. Perhaps she could sympathize with him, and a resolution would present itself.

She plastered on a smile she hoped would appear convincing. "Now, you can clearly see I'm nae in need of protection."

A snicker started like a growl and moved into a haughty laugh. "Balderdash. Lady Rosalyn's attack in Aberdeenshire should serve as a vivid reminder as to how much protection beautiful women like you require. Need I remind you?"

Ursula sucked in a shaky breath, quickly realizing he had set her off balance and was trying to keep her that way. One of his deviant tricks to maintain an upper hand.

Although Ursula hated to admit it, he was right. It had not been long ago, before Rosalyn's marriage, her sister of the heart was attacked on the road to Fyvie after she'd left the safety of the camp, even with Garter knights and her future husband nearby.

Ursula had been silent too long, and when she focused again on Ethan, she found his gaze had wandered to her breasts. She cleared her throat, and his gaze shot up to meet hers.

"Sorry, contemplating your protection," he said, coughing through the feeble apology.

He took one step forward.

She took one back.

"Careful, now, we shan't have you taking a tumble over the wall."

Ursula glanced back briefly, but before she met his gaze again, he was on her like a heavy cloak, hands in places that were too familiar for an acquaintance.

"That is better," he whispered in her ear. "See, this does not hurt."

"But this should," she said at the same time she kneed him in the groin.

Ethan doubled over, gasping and cursing. "Do not think I will be deterred by your antics," he swore. "Makes the chase more interesting," he added, gritting his teeth as he turned his head to look up at her through a strained grin.

She laughed with satisfaction. "Why make yourself suffer, when you can chide your twin here at Fyvie instead?"

"And miss the opportunity to be alone with you in the woods for five days?" he questioned, straightening up with a groan.

"Three days if we travel by ship around the upper coastline, then by horse through the Highlands. I must be back in time for Rosalyn's birthing."

"Either way, I shall keep you warm," he promised, inching closer.

"You mean from harm," she corrected, studying him. Was there more to him than she'd seen as Lachlan's reckless, misunderstood twin brother? She often avoided him, but his warped charisma was alluring in a way Ursula could not understand.

She was the black sheep of her family, too. Shunned by some of her kin. Different was different. Armed with her protection potion, perhaps she could get to know and maybe even like Ethan.

While she had been considering him, Ethan had silently moved close enough to take her hand. "I shall keep you safe," he promised, holding it gently and without possessiveness.

Ursula did not yank her hand away, but let it settle in his, ready to make a pact and a promise. "If you accompany me, we will need rules."

Ethan shrugged his shoulders. "You know me as a rule breaker."

"This is precisely why I require you to promise to abide by my wishes."

"Hmmm . . . Are they rules or wishes?" he asked, a sly smile tugging at one corner of his lips.

She caught herself. The man would take a furlong if you gave him an inch. "Rules!" she snapped louder than expected.

"Everything all right, mi lady."

Ursula threw her arms up in surprise when the deep voice came from behind her.

"Excuse me. I did not mean to interrupt a tryst, but are you in need of assistance, mi lady?"

Ursula spun around to find no words. Her mouth was clearly her enemy as it hung open to her utter embarrassment.

"Alasdair MacLeod, Eighth Laird of Dunvegan, at yer

service," he said in a heavy brogue, then he swung low in an exaggerated bow as if it was foreign to him.

Ursula managed a curtsy but could not stop the heat that no doubt colored her pale cheeks a bright crimson. Perhaps the Highlander could count the cool weather as the culprit? She could only hope as she tried to use her will to overcome the unusual sensation.

"Why are you here?" Ethan asked. His lack of manners did not surprise Ursula. The anger rising inside helped her find her voice.

"Good sir, welcome to Fyvie Castle, the home of Clan MacPherson," she offered and curtsied again out of sheer nervousness. Even though the laird was at least a half foot taller than Ethan and he wore a bearskin cape of the Highlands, she was not afraid. She was intrigued.

Alasdair made the awkward bow again, and she imagined they could repeat the bows and curtsies a few more times as they ogled each other.

"Why are you here?" Ethan repeated his question as if he was a soldier on the castle's garrison and not the laird's brother. A welcome greeting would have been more appropriate. But Ethan never did anything justly.

"To meet with Lachlan MacPherson, the laird of this castle and keep," Alasdair said good-naturedly, clearly ignoring Ethan's snub. "The castle steward pointed to the parapets and said I'd find him here."

"This is his twin, Ethan," Ursula blurted out, gesturing to him. "Shawn must have mistaken the two. It happens often." Her explanation seemed reasonable.

Ethan brushed by the laird. "Since you won't be needing me, I'll wish you a good day." And with that, Ursula was left with the Highlander, her heart pounding and mind racing. An awkward silence followed while she stared at her feet.

"You must have a name."

Her head shot up. "Ursula."

"English or Scot?"

"English? *Och!* Nay! Clan Fraser."

Alasdair's amusement was evident when he asked, "You donnae like the English?"

"I donnae trust the English, that is for certain."

"Nor do I."

"We have quite a bit in common." She paused, searching for what to say next.

He came to the rescue. "You must have important matters to attend to," he said, the burr of his words sounding like velvet. "Shall I escort you to the bailey?"

"*Och!* Nay! 'Tis my error in not offering you escort. I-I-you," she stuttered. While she'd been ogling the Highlander, her manners had abandoned her.

An apologetic laugh rescued Ursula from saying more.

"There you are."

Ursula spun around to find Lachlan behind her, and she quickly curtsied.

Lachlan tossed her a look as if she'd gone too far, but he acknowledged her gesture with a curt nod.

"Lair MacLeod of Dunvegan, I presume?"

"Aye, mi lord, I have an urgent message from our king."

The two hurried off in the direction of the great hall, leaving Ursula shaking her head in frustration.

Tongue-tied, and as daft as a simpleton, Ursula had missed the perfect opportunity. If only she'd had enough wits about her, she would have asked the Highlander of Sky Isle how to find the illusive guelder rose.

Chapter 6

Later that evening, Ursula sat at the head table, dressed in a plum velvet gown. The golden headpiece she wore sparkled with jewels. Simple but regal. Her pale, porcelain breasts, round and proud, were propped up by the crisscrossed laced bodice. Ethan salivated as if she were his feast.

As he walked toward her, he imagined his hands tangled in the dark tresses that tumbled around her shoulders, framing her breasts. A pear-shaped, amethyst pendent hung between her rounded flesh, as if nesting. He yearned to gather that necklace in his hands and brush his fingers through the silky, smooth valley that held it in place.

Only when he stepped up to the dais, taking the empty chair beside her, did Ethan finally raise his gaze to meet hers.

She blushed, his ogling obvious.

Ethan reached for her hand and brushed the top of it with a light kiss. Then raising his head, he asked, “Everything all right, my lady?”

Ursula turned a shade of crimson. What a rare sight, this dark damsel blossoming into an exotic flower. Her once pale skin glowing as if lit by an unseen source.

A slap on the back shattered the moment. Ethan’s sensuous gaze with the devilish beauty disintegrated.

“The saffron-laced soup will be out momentarily, but before you begin your meal, I need to talk with you both,” Lachlan said, nodding toward the castle’s kitchen door.

After begrudgingly following his brother to the doorway, Ethan ducked underneath a heavy platter laden with soup bowls as a servant exited the kitchen.

"What has gotten into you, brother? Not enough help in the kitchen, so you must recruit us?" Ethan said as he rolled up one sleeve in jest.

Lachlan responded by punching Ethan's arm like he had when they'd been lads.

Cursing, Ethan grabbed his stinging arm. His gaze caught Ursula's, and she rolled her eyes.

"Of course, I'd rather we talk in a more private place," Lachlan said as he walked toward the worktable in the center, "but I must make a formal announcement at dinner, and I need your allegiance now."

Fear. The face Lachlan wore when he'd faced his father. Ethan sobered.

"Last night, three more cottages at the outer edge of Aberdeenshire were set to fire."

Ursula covered her gasp, but her eyes bugged wide above her trembling, pale hand.

"As the new laird, I've had meetings with the outlying clans regularly, but one clan, the Keiths, have refused to send representation." Lachlan drew closer to Ethan and Ursula. "My hope is to keep news of this from reaching Rosalyn."

"Gossips are everywhere," Ursula said, her expression somber. "I shall speak to her maid and ask that she cut off any wagging tongues."

Lachlan's gaze narrowed on Ursula.

"Figuratively speaking," she clarified. "I agree that we should keep this from Rosalyn, considering her condition."

They both looked to Ethan.

"You have my word," he promised with his hand over his heart.

"Spare me the theatrics," Lachlan said. "But more important than this, I have a secret request."

But just as Lachlan was about to explain, the serving staff returned, forcing them into the corner by the mops and brooms.

Undeterred, Lachlan pressed on with a hushed desperation. "Yesterday I received a missive from King James, delivered by a Highlander from Skye Isle. In the letter, the king laid out the rules of forfeiture. If I cannot control the uprising clans, particularly the Keiths, Fyvie Castle will no longer belong to the MacPhersons."

Ursula gasped.

The news was dire for Lachlan. The implications were staggering. As much as he disliked his twin, Ethan was concerned about Rosalyn. She had just won Fyvie back. Losing the castle would devastate her.

"You must bring back the Faery Flag from the Isle of Skye to secure our claim," Lachlan offered as a solution.

Ethan balked at the suggestion. "You do not believe in that fable. No, this is a ruse," Ethan said, turning to enter the great hall again until Lachlan grabbed his arm and jerked him back.

"I have never been more serious in my life," Lachlan promised through gritted teeth, the look of fear clearly evident.

Before Ethan could challenge his brother further, Ursula chimed in. "'Tis not a fable. 'Tis true," she insisted, taking Ethan's hand. The gesture sent pulses of pleasure through his arm, softening his demeanor, but not his cock. It went rock hard.

Damn, what that she-devil does to me. I cannot control it.

"Whether you believe or you do not," Lachlan said, directing his words toward Ethan. "You owe me for the loss of Eilean Donan Castle, and as the new ruler, you should be able to demand the flag be presented to you."

"Even if it exits, how will I demand it?" Ethan asked. If his brother did not look so pale, he wouldn't have believed his request.

"Rosalyn said it exists and 'tis hidden somewhere on Skye Isle," Lachlan offered, his eyes wide.

Ethan huffed. "Did you ask the Highlander who delivered the missive?"

Lachlan looked embarrassed, and for once in a long while, Ethan felt sorry for his brother.

"He laughed when I asked him about it," his twin admitted.

When Ethan did not respond immediately, Ursula glanced at him, then squeezed the hand she was still holding as if to offer a truce. Sadly, her attention went back Lachlan's way too quickly.

"We are traveling to the isle for the guelder rose. Regardless, I will search out the Faery Flag. You have my word," Ursula said. "Besides, I'll be among the faeries, and they will validate the flag or swear it off."

"I knew I could count on you, Ursula," Lachlan said, glaring at Ethan.

But Ethan turned his cheek to Lachlan and gave his attention to Ursula. "My job is to get her there safely. I do not talk to faeries."

"You do nae know their language anyway," she responded.

Lachlan seemed satisfied by Ursula's promises, yet Ethan could tell there was more. But he was distracted by Ursula's touch and his stomach. The soup smelled delicious, and he was famished.

"Hear me out. The last is yet to be told." Lachlan took in a labored breath. "I must send you both alone. James has been called back to Windsor." He turned to Ursula. "If you refuse to travel with Ethan by yourself, I will respect you for that. He owes me, you do not."

"I owe your wife. And in turn, I owe you." She blushed that crimson color Ethan thought was only for him.

"Neither Rosalyn, nor I, would ever make a request that could put you in harm's way." Lachlan glanced at Ethan. "My brother is usually more talk than action, but I will have his word that he will treat you with honor. As much as I'd want to send a few of my knights with you, unfortunately, they must stay here to safeguard the castle and surrounding shires. I have little to offer."

"I'm willing to make the journey myself"—Ursula huffed and dropped Ethan's hand—"but everyone believes I need protection."

Lachlan chuckled and put an arm around Ursula's shoulder. "You've become a sister to my wife and a sister to me. Neither one of us underestimate you."

And with that, Lachlan turned her around and gestured toward the kitchen door, leading them back into the great hall, Ethan on their heels as he muttered under his breath, "Lachlan was troubled?" Nothing could please him more.

~ ~ ~

The butterflies in Ursula's belly distracted her as she sat at the head table in the great hall after Lachlan's news was announced. He had explained to the Fyvie courtesans the need for James's return to Windsor and increased security in the shires.

Ursula wasn't anxious about getting Ethan to drink the potion-laced wine. She'd chosen the plum velvet dress tonight specifically to distract him with the low-cut neckline and scandalous fit. But could it be she felt something stir inside her after she'd taken his hand?

Ursula shook her head. No, even though he was handsome and sometimes charming, she still found him repulsive. Heat from the kitchen must have wilted her defenses for a moment. She willed herself to fight the urge to surrender to her emotions.

Although she expected Ethan to join her after the meal and the tables had been cleared, Ursula remained alone at the head table. She glanced over her shoulder, not surprised to find the twins still in a heated discussion by the servants' table outside the kitchen.

Ethan had promised to share wine with her after the meal. Yet she was thankful for the current distraction. It gave her the opportunity to add the potion to Ethan's goblet under the table now that the great hall was empty.

While the twins continued debating her future, Ursula muddled through her thoughts and emotions alone. As she considered the comments Ethan had made in the kitchen, she was taken aback by what he had said about the famous flag.

Even though she had not let on to Lachlan, Ursula was well versed in its powers and was surprised Ethan had dismissed its existence so quickly. Perhaps he knew even more about it than she did? He had lived near Skye Isle and should have been familiar with its reputation.

She sighed. Oh, the stories her mother had told of the Faery Flag, *Am Bratch Sith*. When Ursula had been a wee lass of three summers, sitting on her mother's lap after taking a big tumble, she'd been distracted from the pain by a square of yellow cloth her mother brought out from a jeweled-covered box. It was the softest, silkiest material she had ever touched. So small it had fit in the middle of her child-sized palm.

With wet eyes, Ursula had looked into her mother's face and thought the fabric to be special. "A faerie trade, a piece of the magical Faery Flag," her mother had told her.

"Dreaming of me?"

Ursula bolted upright and spun to her left to find Ethan with his chin propped up on his arm as he leaned on the trestle table and grinned at her as if he had already consumed his wine.

Instead of answering him, she scooped up her goblet brimming with mead.

Ethan mimicked her, raising his goblet, the altered wine sloshing over the rim and onto the table.

"To a successful journey. May we bring back the guelder rose for Rosalyn and the Faery Flag for Lachlan," Ursula said.

"May I find a way into your heart," Ethan said over the top of the dark liquid. Then he tipped his head back and drained the goblet of its contents.

Her heart skipped a beat, and the butterflies returned. No, not Ethan, she told herself as he remained grinning like a fool at her over the empty cup. She only had to remind herself how he had treated his twin to realize he was not a man to give her heart to. In the meantime, she would tame him, so she could trust him.

"Have you nae learned anything in my company?" She gave him a piercing stare. "I break hearts, and so do you."

Ethan's head tipped back, and his laughter filled the air. "You may never love me, but you have met your match, Ursula, the dark witch."

"I shall take that as a compliment, for I do nae want to be coddled."

He raised one brow. "What about cuddling?"

Her back stiffened, and she remembered they still had rules to discuss.

"Rule Number One. Obey all my rules."

Ethan nodded obediently. Perhaps the potion was already working? If not the concoction, the goblet of mead was making an impact.

"Rule Number Two. Do not do anything I ask you not to do."

"Is that not a trick question?" he asked but seemed agreeable.

Powerful potion. Perhaps she should let Lachlan in on her secret. On second thought, the less anyone knew about her potion skills, the better.

"Agreed. Only two rules, that makes it easy to remember," he replied, grinning.

Clearly, he was under and would stay so for at least four days. Aye, she was thankful for the strength of the concoction. Any emotion-controlling potion had to last at least that long. Especially love potions. Wedding proposals and the like were events that could not be rushed, unless there was an angry father at the helm.

She crossed her arms in front of her chest and sat back, quite satisfied with herself. Perhaps she could speak to him now about the Faery Flag with more cooperation.

"You said in the kitchen that you did not believe in the Faery Flag. Was that for Lachlan's sake, or did you mean it?"

He shrugged his shoulders. "Eilean Donan was my home for seven years. Was the Faery Flag a legend? As a young boy my mother would speak of it," he said with heavy lids, eyes dropping and words slurring.

Could the side effects of the potion and the wine together serve as a short-term truth serum? This man whose thoughts were blocked to her might prove to be readable after all. If not, she would get her answers through her questioning.

"What did you learn about the myth of the Faery Flag when you lived at Donan? Even if you did nae believe, you must have heard about it?" Now it was her turn to prop her head on her hand and give her full attention to him.

Ethan cocked a grin and leaned back into his massive chair, the great hall empty except for a few servants sweeping the floor.

He stared past her, as if looking back farther than he had in a very long time. As if he was opening a closed door to his memories.

"It's been said that the fourth MacLeod clan chief of Dunvegan married a faerie with whom he had a son," Ethan said as if describing a dream. "On the boy's first birthday, the faerie told her husband, Iain, that she could no longer live with the mortals and must return to the faeries.

"Iain loved her and asked her to stay, begging her to help him raise their son. But it was not to be." His gaze shifted back to hers. "As father and son followed her to the border of the faerie glen to say their goodbyes, she rose above them on her wings and dropped a piece of yellow silk, saying, 'Keep this flag and unfurl it to the wind whenever you are in real danger, and it will protect you.'"

He blinked hard, as if he might be saddened by the tale. "Then she was gone, never to be seen again."

"Never?" Ursula asked through a sigh, closing her eyes. The story was heartbreaking. After all the birthings and the special bond created between a mother and child she had witnessed, she couldn't imagine having to leave a child behind.

She opened her eyes, and her breath caught from Ethan staring at her longingly.

"Never is a very long time in faerie tales," he muttered in a dreamy kind of way.

Ursula chuckled. Now she had the lore.

Chapter 7

Powerful magic, it has been said, could be conjured by the bearer of the Faery Flag. Ursula was not interested in sharing all she knew about the flag's properties, and as far as she could detect, Ethan had told her all he knew.

The potion had started working immediately after he'd guzzled it down. No doubt the rate at which he drank the sweet wine easily counted as an excuse for his loose tongue. But after they both lingered at the table and became the last ones to leave the great hall, she was convinced she would lose her heart to him if his was not naturally black.

She knocked softly before entering Rosalyn's chamber, smiling at the compliment Ethan had given her when they parted. He'd said it in Gaelic, which had surprised her.

But considering he'd lived near the Isle of Skye for seven summers as a young lad, he would have had to learn the old language to survive.

"How am I to survive? That is what you should be worrying upon," Rosalyn said so loudly Ursula was certain anyone in the outer corridor would have heard her.

"*Shhhhh!*" Ursula scolded. "You do nae want all of Fyvie Castle to hear my private thoughts." Then she walked over to her sister of the heart and laid a hand on Rosalyn's bulging belly. "You're concerning me now."

"That I can hear your thoughts or because of my rapidly expanding girth?" Rosalyn smiled despite her discomfort.

"Both," Ursula said before she thought better of it. "You should be asleep."

"I cannae sleep thinking that you will be sleeping with Ethan in the woods, and I shall be at least a sennight without you," Rosalyn moaned like a child.

"At least you did nae say that at the top of your lungs," Ursula said softly, tsk-tsking after. "I willnae be sleeping with Ethan. Wipe that vision from your thoughts right now," she said through gritted teeth, placing her hands on her hips.

Rosalyn let out a huff. "You clearly know what I meant."

She studied the woman who had given her a home at her darkest hour. Rosalyn's fiery, auburn hair suited her passionate personality. Her blazing amber-hued eyes burned like hot embers while she tried to get comfortable lying in the bed with a belly full of not one, but two babes.

Ursula reached for a pillow at the other side of the headboard. "Here," she offered, "turn on your side and rest your belly on top of this." She pushed the soft feathers inside the casing around until it created a nesting spot for Rosalyn's belly. "There," she said, finally satisfied and stepping back.

When her friend let out a long sigh, Ursula took it as her cue to get to work on the evening herb mixture. A pinch of cat's claw and boswella, with white willow bark, would numb Rosalyn's discomfort and give her a much needed rest.

"Ursula, you cannae leave me." The words came out like a whimper.

"Hush now," she said, choking back her own emotion. "I will teach your maid and Lachlan how to make the mixture."

"'Tis more than that."

"I would nae be leaving without a plan," she said as she glanced at Rosalyn and gave her a reassuring smile.

"Do nae smile at me and think that will placate me," Rosalyn said.

Ursula frowned, and that made Rosalyn laugh loudly. "You are more beautiful when you smile."

Ursula ignored the compliment. "I mean that I have found my replacement. A woman in the village named Thea.

She is a distant cousin," Ursula explained as she walked with the potion to join Rosalyn on the bed. "And I trust her," Ursula said, taking a seat.

Rosalyn looked at her with doe eyes. "Tell me again why Ethan cannae do this deed for you?"

Ursula hesitated to answer. She struggled with how much to share. Finally, she decided some of it had to come out. Taking her arm behind Rosalyn's neck, she directed her forward so she could easily drink the potion.

After a few long sips, her friend rested back on her side, and Ursula scooched over to smooth back the stray, wild, red bangs that were forever falling into Rosalyn's eyes.

"Ethan would never find the faeries on his own," Ursula said softly, stroking her friend's brow.

"You do nae believe he can find the guelder rose you seek without the faeries?"

Ursula threw her head back and cackled. "You do nae know faeries."

Rosalyn's eyes flashed with a spark of competitiveness, despite her encumbered position. With a huff, she said, "Ursula, you're nae the only one in the room who's talked to the Fae."

"In Faery speak or Gaelic?"

"*Och*, they have their own language?"

"Aye, and this is why I must go." Ursula put her finger to Rosalyn's lips when she appeared to protest. "Faeries can be quite evil when they want to be. I've known them to lie and lead mortals off into caves never to be seen again."

"Well, Lachlan was looking for a way to rid himself of Ethan," Rosalyn admitted with a look of hope in her eyes, but she frowned, too, as if conflicted. "But there would be no one to bring back the flower . . ."

"Unless I go."

"Go."

"There does not appear to be another way."

"Unless, Lachlan goes with you . . ."

"That is inviting trouble. If the rebel clans get wind of Lachlan's departure and your incapacitation, you could have an uprising on your hands."

"I already invited trouble when I agreed to Ethan's escorting you. But that was before James was called away," she added wistfully, as if having a Garter knight at Ursula's stead had given Rosalyn peace.

"He's nae far and will respond if needed. Lachlan has James's word. And a Garter knight's word is as important as his life."

The potion must have started to work because Rosalyn's eyelids were drooping.

"He's nae far. That should give me some comfort," Rosalyn said, then raised her head. "I almost forgot. Did you poison Ethan?"

Poison? Ursula struggled to keep from laughing. In the past that would not have been funny, because she had tried, with good reason. Not permanently. Well, that was another story.

Ursula choked on a giggle before she said, "You mean, did I give him a potion to make him into someone he's not?"

"If you could change his black heart to gold, that would be a miracle. But aye, I meant have you changed him for the better, even if temporarily?"

Now it was Ursula's turn to be wistful. If she could change Ethan permanently, would she? 'Twould be a noble cause. Make the world a better place.

Rosalyn murmured something Ursula could not make out. As sleepy as her friend was, she must have been reading her thoughts. "Too bad you cannae make it for keeps," Rosalyn mumbled more clearly as she appeared to nod off, but then her friend perked up again. "But how will the Faery Flag help you?"

"What?"

"The yellow flag," she asked as if she was talking in her sleep. "Why must you bring it back?"

"Sleep, Rosalyn," she soothed. "You are dreaming about faeries. Those are nae my thoughts."

"Well, I better wake up because dreaming of Ethan in my bed would be a nightmare."

Ursula chuckled as her friend finally succumbed to sleep. She tucked Rosalyn in as best she could, grateful that she had not let on about the attacks. She'd come too close in the heated moment and almost gave away the reason for the flag.

Ursula walked over to the extra bed that had been brought in for her. Lachlan had moved out a sennight ago. Between Rosalyn's flailing and his undeniable snoring, neither were getting any rest.

Besides, even though they were newly married, any natural inclinations to rutting were discouraged and, furthermore, could be damaging.

Initially, Lachlan snorted and stomped about like a lusty bull, but Rosalyn was able to get her way.

As if on cue, after a light knock outside the chamber, Lachlan's grinning face appeared between the jamb and the door.

"Where's my love?" he asked sweetly into the warm and darkened bedroom. The hearth was burning low, giving off long shadows that reached to the ceiling. The embers emitted plenty of heat but not much light as they glowed, giving the sleeping beauty an ethereal coloring as she lay facing the warmth.

Almost tipping in on his toes, Lachlan moved his feet with exaggerated movements, knees drawing high with each step, as he walked with care across the chamber to Rosalyn's side.

"Ah," he said as he bent to one knee and took one of her hands in his. "Here's my love."

Rosalyn let out a sleepy groan and batted her lashes, but that was all she could muster for Lachlan under the influence of Ursula's concoction.

Lachlan harrumphed and hung his head, no doubt disappointed she was so sleepy.

After a few long moments, Ursula cleared her throat, and Lachlan's spine stiffened. He reached for the hilt of his sword.

"'Tis only me," Ursula whispered with a shaky breath.

"I'm grateful for that," Lachlan answered back in his own whisper, releasing his hold on the weapon.

She rubbed her throat absentmindedly. Having been called a witch much of her life, Ursula had become accustom to being misunderstood.

Lachlan stood, giving his wife a last glance before he strode across the chamber to where Ursula sat on the edge of her bed. He had carried the stool with him and set it down beside her.

She smiled broadly. They'd always gotten along, both hating his twin. She'd been protective of Rosalyn and wary of Lachlan until he saved her friend's life more than once.

Lachlan and Ethan were identical twins. And before Rosalyn had fallen in love with Lachlan, she'd been wary of both men. They were half English, and neither Rosalyn nor Ursula had ever trusted the English.

Lachlan scattered her thoughts when he took her hand in his like a gentleman would a royal. "My lady, Ursula." He bowed his head slightly over her hand. "You know more than you say. This I've observed over many weeks. 'Tis your eyes that give you away," he admitted, letting go of her hand and sitting back to study her.

Ursula's grin turned smug. She, too, had observed Lachlan over many weeks, and he'd become like a brother to her.

"When you know more than you should, your eyes become glittery dark pits where observations go to be cataloged."

Her smugness disappeared because there was truth in his words.

"And you, brother, know more than you reveal."

Amusement sparked in his eyes. "Is there no way for me to keep secrets from you?"

His question was provocative. She cocked a brow. Should she tell him the truth?

After a long silence, Lachlan waved an imaginary flag over his head as if to surrender.

"The Faery Flag," she said, knowing what was on his lips.

"Aye, you do have a gift."

"Some would say a curse."

"A cursed gift, and I must mind my thoughts."

She gave her head a brisk shake. "'Tis almost impossible to control your thoughts." She blinked, and a soft spot in her heart ached, as did his, for they both loved Rosalyn. "Aye, I fear for her, too," she reluctantly confessed.

After an awkward moment of silence, Ursula took his hand. "I would nae be leaving her unless I was certain it was the right thing to do," she admitted, and before he had time to object, she said, "I have a healer from the village ready to take my place. She's verra smart, and I trust her."

Lachlan relaxed his shoulders and squeezed her hand before letting go. "I hate to admit it, but I trust you."

She nodded, happy she would not need to argue with him.

"But I do not trust my brother."

"Trust me there, too."

Lachlan studied her like an art object, tilting his chin up as if inspecting her intentions, turning his head from side to side. She would have laughed out loud if Rosalyn had been awake.

Ursula started to speak, but Lachlan put his finger against her lips. "My turn to read you."

She crossed her arms, about ready to tell him she was like a book and he should read the disgusted look on her face to know what she was thinking.

He chuckled. "You shall do what you want regardless of what I say."

Ursula's mouth snapped into a taut pucker, and she let out a tight little laugh, too, embarrassed he'd gotten it exactly right.

"Good guess," she muttered, not wanting to give him any satisfaction. Clearly, her face had said what her mind was thinking.

"I know you have put a spell on Ethan. And I trust you know what you are doing. The flower and the flag can only be found by you and released to you by the faeries."

Her spine straightened, and she peered at Lachlan through one squinted eye as she turned her head to one side, surprised again that he was so spot on.

"We need the flag because we cannot fail." He swallowed hard. "I cannot fail my wife or the clans."

She nodded.

"I can only hope it has at least one unfurling left."

Rosalyn yawned and mumbled, "Bring back the Faery Flag for Fyvie."

Ursula shuddered. It was up to her to save them all.

Chapter 8

Ursula faced west, her back warmed by the rising sun as Ethan checked his destrier's foreleg. The warhorse had limped slightly when it walked from the stables moments ago, saddled and ready for the journey to Skye Isle.

Rising from his crouched position, Ethan ran his gloved hand down the chestnut's withers. His warhorse was a magnificent steed, muscles rolling under a supple coat, but a bit standoffish like Ethan.

"Any idea what's troubling Bayard?" Ursula asked, anxious to start the day's ride and hoping they would not be delayed. They had a ship to catch.

"We've weathered many rough roads and smooth cobblestones together," he admitted, lovingly stroking the horse's mane. "He's my confidant, companion, family. For when no one else would stand by me, Bayard would."

Ursula understood what it was like to be an outcast. She wished she could say the same as he about her palfrey, Tempest. But she had more of a connection to plants than animals. She talked to her herbs when she made potions. They were a comfort, for she could count on their results to build her confidence.

"Come, come, beast," Ethan said in a soothing way, "you may not quit your service to your master now." Taking a ripe, red apple from his saddle's satchel, Ethan offered the sweet treat to his horse. "You have a few more good years left in you, and now is not your time to pasture."

Raising his massive, majestic head, the warhorse snorted. Its gaze seemed to drift to the pasture for a moment before he shook his head from side to side as if to agree his time was not now.

"Aye," Ethan said, hoisting himself into the saddle and taking the reins from the groomsman. "You have the heart of a champion. Heart over head will win every time."

Ethan rode his warhorse to the track by the stables and put him into a gentle trot. Ursula followed. She'd need her mount soon, too.

After a few rounds, the warhorse behaved as if he'd never taken a faltering step. His ears stood at attention, nostrils flared, and he pawed the ground like he wanted to race.

Once it appeared the horse's confidence had returned, Ethan took Bayard into a full gallop around the track. Looking satisfied once he'd finished the exercise, Ethan steered his horse toward the gate where Ursula stood.

She took a few hurried steps backward when Ethan reined his warhorse into an abrupt stop in front of her instead of passing by.

She tilted her head up and eyed him suspiciously. "Will you mow me down before the journey has started?" She shook one finger at him. "Did you nae promise to protect me on our journey to Skye?"

"Testing your mettle." Then he grinned at her. "You look beautiful."

She spat on the ground.

"Less beautiful now."

"Good," she said, turning her back on him and walking toward the stables, expecting him to follow. "There's been a change of plans," she said tersely. At the very least she hoped the potion would not only make him less devious, it would make him more agreeable to her suggestions. Now was the time to test it.

With her back still to him, she said, "Lachlan has come up with a way to cut our journey's time in half." When his reply was only silence, she turned to face him and stopped. "We will travel to Inverness by ship with Rosalyn's Uncle Quinn. Conveniently, he'll be making a trip to that Highland port for a wool exchange."

"The sea and I do not agree," Ethan said.

She hid a smirk. "I have a potion for that."

"Of course you do." Ethan's face twitched as if he wanted to say something disconcerting, but he did not.

"I shall make it taste like your favorite food," she offered, hoping to get the confirmation she needed and get past his reluctance. At least he hadn't refused.

"Mince pie?"

She stifled a laugh. "Aye, I can make the potion taste like pie."

"For my warhorse, too? He and the sea, neither agree."

This time she did chuckle. "Apple flavor for Bayard?" She clapped her hands together. "Consider it done," she promised, then turned when she heard her name called.

Lachlan and Rosalyn were approaching, followed by the groomsman with Tempest. They would have a short ride to the harbor before they would board the ship.

Lachlan was guiding his wife with care by her elbow. Ursula watched Rosalyn with compassion as she hobbled toward her, pleased Lachlan had come up with the amended path for the journey to Skye.

As they talked late into the night yester eve while Rosalyn slept, Lachlan had outlined the plan for the new itinerary. Although Ursula had not sailed much, she was willing to make adjustments to shorten travel time.

When the group reached them, Ursula rushed to Rosalyn and began to fuss.

"Out of bed?" She shook her head in frustration. "I've yet to leave the castle grounds, and you're already misbehaving?" She wagged a finger at Lachlan, and her brows scrunched together. "You must not let her manipulate you."

Lachlan shrugged sheepishly, while Rosalyn looked guiltlessly at him. The two were so perfect for each other in their own imperfect ways. Ursula dared not to dream she would ever have a love like theirs, for she was a mix of Fae and Highlander. Magic and mist. Born to heal, not to be loved.

Well, Joshua had professed his love for her, but she'd never been able to test it like these two had. That was another story.

She sighed before she spit words again. "This time is the last time. No more walking for you, lassie." Despite her terse tone, Ursula gave her pregnant friend one last hug with all the love and tenderness she could muster.

Once Ursula released the sisterly embrace, Rosalyn's eyes clouded with tears. Ursula forced her own tears back with a trembling grin and bit her lip to steady it before she reiterated her warning. "A walk to the privy or to the window, not much more than that."

Rosalyn pouted and looked up at Lachlan. He patted her hand. "You know Ursula will be able to use some kind of magic to spy on you, so I suggest you agree to do her bidding."

Lachlan glanced over and grinned before he said, "Ursula has a way of getting her way."

Everyone laughed, even the groomsman, although he did his best to hide it as he gave Ursula a boost up to her saddle.

"Nothing will keep me from getting my way, that's for certain," Ursula promised.

After the last tearful wave goodbye, Rosalyn turned toward her beloved castle, and Ursula coaxed her palfrey in the other direction toward the gate.

Ethan's warhorse fell in step beside Tempest, and they traveled side by side through the castle gate and out to the surrounding glen toward Petershead, where they'd meet Rosalyn's Uncle Quinn and later board his ship.

She hadn't intended to silence him but gave the potion credit for the pleasant half-day journey to the coastal town.

The hours rolled by, peacefully and uneventful. Although Ursula was pleased with the dramatic change in his persona, from the potion she'd concocted, the elixir did not break down the wall that blocked his thoughts. Perhaps he didn't have any?

She laughed out loud at the idea of Ethan having an empty head as they came through the clearing into Petershead late that afternoon.

"This pub here will do," Ursula said, pointing to the first building on the town's outskirts. "For a strong ale to wash away the taste of the road."

Ethan reined in his horse and waited until Ursula caught up with him. "Why stop and delay when we have ale with us?"

She didn't want to appear weak when she'd promised Ethan she could travel like a man, but all she wanted right now was a basin of fresh water to wash away some of the road grime, and to quench her thirst with a cool drink, not the warm liquid they carried in the goatskin pouches. She had more dust in her throat and eyes than a wayward sheep.

"If you were a woman, Ethan, you would nae ask that question," she sputtered.

Ethan grinned. What a handsome man he was when he smiled.

"I thank God every day I am not a woman," he said in his own straightforward way. But he gave her a wink and said, "Ursula, you refrained from nagging while we traveled today, and for that I shall grant you a respite before we push on to the harbor."

She kept her snide reply to herself and just nodded in agreement before she spurred her palfrey forward toward the tavern.

It was not long before they had dismounted and were standing in the welcoming entryway with their traveling satchels. They were greeted by a man with eyes the color of the bluest sea and skin like tanned leather.

"Welcome ye now to the Crooked Billet," he offered with a bow while leaning slightly on a carved walking stick. "Name's Finn. Who do I have the pleasure of making an acquaintance?" he asked, straightening up.

Ursula had not thought about accommodations and needing separate rooms. But before she had a chance to explain, Ethan blurted out, "Good sir, we are newlyweds on our way to Inverness to celebrate. Taking a coastal voyage, rather than land travel, seemed more romantic, so please show us to your best room before we are seabound on the morrow."

Ursula grunted under her breath but smiled through gritted teeth. Could the potion be wearing off? Although she expected it to assist her with Ethan's wanton ways, apparently it could not produce miracles.

Without protest, she and Ethan followed Finn up the narrow steps, then down a long hallway to its end. Stepping through a doorway on the right, he motioned them inside.

Ursula sucked in a sharp breath. The room was beautiful, with a fire burning in the hearth and walls paneled in timber. Ornately carved furniture and red woolen plaid bedding made the room a warm and cozy retreat. Although Fyvie Castle was well-appointed, there was nothing cozy about it.

Ursula sighed when she noticed the wash basin under the charming window that was framed by drapes in the same plaid that covered the bed. All she wanted now was a wash and a nap in that bed. Ethan could go down to the pub or the wharf. She did not care if he sailed off without her.

"Perfect," she said to Finn.

"It will do," mumbled Ethan, perhaps undone by

the charm of the place. She was happy after all to have a comfortable bed before they embarked.

Finn nodded. "With the room comes dinner or breakfast. Should ye be needing either?"

"Dinner," they answered in unison.

Thinking about the journey ahead, Ursula came to realize how easy life at Fyvie had been the past few months. No doubt Rosalyn's uncle would see to her welfare, but her sister of the heart had warned her about the food aboard the *Merry Maiden.*

Ethan gave Finn a few shillings, and after a handshake, the proprietor left.

Once the door closed, Ethan leaned against it and raked his eyes over her with a devilish grin. "Why fight me, when you can love me?"

Why? Why hadn't she insisted on separate rooms? His charisma made her knees weak. Tall, dark, and charming, but with a madness that was disturbing, Ethan contradicted proper behavior with his actions. Erratic and erotic, he was tempting like an exotic warlock with spellcasting powers.

While she stood there spellbound, he was on her, kissing around her ear, his one hand splayed across her arse.

Her only defense? To scream.

Chapter 9

As one might expect, the proprietor was at their door in moments, asking if everything was all right.

"You misjudged me again," Ethan whispered to her harshly, then yanked open the door to greet a confused-looking Finn.

"My wife thought she saw a rat," he explained, shrugging his shoulders with his back to Ursula, "but it was this black rock you have here to hold the door open."

Finn laughed, looking down at the rock. "We keep a tidy tavern, you know. Not likely you'll be finding any varmints in your room."

"She's a fragile one, and the road travel has her on edge," Ethan offered. "Down to the harbor for me to see the ships while she rests," he told Finn, joining him in the hall and closing the door behind, leaving Ursula alone.

She took in a big sigh. Ursula hated to admit that Ethan's advances, although inappropriate, were thrilling. Yet, she scolded herself for accepting the momentary pleasure. She was above primal urges and had more pressing personal needs.

Relieved to be alone for a while, Ursula wasted no time in finding her way to the wash basin, delighted to find the pitcher full. She poured about half of its contents into the sky-blue and white patterned porcelain bowl, then dipped a soft linen cloth into the cool liquid.

After twisting the excess water out, she closed her eyes and ran the cloth up one side of her neck, around her face, and down the other, sighing all the way. The water was delightful. But the rest of her body demanded attention.

Without a care, she opened her eyes and bent down for the hem of her travel dress, then yanked the stifling fabric over her head. Shaking her long locks free, she let the dress fall to the floor.

Ursula stretched both hands above her head and gazed out the window facing the woods, certain a few moments without the restrictive, overly warm garment would be worth the risk. A gentle breeze drifted in, kissing her bare skin. But just as she reached for the cloth again, a sharp whistle sailed through the window.

"*Och!* Nay." Ursula ducked, covering her breasts, mortified when she spied Ethan ogling her through the window.

She screamed and threw the cloth at him before ducking below the sill.

How could she be so foolish? But Ethan's behavior? Juvenile. Another catcall like that and half the men in the sleepy, seaside town would be outside her window.

Even though her potion had altered Lachlan's twin to her liking, the spell clearly had its limitations.

Aye, he had a good look. This risk that went awry would either appease Ethan for a while or send him into an obsessive pursuit.

Why had she been so careless?

Ursula snatched a fresh dress from her travel satchel. Once the hem hit the stone floor, she breathed a sigh of relief, rushed to the door, and turned the key in the lock.

Stepping slowly backward, Ursula trained her eyes on the door, wondering if he'd come back to make intimate demands.

After a few moments, she walked to the window to peer out.

Gone. And with that realization, she collapsed on the soft bed and closed her eyes.

~ ~ ~

After seeing Ursula in the window and catching an eyeful of her natural, naked beauty, Ethan walked toward the main road in a daze.

Where was he going?

But the early evening breeze cleared Ethan's head somewhat, as he stumbled along for a while until he remembered his plan to find the *Merry Maiden.*

Yes, Ethan was anxious to take a powerful position in the Scottish Highlands, and the journey to Kyle of Lochalsh could secure it. As the son of a Scot and a Brit, he'd been called a bastard by most. Not that he cared, as long as he could take command and demand the respect he deserved.

'Twas so many years ago when his mother died at Eilean Donan, while his father ruled from his English castle during the War of the Roses. For reasons Ethan didn't understand, his father delayed his return six months after her death.

Even then, Nicholas did not mourn her passing, his final words about her death still haunting Ethan. *You delivered me from evil.*

"Deliver me from evil." The words were whispered in his ear.

Ethan spun around.

While lost in thought about his past, Ethan hadn't noticed where he had walked. To his right, the ocean was in view, but he'd need to walk a bit farther to reach the wharf.

To his left was a church. Even though the action went against his instincts, he strode in as if he belonged, as if something or someone was guiding him.

Ethan took a seat on an empty bench, closed his eyes, and wondered when he'd last set foot in a place of God. *Lachlan's wedding?*

"You need not be in God's house for him to be with you."

Ethan turned around in his seat. He twisted back the other way, then faced the altar again. He blinked quickly a few times, listening. *Was that a woman's voice?*

"Do not be afraid."

It was a woman's voice, and it sounded strangely familiar.

"I am not afraid," he answered back, expecting a nun or acolyte to step out of the shadows after having pulled a clever ruse on an outsider.

"Good. For I am with you always."

Is God a woman?

"Ethan, I know it was an accident."

"Mother?" He sucked in a quick breath and spun around in his seat again. "Show yourself," he demanded.

To his surprise, a soft form began to materialize in front of the altar, and in mere moments, a woman floated before him.

"Mother?" The ethereal figure matched Ethan's memory—soft, warm, amber-colored eyes and long, golden hair about her shoulders. A faint halo hovered above her head.

"Mother?" he asked again.

"My son," she whispered. "You have grown into a handsome lad. Aye, you have," she said.

Ethan wanted to rush to her. Hug her. Cry on her shoulder and tell her how sorry he was.

"Nay, my son, 'tis not your fault. I never blamed you. For now I see you saved me from a more gruesome end. Your father was plotting my demise the day I ate the berries. He was going to have Rudolph end my life. I only became aware of the plan when I traveled to the other side, where thoughts are as loud as shouting voices and prayers are like angels singing."

Ethan stared at the image, not certain what to do or say. He could see through her. A cold chill raced up his spine. He could dismiss a mysterious voice, but this angelic form claiming to be his mother was quite another matter.

"'Tis a lot to take in, my son. But there are rules in the other worlds, and well . . ." She hesitated. "Some debated you were not worth saving."

Ethan laughed. "No, spirit, most would say I'm not worth saving." Some of his trepidation dissolved, for if this was not real, it was an elaborate hoax.

The form moved toward Ethan, gliding over the slate floor. His smile faded, and he sat erect as the shape of a woman came toward him. When her hand reached for the top of his head, he shivered from a cool flick of air passing through him.

"You are worth saving, and you have important work to do."

"Mother." The scent of lilacs filled his nostrils, triggering his memory of her.

Ethan bowed his head under the gentle pressure of her hand. She stroked his hair while a waterfall of genuine love poured over him.

Ethan choked up. He wanted to ask her about the important work, but he could not find the words.

"Ethan, life is not about owning land, but owning your actions. You are too much like your father," she chided. "Still, you have the power to change."

Ethan shrugged his shoulders. "Sounds like a motherly thing to say."

When she glided away from him, Ethan could sense her touch leaving, creating a void. He looked up.

"Ethan, my visit is not an accident. Somehow your heart has been softened enough to see me. I've been at your side all along, but you have not heard me."

The last words stung. *She had been by his side all along?* Aye, he'd been called black-hearted, even by Lachlan. *Especially by Lachlan.*

He smiled at the image. "Well, if you are my mother and not an angry angel here to strike me dead, I must say I'm pleased to know I have a higher purpose than land-loving, clan-clashing, and wench-watching."

The ethereal image smiled.

"Time is precious, and life can be short. You, my son, can leave a better legacy than your father."

Ethan sobered. His father had been gone a few months. Ethan realized the power Nicholas had over him. He'd been his puppet on strings.

"Aye, Ethan, you can be selfless instead of selfish." She paused and looked behind her as if startled. "Others are coming. I must be quick." She wrung her hands. "Help the girl, the one with the black hair. She has a gift and a purpose. Do what you can for her."

A loud bang sounded behind Ethan just then. He jerked around to find an old couple walking into the nave. When he swung back around, his mother was gone.

Ethan sighed and closed his eyes. He wanted to let his mother's words take hold.

Clearly she was speaking of Ursula. *Be selfless?* That wouldn't be easy.

Chapter 10

As the bell finished its eighth ring, Ursula opened her eyes. *Where was she?*

The first thing she spotted was the fire in the hearth beyond her feet. It still glowed with embers stoked hours ago.

A cheery room greeted her as she sat up in bed. *The cozy tavern?* Aye. Last night she'd collapsed into bed after a generous supper of lamb stew and ale.

When her mind cleared even more, she glanced at the spot beside her. *Ethan?*

Nay, she'd slept alone.

Eight bells? Wait. The Merry Maiden was due to leave port at eight.

Ursula flung off the plaid covers and made a direct line to her satchel by the hearth.

"Holy Mother of God!"

"*Och! Diabhal!*" Ursula went down fast and hard.

When strong arms grabbed her around the middle, she couldn't breathe. Either from his squeezing or having the wind knock out of her in the fall.

Ethan chuckled into her neck, but she bit his ear in return.

"You are feisty in the morning," he said, smacking her arse. He turned his head and started to kiss her.

Maybe it was her anger that set her breathing back in motion, but it came back as quickly as it left, and just in time for her to bite his lip, breaking his hold.

Ursula scrambled to her feet. "Get up," she shrieked, and before she realized how inconsiderate that was, Ethan was on his feet, too, swearing loudly.

At least she hadn't screamed like she had yesterday. The last thing she wanted was the tavern owner at her door again.

"God's teeth, woman," he spewed, looking at her incredulously. "I shall leave you here and retrieve the faerie items myself if this is how I'll be greeted upon waking," he grumbled, rubbing his eyes.

Ursula sucked in a breath. Ethan was naked.

"If this is how I shall be treated upon waking, then I shall leave you here and retrieve the faerie items myself," she mimicked, tamping down a snicker and eyeing him.

It took him a moment to realize what was up. Then he shrugged and met her gaze with a devilish grin. And with quick movements, he yanked the blanket off the bed to cover himself and his reaction.

The potion is still working.

He cleared his throat. "Some privacy."

Ursula spun around to face away. "So modest," she declared, but she appreciated the courtesy. Without the potion, she might have had to fight him off to protect herself.

Thankfully, Ethan had been a gentleman last night, or at least she had no memory otherwise.

He'd sacrificed his own comfort for hers?

A few minutes passed while she waited, until she remembered why she should not be waiting so patiently. "The boat," she shrieked. "We missed it."

Expecting a panicked reaction from Ethan, she was surprised he chuckled instead.

"No alarm necessary," he said. "You can turn around now."

When she complied, she found him looking dapper in his traveling clothes and cape, sword secured in its scabbard at his waist.

"*Och!* We have missed the *Merry Maiden's* sailing. The bells tolled eight."

"No, the ship sails at ten. If you'd followed me to the harbor rather than dining in the tavern, you'd have found out about the delay."

While her mouth remained agape, he filled the silence. "You are welcome." Then he bowed. "I shall meet you at the stables shortly."

And without another word, he was gone.

She shook her head in disbelief. *Damn, her concoction was working wonders.*

So instead of needing to make another batch of it, Ursula set about tiding up the room before she thanked the tavern owner.

When she met Ethan by the stables, he had her palfrey ready and even offered a boost into her saddle.

She agreed in spite of herself, and in no time, they were riding their horses through the cobblestone streets of Petershead.

Ursula had spent time in portside villages before, but this one was more charming than most, with cheery, modest-sized thatched roof cottages and window boxes filled with bright flowers. The dew on the patches of green between homesteads looked like rows of glistening emeralds.

After Ursula and Ethan reached the hilltop at the village's center, she had a good view of the port. Flat, clear blue water stretched as far as she could see. Her heart skipped a beat for a moment, though, when she thought the harbor was empty, until she finally spotted the *Merry Maiden.*

A three-masted ship with lateen sails floated on the eastern edge of the calm waters. Even from this distance, she could spot the riggers tightening ropes and the boat testing its anchor.

Ethan said they had plenty of time, but she was anxious to board. She'd been fidgety in her saddle most of the ride, Ursula was pleased they'd made their way efficiently down the winding path, and once at the wharf, they handed their horses over to the crew. In no time, Ursula was on deck talking with the captain.

"Yer to be bunking in my cabin," Rosalyn's uncle said after introductions were made. "It be above board rather than below."

Ursula gave Captain Quinn a concerned glare.

"Without me in it, lass," he amended.

Ursula curtsied. She often traveled in the company of men, but as long as there were boundaries, she rarely worried about the accommodations.

"'Tis good for a captain to sleep with his mates from time to time," Quinn admitted, then made a grand gesture, sweeping his arm across the deck before them. "My *Merry Maiden* is a fine gal, and she's not had any lady friends to visit. I'm sure if she could talk, she'd insist you have my cabin."

"I cannae turn down your offer," Ursula said with another curtsy. "'Twould be disrespectful of me."

"Good, 'tis settled," Quinn said. Then he grinned. For a moment, his smile blinded Ursula, the sun's rays gleaming off his front gold teeth until he spoke again.

"Best you take your meals in yer cabin as well. The talk amongst the men will nae be for a lady's ears."

"No reason to sidestep around me, captain. I do nae want to feel like a prisoner." But when he frowned, she added, "I mean no disrespect."

"See for ye self, lass," Quinn said. "And ye will fend for ye self, too. The men get to grabbing."

When her eyes opened wide, he added, "For the food."

Ursula laughed.

"Captain! Captain! We have a request for permission to come aboard. Chap says he needs a passage to Inverness."

Quinn strode to the starboard side and peered over, no

doubt getting a good look at the chap. After the newcomer apparently passed inspection, Quinn waved him aboard.

More like a giant, the new passenger strode across the deck. He moved with a bit of a limp, but that did not diminish his grandeur. When he reached the group, the voyager stopped across from Ursula. With his massive hands at his waist, the man reminded her of one of the sturdy masts rising behind him.

Unmistakably a Highlander, sporting a gold-and-black tartan kilt and sporran. The massive black bear fur covered a beaten mustard-colored leather vest, but it was the face of a warrior that told his story. His highbrow, chiseled jaw, dark-hazel eyes, and burnished red hair to his shoulders made him appear as wild as she imagined he'd be.

"Alasdair," he offered. "Alasdair MacLeod."

"MacLeod of Dunvegan?" Rosalyn's uncle asked as Ursula swallowed hard, remembering the Highlander.

She blushed and curtsied.

Alasdair bowed but kept looking at her, sporting a wry grin.

She welcomed an immediate distraction from the crew as they dragged the gangplank aboard and weighed anchor. She imagined once they were underway, the men would want her off the deck.

Ursula blushed after she realized she and Alasdair were still staring at each other while the captain began his story of the ship's history.

"She's as nimble to steer as a warhorse. Built for cruising close to the shore and close to the wind. My *Merry Maiden* can outrun any square-rigger," Quinn boasted like a proud father. He grinned as he swept his arm above his head in a flourish. "She's Portuguese, but that does nae bother an old Scotsman like me."

Ursula twittered while the giant studied her even more. Glancing his way periodically under her lashes, she was surprised by the boldness of his ogling. She should have been appalled, but it thrilled her instead.

Nay, having Alasdair MacLeod aboard was a fortunate coincidence, although Ursula never believed in coincidences. Ethan had said the Faery Flag had been given to a MacLeod, the fourth laird of Dunvegan. Alasdair was a decedent. No doubt he could speak on the matter.

When they'd met at Fyvie just three days ago, their time spent together was much like this, bowing and curtsying. After Ethan had rudely abandoned Ursula, Lachlan had rescued her. But he'd whisked the Highlander off to a secret meeting. It would have been odd for her to ask Lachlan about the Highlander, so she hadn't.

Fortune smiled on her now. Alasdair MacLeod could be the key to getting everything she needed on Skye Isle. Now, if only she could convince him to help her.

"What is a lass like you doing aboard a ship full of cussing sailors bearing for the Highlands?" Alasdair asked.

The question startled Ursula out of her musing. She found him standing beside her.

Ursula remained silent as she struggled to come up with a plausible answer for the provocative Scotsman.

"Reuniting with my family in Kyle of Lochalsh," Ethan interjected.

"Yer family and mine would be near neighbors," Alasdair said. He studied Ethan. "You do nae look like a MacKenzie, but you do look familiar." He sounded suspicious as he eyed Ethan up and down.

Ursula cut Ethan off before he could answer. "You may remember us from Fyvie Castle where you delivered a missive to Ethan's brother. We are newly married, and 'tis my family we be visiting, Clan Fraser."

Alasdair's face brightened, and he flashed her a dazzling smile. "Well now, lass, that be a might better, for there's been much fighting over the tidal home of the MacKenzies.

'Twould be a bit dangerous for a lass to visit Eilean Donan Castle until the ownership is settled." Then he paused and shifted his weight. "'Tis at least how 'twas when I passed through Kyle of Lochalsh on my way to Inverlochy a fortnight ago."

Ethan moved to Ursula's side and placed a possessive arm around her waist. "She willnae be in danger, sir. I protect what is mine."

Ursula raised a brow at Ethan's attempt to sound Scottish. *God help him.* But at the same time, she realized the implications of her actions. Although Ethan was still under her potion's influence, he might consider taking liberties as they posed as husband and wife. Even though he'd left her alone last night, the morning tussle on the floor left her uncertain.

Now she regretted resorting to the same excuse Ethan had used with the tavern owner. Perhaps the clan leader would assume their marriage was one of title convenience like most. She wished instead she'd told the Highlander she was Ethan's sister.

Rosalyn's uncle broke the awkward silence. "'Tis customary on my ship to toast to the voyage. To my cabin." He pointed to the back of the ship and a set of stairs leading to the upper deck beyond the masts.

Ursula slid out from under Ethan's arm as he turned toward the stern of the boat. While he and the others followed the captain, Alasdair stood transfixed in his spot as did Ursula.

The Highlander took her hand, then bowed low. "Are you in need of assistance, mi lady?"

She swallowed her gasp. *The first words he'd said to me on the parapet at Fyvie.* Her stomach did a flip-flop.

"Ursula!"

Ethan's shrill yell broke whatever spell had been cast, and the Highlander released her hand. With an apologetic grin, Ursula curtsied one more time, then rushed to catch up with Ethan.

When she reached the captain's quarters, she glanced back, expecting Alasdair to have followed, but he was nowhere to be seen. The main deck was empty. She shrugged, perhaps he'd seen this all before.

Quinn led them into the well-appointed cabin. Never having set foot in a captain's quarters before, Ursula was intrigued by the maps and navigational instruments on the massive table in the center. Curious, she walked over to examine the navigational tools and was dazzled by the inked markings on the map outlining the northern coast.

While the men gathered by the bar and poured generous servings of amber liquid into weighty pewter mugs, Ursula studied the arrow markings. She assumed they represented either wind patterns or ocean currents.

Glancing briefly at Ethan when he called her name, Ursula waved off the offer of a morning ale. Instead, she went back to studying the parchment before her, intrigued by a map of her homeland.

Tracing a finger along the northern coast, Ursula drew along the path of the shore to the village of Inverness. Fascinated by the distance they would cover in half the time than by horse, Ursula decided Alasdair would likely be traveling with them all the way through to Inverlochy. She immediately hatched a plan.

Chapter 11

The moon shone brightly on the placid ocean water as the *Merry Maiden* snuck through the darkness and cut through the waves like a silent thief. A gentle rocking motion and a soft breeze made Ethan's eyelids heavy. He was ready for sleep.

But Ursula had shut him out of the cabin with threats of dismembering his manhood. She had made it clear he wouldn't be sharing the captain's quarters with her. So he'd slammed the door and descended a short flight of stairs to the wardroom.

Quinn did not appear a bit surprised when Ethan joined him. Some of the crew had gathered in the cramped quarters, too. They sat drinking and laughing at tables made from storage barrels.

"Marriage troubles?"

Ethan grunted.

The captain doubled over with laughter, and when he regained his composure, Quinn recruited a young lad to bring a tray of tankards to the table.

Ethan took one for himself and opened its lid. The boy filled it to the brim.

After a few long swigs of the ale, Ethan's anger diminished, and he relaxed a bit.

"She's a witch, you know."

Quinn cocked his head to one side. "She does nae look like a witch."

"Looks can be deceiving."

"Does she turn into a hag after the sun goes down?" Quinn asked. "Is that why you are here with me rather than in her bed?"

It was Ethan's turn to laugh.

"Hag, no. Nag, yes," Ethan told the captain after he'd caught his breath.

Quinn slapped his leg. "All women are nags, Ethan. That's why I'm married to the *Merry Maiden* here. We coexist peacefully in our ocean home. I tell her what to do, and she does nae talk back."

Quinn was an amiable man. Ethan admired that kind of logic. "Well, you are lucky to have such a lovely lady in your life," Ethan said. "Have you two been together long?"

"We met about five years ago when a Portuguese captain was down on his luck," Quinn said. "He'd sailed her into Aberdeen's port with just a two-man crew."

Quinn shrugged his shoulders. "How they managed the fourteen sails, I do nae know." He took a long swig of his ale, then leaned forward so only Ethan could hear.

"But I happened to be on the pier when he threw anchor, and I helped ease her into the wharf," Quinn said. "Once the gangplank was in place, the captain raced down the wooden ramp and kissed the ground. The two crew members scurried down moments after."

Quinn stopped, and after a quick glance around the table, he leaned in even farther.

"The two crewmen took to running," Quinn said. "Their legs pumping as fast as they could, they flew from the wharf as if something . . . or someone was chasing them."

As Quinn took another swig of ale, Ethan wondered whether the captain was spinning a yarn to take his mind off of Ursula or confiding in him about female troubles of his own. The captain's words drew Ethan in.

When Quinn looked around the table again, Ethan leaned closer.

"A strange sight to be seen I tell you," Quinn said. "I helped the captain up, who was as white as a ghost, and I offered my assistance.

"With eyes full of fear, he told me he needed a buyer for his ship immediately.

"Well, Big Douglas had just died, and I was helping Rosalyn and her mother with the wool trade. A new ship seemed like a good idea, until he told me a woman came with it."

Ethan laughed. "Sounds like an awkward marriage proposal if you ask me."

"I thought the same and asked the captain to explain," Quinn said. "The man shook his head as if he couldn't, then told me, 'I'm asking but twenty pounds for her.' I assumed he was speaking of the ship, not the woman."

"Twenty pounds would be the price of a horse, not a ship," Ethan said. "I'm assuming that's why you're now her captain."

"Aye, that price for the ship was worth any entanglement with a female that would come along with it," Quinn said. "So I shook hands on the offer right then and there.

"The captain promised to meet me at the harbor the next day, and we'd settle the deal. I agreed, half expecting he wouldnae show up or would quadruple the price.

"But the next day, there he was, and he took me aboard," Quinn said. He made a large sweeping gesture in the wardroom and added, "There was nae a thing amiss. No damage from storm or raid. All the below board spaces pristine. Just as you've seen above board."

Ethan was intrigued. "The woman? Did you finally meet her on the ship?"

Quinn shook his head. "That's the thing. When I asked him about the woman that came with the purchase, he said I'd meet her in good time." As he said it, his gaze was hollow and distant."

"Now that sounds like a fine deal, a woman with a purchase," someone said. "Where'd you be doing that kind of trading?"

Alasdair?

Ethan spun around. It *was* the clan leader. Unbeknownst to him, the sturdy Scot had found a seat on a nearby barrel. When Quinn turned, he looked just as surprised to have the giant's company.

"The east coast of Scotland has an extensive and unconventional trading history. Verra different from your western Highland isle," Quinn said affably. "Have you ever bartered for a woman?"

Alasdair had a likeable laugh, and Ethan couldn't help but join him. Although their cozy conversation had been interrupted, Ethan was more interested in using the clan leader as a resource to learn about the current state of Eilean Donan. The rest of Quinn's distracting yarn could wait.

"On Skye Isle we do nae barter for women. We respect them," Alasdair said. "Yet, I can admit more than a few of our womenfolk prefer to live alone and fend for themselves. We are a mix of Scot and Viking blood, and our women are more Valkyrie than lassie."

Quinn seemed amused by that and said, "Aye, I have met some of yer clan's women in my travels, and they're more intimidating than your men."

Alasdair chuckled, seemingly not offended by Quinn's comment.

Ethan hesitated before he spoke. Even though he was half-Scot, he'd assumed he'd make a better impression on the Highlander by keeping his English roots to himself. Englishmen were barely tolerated in the Highlands, and Ethan had personal proof of that.

"My mother, Colleen MacKenzie, was an elegant lady, but her sister, Bonnie, could have led an army. Aye, she could have," Ethan said.

Alasdair nodded as if he could make a comparable claim. He grabbed a tankard from the young lad's tray and said, "The MacLeods and MacKenzies are nae allies or rivals. But one thing is for certain, we both despise Clan MacDonald."

Alasdair opened his tankard and drained it while Ethan admired the Scot's thirst.

"Ye said there was some unrest in Kintail," Ethan said. "At Eilean Donan?"

The Scot peered at Ethan over his empty tankard before he set it down with a thud and signaled the lad for another round.

"My new wife is Clan Fraser, and this will be her first visit to the castle," Ethan said. "My mother died over twenty years ago, and my family has had their challenges."

"That be as much as saying a woman who is ugly is almost pretty. Let's call a sheep a sheep," Alasdair said politely.

"Or the ugly woman a sheep?" Quinn piped in as the boy appeared with a jug. Holding it tightly with both hands, the lad poured more golden liquid into Quinn's tankard. Then he moved to Alasdair and did the same, distracting the clan leader for a moment until he had another tankard full of ale.

Ethan waved the boy off as he said, "I'm not a sheep farmer, but I know a sheep when I see one."

The muscles in Alasdair's face relaxed into a grin. "If we be using sheep farming as an analogy for your family's circumstance, I'd say the gates have been open far too long and most of your loyal flock have strayed."

That was the friendliest way Ethan could have been told he'd have his hands full when he arrived. "Well, sir, I appreciate your candor."

Alasdair's cheeks reddened. "In my estimation, you could be walking into a massacre. I could nae let that rest on my conscience, especially after meeting your lovely new wife."

Ethan's ire rose. Clearly, Ursula had made an impression on him as she did all men. They'd have to be dead otherwise. And this barbarian was calling Ethan's attempt to visit his clan's home a mistake only an idiot would make.

"Come with me to Dunvegan, and we'll assemble my warriors. Then we'll march on to Eilean Donan. The MacLeods have no quarrel with MacKenzies, but if we find a MacDonald at the seat, then we shall have a score to settle," Alasdair promised.

The Highlander rose, no doubt ready to bunk down for the night, but added as he turned to go, "Killing a few rival clansmen will give keep my warriors' battle skills sharp for when I must defend my home, and 'twill send the message . . . *na cuir stad air mo thir.*"

Ethan nodded as if he understood the Gaelic. He was pleased they could agree on something besides lusting after Ursula.

Chapter 12

It was easy to eavesdrop on the conversation, and Ursula did not feel guilty one bit. The captain's cabin was above the wardroom, and Ursula had put an ear to the floor when she'd recognized Ethan's voice last night.

Now as Ursula dressed and prepared for her breakfast to arrive, she pondered Alasdair's initial concern for her welfare. She had taken a keen interest in the Scot. There was something a bit dangerous about him, but approachable at the same time, like a Scottish deerhound. They were a breed of fierce protectors, but docile toward their masters.

The *Merry Maiden* was docked, and Ursula had observed the early morning activities from the captain's window overlooking Lossiemouth.

Rosalyn's uncle and several of his crew had loaded the ship with what looked like huge bales of raw wool, no doubt brought in from the countryside by the farmers nearby.

This was part of Rosalyn's world. Her Uncles Quinn and Angus collected the finest Scottish wool from the rural parts of Scotland, then brought it back to Aberdeen to be woven into goods or shipped to France for production. No doubt her sister of the heart had become easily accustomed to sailing.

They'd travel close to the shore. Still it unnerved Ursula to be out in the ocean. She had heard tales of her Viking cousins who had ruled the Orkney Islands and later the Highlands. They were a people who were more at home on the North Sea than on their own land of Norway.

Ursula decided she could not be of Viking bone and blood as she rubbed the back of her neck, sore from the lack of a pillow. Rosalyn had teased Ursula before she had left, claiming she had become too comfortable at Fyvie. After last night, she'd agreed.

But Ursula hadn't stayed awake fretting over cruising the ocean. She'd been awoken by a . . . by something.

By a ghost?

For a healer and seer, visions were commonplace. Witnessing ethereal shapes and unusual sounds or the presence of otherworld energy were all natural experiences for her. But last night had been different. No doubt if she tried to explain it, she'd be laughed at by Quinn, Ethan, and even Alasdair.

She was still gazing out the window when the cabin door slammed shut.

Ursula screamed, almost falling off the bed in her rush to turn around. "*Och!* Captain Quinn!" She scrambled to her feet. "'Tis only you."

"Aye, and a fine breakfast almost dropped when you attacked me with your screeching. I would have expected more of that last night when Molly made her rounds."

"Molly?"

He set the tray full of cooked eggs, scones, jam, and cream on the empty navigation table, then crossed his hands over the center of his chest. "You near made my heart stop. I thought I was dead in my tracks."

Ursula walked to meet him at the table, smiling. She could not help it with Quinn looking so serious. Stomach growling, Ursula grabbed a scone and slathered it with butter and cream.

"Does Molly have long, wavy, strawberry-blond hair and green eyes?" Ursula asked, bringing the captain back to his earlier comment about last night.

"Ye met her then. Aye, my bonny bride."

"Captain, you said you were married to the *Merry*

Maiden." She shoved a chunk of the delicate treat into her mouth, mumbling at the same time, "This is delicious."

"Not made by my crew, mind you. The eggs, aye," Quinn admitted when her eyes grew wide. "The scones were from a bakery cart on the wharf."

She curtsied.

"I promised Rosalyn I'd take care of you."

Ursula blushed. "Aye, you have. Let me sleep in your bed, kept Ethan at bay, and served up cream and jam with scones fresh out of the oven. But you did nae warn me about Molly." She waved a scolding finger at him before she finished off the first of the fruit scones.

"Aye, Molly. She's as much my wife as the *Maiden*," Quinn said. He paused and searched for the right words. "She came with the ship, you might say."

Ursula cocked her head to one side. "You might say?"

Quinn grinned. "I was telling Ethan the story last night, but I had nae got to the best part because of Alasdair."

"What did Alasdair do?"

"Nothing other than interrupt the story before I got to Molly. I wonder if Molly got to Ethan?" He chuckled. "She usually leaves the women alone."

"But I am a witch."

"You do nae look like one, and I daresay you'll nae want to be admitting that around my men. Molly's enough, and she's promised to leave the crew alone and only visit the guests."

"Well, that's quite hospitable of her," Ursula snickered.

"Now, you must know what I mean," Quinn said. "When I purchased the ship from the previous owner, the man near gave the *Merry Maiden* away. What was left of the crew, the last of 'em, abandoned him once he'd reached Aberdeen. None of the local seamen would hire on, and her captain had no means to return home to Portugal with his ship." He paused. "I made a deal with her."

"You made a deal with a ghost?" Ursula mumbled through another bite of scone, jam, and cream.

"One might call it an arrangement," Quinn said. "My granny was a witch, too."

Ursula came around the table to give him a hug. He'd been kind to give her his bed and a fine breakfast. Quinn's comment about his granny being a witch also gave her proof that Rosalyn may have acquired *sight* abilities through inheritance, and the pregnancy had heightened them.

"Molly is nae so bad. I just wish you had warned me first," Ursula said. "I could've used some herbs to make her presence less frightening."

"She is frightening," Quinn said, eyes wide. "Mayhap she is jealous of you?"

He raised a knee and slapped it. "Aye, that is the problem. I had another beautiful woman who'd bunked in my cabin two years back who demanded we let her off the ship when we docked after the first night." He scratched his beard. "I had forgotten about that."

Now that Quinn was talkative, and had spent time with Alasdair last night, perhaps she could learn more about the Highland chief of Dunvegan and steer away from the ghost.

"You were saying Alasdair interrupted your time with Ethan yester eve. Was he angry about something?"

Quinn appeared surprised by her question. "Why do ye think Alasdair was angry?"

"Aren't all Highlanders angry?"

She hadn't thought her question funny, but her response sent Rosalyn's uncle into fits of laughter as he slapped his leg again. The chuckles finally subsided to snickers, then he took in a deep breath before answering her. "Aye, Ursula, Highlanders are angry much of the time, I'll give you that, but Alasdair is quite charming for a clan chief."

Charming? Alasdair had been charming in her company thus far. But she doubted he would be so when he led his soldiers. It was his quiet demeanor that had her unsettled. She would have a difficult time asking the clan chief questions directly. "If he was nae angry, what was he doing interrupting you?"

Quinn looked at her quizzically for a moment, but finally it appeared he understood her question. "Bad choice of words on my part," he said. "He was being . . . what you call . . ." He struggled for the word.

"Sociable," Ursula suggested.

Quinn hemmed and hawed, then said, "'Tis close enough."

They stared at each other through a long silence.

"Scone?" Ursula offered when he turned to leave.

Quinn eyed the fluffy half scone smothered in sweet toppings in her outstretched hand. "Looks delicious," he said.

"I would nae tell your men you partook in a bite of breakfast with me," Ursula said. "You, being the gracious host, should enjoy more than just your galley's fixings."

He quickly snatched the sweet from her hand, and while he took generous bites, she queried him further.

"Do nae be telling Alasdair I'd be asking about him, but do you know that he's offered to escort Ethan and me to Dunvegan, then have us march with his warriors to Eilean Donan?"

Quinn's mouth was full, so he acknowledged her question with a nod of his head.

"I'm interested in knowing more about him before I leave the protection of your ship and travel with a man who purportedly could be dangerous." She leveled her gaze. "Do you know him well?"

Quinn swallowed the last of the treat and licked his fingers before saying, "Nay, I've ne'er set eyes on the man before he walked aboard the gangplank yesterday."

"Of course, you understand my concern," Ursula said as she walked around to the other side of the navigation table. "Although I was born on the fringe of the Highlands, I've been on my own since I was six and ten, spending my time working as a healer for the royals in Berwick upon Tweed and the eastern coast of Scotland," she added.

Ursula faced Quinn from across the table. "What I know of the Highlanders may be more myth and legend. You have traveled with them, eaten with them . . ."

"Slept with them aboard my ship," Quinn said, finishing her sentence. "Aye, I have had much experience even though I grew up on the eastern coast in Aberdeenshire. This Highlander, though, appears to be approachable and amiable. He asked us to call him, *Crotach*."

She paused as she attempted to translate the Gaelic. "Humpbacked?"

"Did ye nae get a good look at him, lass?"

Ursula blinked hard a few times and pursed her lips.

When was she not observant? "Was he disfigured?" she asked.

Quinn looked at her sympathetically. "You didnae see he was hunched over and limping?"

She shook her head. Ursula could only remember him standing on the deck of the ship as the sea winds swept back his shoulder-length, burnish-red hair to reveal a noble face. His broad, handsome forehead accentuated his deep-set, dark-hazel eyes.

Perhaps she was smitten.

And his gaze. She remembered it roaming over her as if she'd been gently groped with her permission. His demeanor, unshakable and perceptive.

Humpbacked? Limping? Not Alasdair MacLeod.

"My guess," Quinn proposed, "is he wanted to get the story out before others asked. About his physical appearance, that is."

When she gave him a quizzical look, he addressed it. "He's a bit crooked. Can nae stand up straight."

That made Ursula reflect again. "I've looked up at him from below. No doubt I would have seen the condition if I were your height," she said, not wanting Quinn to think she was daft.

He scratched his beard again as he carefully chose his next words. And she was not surprised when she heard them.

"You may be smitten with the man, I'd be supposing."

"Bite your tongue," Ursula said. "I'm a married woman," she sputtered when he snickered.

"I am . . . pretending to be a married woman," she amended.

"Does nae changed the way you look at him."

She was aghast, perturbed, and shocked—because it was true. She raised a finger as if to object with another reason, one she searched for but could not find.

Quinn shook his head at her as if she'd be a fool to deny it.

She turned her back on him, embarrassed. But as she searched her heart, she was certain. She had settled on Joshua. Gentle, kind, Joshua. And she had settled on thinking if she changed Ethan . . . No, she could never live a lie. Only be distracted by one. Sad but true, a seer could never see herself. She saw only for others.

Coming out of her musing, Ursula spun back around to find Quinn eating the last of her scones.

Now it was his turn to be embarrassed. After choking down the last morsel, he said, "The Highlander seems to be a man of his word. Call it merchant's intuition, but I believe his story."

Finally, Ursula was closer to her goal. "Captain Quinn, surely you have a ship to attend to, but seeing as you've eaten half my breakfast, please give me a morsel of his story to feed my curiosity," she said with her hands clasped together. She was not too proud to beg.

Quinn nodded sheepishly, plopping down on a stool by her cooked eggs and picking up her fork. She joined him on the other side. Between bites of her eggs, he began to tell her Crotach's story.

Chapter 13

The captain had replaced the breakfast tray with a map of Skye Isle, and he'd added miniature ships on the navigation table. When a commotion outside the cabin door disturbed his demonstration, he glanced up but waved off Ursula's concerned look.

"As captain, I hire a crew to do the work. If I'm needed, they can find me." He shrugged his shoulders. "Right now, I'm not needed."

Apparently pleased with the explanation, Quinn got back to the map and pointed to the western coast of Skye Isle.

"Dunvegan is the home of Clan MacLeod. The castle can only be approached by a sea gate from the loch. 'Twas a Norse fortress first."

He looked up from the map, as if expecting her question before she had formed it.

"Aye, he's of Norse blood," Quinn said. "Captains have a way of getting information from their passengers."

Ursula shivered. The stories her mother had told her about the Vikings had put fear of them in her heart.

"Last night, Crotach explained how the bloody battle came about," Quinn said. "He told me it was three summers past, at a time when John MacDonald was chieftain of Clan MacDonald, Lord of the Isles, and had a secret treaty with the king of England." He paused and squinted at Ursula with one eye. "This piece of history I can confirm as true."

"That could not have boded well with the king of Scotland," Ursula said.

"Nay, it did not, and John was ejected from the clan when our Scottish king found out. But John fought back," Quinn said. "Fought back against his own son, Angus, who had forced him from his home and taken over leadership of the clan.

"Then Alasdair's father and his clan joined forces with John MacDonald. They supported his leadership and wanted him reinstated," Quinn said.

When Ursula yawned inadvertently, he shot her a frustrated glance, but she waved him on apologetically.

Quinn appeared perturbed by her gesture, but also anxious to tell the story. "Alasdair was brutally attacked with an axe to the shoulder in his support for John, before the battle called Bloody Bay."

Quinn placed the miniature boats in two opposing lines near the coast of Mull. "A few months later, the MacDonalds and the MacLeods gathered in the bay near Tobermory." He pointed to it on the map.

"Did Alasdair speak of the Faery Flag? Was it unfurled in the battle?" Ursula asked. She didn't want a history lesson. Although she did pick up on some of their conversation last night, most of it had been drowned out by the wind when the sails flapped and the masts groaned.

Quinn glanced up from the navigation table with a pout, like a lad who'd been told it was time for bed. He grumbled under his breath while he moved his miniature ships aside and rolled up his map. "'Tis what you wanted to know all along, I imagine?"

"Nay, all of what you have said has been helpful." She kept her eyebrows raised, hoping she had asked the question as directly as she could.

"Aye, he did speak of the flag. But he did in such a way I would say 'twas more lore than not."

"Tell me anyway," she pleaded.

"Who would validate a Faery Flag unless you spoke to a faerie?" Quinn asked, his lip and face twisting up. "I was telling you about concrete history. Do nae tell me you have nae heard the story of the Faery Flag?"

"There are many," Ursula said, exasperated. Perhaps she should just ask Alasdair herself.

"Perhaps you should ask Alasdair yourself."

She sighed. "I will nae be asking Alasdair any such thing." The idea of even talking directly to him made her stomach flip. "The important parts. The magical parts. The unfurling," she prompted.

Quinn appeared as though he'd had enough. The food was gone, and so was his patience. He scooted back on his stool, preparing to rise, but she stopped him.

"Please stay," Ursula begged. "You have been so kind to me, and I appreciate everything you've told me. What I want to know is how it was used in battle." If she brought it all back to the bloody battle, he'd stay.

And he did, telling her the flag had been left by the Faery Queen. And Alasdair confirmed what Quinn had heard. The flag could be an aid in battle, multiplying or rallying the troops, even aiding in the outcome. But the flag could only be unfurled three times, or it would become useless or vanish.

Of course, she had to ask. "How many times has the flag been unfurled?"

"Did you nae hear me, lass?"

Her cheeks heated. "I promise I've been listening."

Quinn smiled kindly at her and went on, even if he was repeating himself. "Only once. After Alasdair's father was killed by a MacDonald. But by then, even though the flag was given credit for making some of the MacDonald clan supporters switch sides, the outcome of the battle had already been determined, and they were all on the losing side."

"Only once," she muttered to herself.

Quinn snorted. "Ye nae be thinking of asking for the Faery Flag?"

Ursula's eyes glowed. "Nay, I would nae dare ask for such a thing," she told the captain, knowing full well she didn't mean a word of it.

~ ~ ~

Alasdair was up early and in the wardroom for breakfast with most of the crew. He'd not slept much at all because of a strange disturbance. A disfigured woman had appeared and floated over his bed. She seemed to have no arms, as her long flowing sleeves had hung dormant from her shoulders. Her grotesqueness hadn't bothered him, nor the fact she was a ghost, but her incessant moaning had kept him from sleep.

After polishing off a pint of stale ale, Alasdair decided it was time to see the captain about important business.

He made his way the short distance to the cabin, then knocked on the captain's door. When the beautiful Scottish lass opened it instead, he lost his words. But she did not.

"Och! dè tha thu a 'dèanamh an seo? Chan eil seo iomchaidh!"

Her Gaelic is beautiful, too.

He cleared his throat and retreated a few steps backward, then bowed. "I beg your pardon, my lady, Titania." After a few beats, he looked up, still bowed with his arm across his chest. "May I rise?"

She softened her glare. "Aye."

As he complied, he told her, "You must forgive me, for I expected the captain behind the door, nae a faerie." She did remind him of the legend, her appearance strikingly similar to the artwork he'd seen of Titania.

Ursula blushed, and her words were softer. "Good sir, you flatter me," she said as she curtsied, "the captain was gracious enough to insist I take his cabin for the voyage. For privacy."

"Your husband is lucky on many accounts." He leaned forward and glanced behind her into the cabin. "May I have a word with him as well?"

"My . . . my husband?" she stammered.

"I was introduced to one yesterday . . ."

"Oh, him." She appeared confused and embarrassed.

"If I have come at an inappropriate time, I apologize again." Alasdair began to turn away, but to his surprise, she grabbed onto his sleeve.

"Come in," she offered apologetically, "but keep the door open, so no one thinks ill of it."

Ursula ushered him into the cramped cabin. Expecting it to smell of leather and sea salt, he was surprised to find the aroma of a spring garden. She looked out of place in the masculine cabin with its dark shiplap walls and brass instruments. A delicate flower amongst bracken.

Ursula gestured for Alasdair to take a seat at the navigation table and blinked nervously before she spoke. "You mentioned the name, Titania. Who is she?"

Alasdair had almost forgotten he'd spoken the name. "I will tell you," he said, "but first I must understand why your husband is not here guarding you."

She almost spat. "Alasdair MacLeod, I need no man to guard me." Her eyes flashed. "This you should know first and always remember."

He grunted, and his nostrils flared slightly. What had begun as a hunt for the captain had turned into his capture and an inquisition by a faerie-like lass. A damn distracting one.

Where was her husband?

While he sat in silence, sizing her up, her demeanor softened. "Excuse my outburst," she said as she cast her gaze downward. "I have been on my own for a verra long time."

Clearly Ursula was not going to address the comment

about her husband or the lack of chaperone in the room, but as she'd said, the door was open.

She wants to know about Titania?

Alasdair pondered which answer to give her, but he was certain he'd not be bullied by a wisp of a woman even if she was enchanting. He'd offered to take her and Ethan to Dunvegan, his home, then rally his troops to escort them to Eilean Donan. He needed to know more about her.

"You're of Clan Fraser? Who was your father?"

She hesitated until his intense stare forced her answer. "I do not know," she said, appearing to answer honestly. Rising, she began to pace. "I was ten and six when I was sent to Berwick upon Tweed as a healer to the royals."

"A comfortable royal bed? Why journey to the Highlands if you do nae have a family to call yer own?"

She bristled but did not lash out as before. "For Ethan. He wants to reclaim Eilean Donan."

"So what he said on the deck yesterday was a lie. You do not want to reunite with your family?"

"My family is what I make it. Who I include and who I do nae. Simple as that."

Her honesty made Alasdair laugh and in so doing broke the tension that filled the room.

"Wise words from a wise lass," he said, then added, "Although I am clan loyal through and through, my family has been both friend and foe. My brother's ambition broke my father's heart." After Alasdair made the admission, he was embarrassed to have confessed it, but he added, "They're both dead now."

She paused, reflecting what he said but did not ask for explanation. Instead she offered her own apologue, "Our ambitions can be grounded in good or selfishness," she told him. "I've ne'er wanted land. It appears to be the bale of all evil and dissention."

"That and love . . ." Alasdair stopped before he revealed too much. Here he was trying to find out more about this vexing, black-haired beauty, and instead he was baring his soul to her.

Had this faerie woman put a spell on him?

Ursula ignored his last statement and took a seat across from him at the navigation table. "Tell me about the Faery Flag."

She asked him with such directness he was taken aback. The last time he'd been queried in such away, he'd been in a court on an issue of border property with the MacDonalds.

After Alasdair got over the initial shock and could no longer endure her direct impatience for information, it was his turn to rise and pace.

She could have the lore.

"Titania and the Faery Flag are oft named in the same sentence," he said. "So you are a clever lass to ask about both." He turned and smiled at her. "How do I know you are worthy of such secrets?"

"I'm nae a faerie, but I can understand them," Ursula said. "My sister of the heart is in dire need of a flower that only grows near Glenbrittle on Skye." She clenched her hands together on the table in a prayer-like manner. "She could die if I don't bring back the flower."

Alasdair had forgotten her name. "What do they call you?"

"Witch," she confessed without flinching.

He put his hand on his left side, just under his arm, where it always felt as if daggers were piercing his skin. Alasdair held his side as he laughed out loud at her admission.

He shook his head. "Nay, your birth given name."

Her shoulders relaxed. "Ursula."

"Aye, that's it," he said, and she raised a brow. "Ur-su-la." He said the name slowly, wishing he could unlock all her secrets by doing so. *Was this the name whispered in his dreams?* He'd ne'er known an Ursula.

With the taste of her name still on his lips, he gazed at the beauty as she sat perched on her stool, leaning on the table with piqued interest. Now he knew Ursula had another reason to travel to Skye.

He took a seat across from her again, his side still aching, a constant reminder of his battle scar.

"I know the faerie pools at Glenbrittle, near the Cuillin hills. 'Tis a place no mortal can walk," he said. When she appeared to protest, he cut her off. "However, we've been in need of the faeries help at Dunvegan, and we've been blessed by the wee folk." He gave her a wink. "Most mortals cannae walk the glen, but perhaps a Fraser witch can."

"Aye, good sir, I've walked that glen. I need only escort to the place on Skye Isle. I was just a young lass when I set foot there the first time with my mother." When his eyes went wide in disbelief, she added, "My mother was a witch, too. Burned at the stake in Edinburgh."

Faeries and witches, he was not sure where one began and the other ended. Most mystical folk on Skye Isle, where centuries of MacLeods had flourished, were revered as well as feared. But not by Alasdair. Titania was his great-great-great-grandmother. The prophecy she left said 'one of her kin would marry a Fae, one who would have no father to protest the union.' That would give Alasdair much to think upon in the coming days on the *Merry Maiden.*

Chapter 14

After Ethan had broken his fast, and while the *Merry Maiden* bobbed in the quiet waters next to the wharf, he roamed the pier while the wool was being loaded.

Walking toward the center of Lossiemouth, he found the sleepy village had one main street and one Protestant church at the center. Other than a few taverns, there was not much to crow about.

The *Merry Maiden* dwarfed the other vessels along the wharf. No doubt there were ships her size in and out of the port, but for now, the streets were empty except for a few eccentric hens.

That was why after Ethan returned to the gangplank and began his walk up, he was surprised when someone called out to him.

"What's her destination?"

Ethan spun around and found a regal man dressed in fine silks rushing up behind him on the plank. The man was very much out of breath, as if he'd run the whole length of the village to get to the ship.

"Inverness," Ethan replied, trying not to show his amusement. The regal man was sweating profusely and was almost as wide around as he was tall. Every one of his fingers was glorified by a gemstone ring.

"Hold the ship," he shrieked.

This time Ethan could not retain his laughter and let it go despite himself.

The uppity, titled man huffed. Then in an effeminate way, he lifted a lace kerchief from inside his vest, blotting his forehead. "Sir, this is not a laughing matter, but one of life and death."

Ethan sobered. "My sincerest apologizes," he amended with a curt bow. "The ship is not scheduled to sail until the sun is high in the sky."

The man glanced over his shoulder, not toward the rising sun, but the other direction, as if he was expecting someone to meet him.

"Well, I don't care when it is scheduled to leave. It cannot leave until I say so."

"And who pray tell are you?" came the question from behind Ethan. He recognized the voice of the captain.

"And who pray tell are you?" the effeminate man asked in just as bold a voice, fanning himself with his kerchief.

"The one who makes decisions on when this ship sails or not," Quinn replied calmly.

Apparently, that was all the man needed to know before he rushed up to the captain and began to toss his kerchief about.

"Oh, captain," the pretentious man fussed. "My mother, well, she is the eldest cousin to King James the Third. And that makes me . . ."

A pompous arse, Ethan thought as the man began to recite his linage to the Scottish crown. Even before he finished listing his family's heritage, a procession began to snake from the center of town toward the wharf. It consisted of an ornate, curtained cabin, carried on crisscrossed posts by four guardians. An entourage of knights on horseback followed the raised cabin bearing the family's coat of arms.

"Here comes the princess! Finally!" the rotund man screeched.

Ethan caught Quinn's attention, and the captain rolled his eyes upward. No doubt he was praying to the Almighty for some assistance.

With the village as modest as it was, it didn't take long until the group came to a stop on the wharf before the gangplank and the knights set the carriage down.

No sooner had all but one stepped back at attention did the red velvet curtains part and a withered hand reach out for assistance.

When a white-haired woman emerged, wearing a shimmering, jeweled crown, Ethan's jaw dropped. Although he hadn't listened to the effeminate man's details, this woman could be royalty.

The captain coughed. "My ship is a merchant vessel," he said, shaking his head. "As much as I would like to help you, I cannot. I do nae have the proper accommodations for your mother," Quinn explained and patted the man on the shoulder, turning to go.

If Ethan had been the captain, he'd have hightailed it even before the procession had reached the wharf. Any man wearing hose, crisscross leggings, and smelling of perfume should be avoided. The crew had already found Ursula distracting and now this?

"No, sir, you cannot deny Princess Margret," the man told Quinn, finishing with a false smile. "You cannot deny royalty, or you shall lose your ship and"—he snickered and put his hand to the side of his mouth—"your head."

Quinn took a measured step backward, then with a quick bow, he said, "Your mother is welcome to my cabin. 'Tis the best I can offer."

The snooty man smiled his wooden smile again, apparently pleased with Quinn's change of heart.

This shift in accommodations would put Ursula out of the captain's quarters. He sighed with satisfaction. Now he might have a better chance of convincing her to sleep with him.

With that goal in mind, Ethan ascended the gangplank

and made his way to the cabin. When he reached the door, he was surprised to find it ajar.

Ethan's heart beat frantically as he withdrew his sword from its scabbard. Could one of the crew have compromised Ursula? He swore as he rushed into the room with his weapon at the ready.

It took a few moments for his eyes to adjust to the darkened room, but he heard Ursula's harsh words before he saw her.

"Ethan, put down your sword. 'Tis nae what you think."

What he thought and what he finally saw were one and the same. Alasdair was alone with Ursula, and the Highlander had drawn his sword as well.

"Why should I lay down my defense, unless you have something to be ashamed of?" Ethan shouted. *How dare this Highland brute assert himself in such an intimate way?*

"Do nae be a dimwit. Alasdair has offered to help us," Ursula shouted.

"Help himself to my wife," Ethan shot back.

"You are nae my husband, so stop pretending."

"Is that what you told Alasdair?"

"I told him the truth."

"That you are a witch and you trick men into falling in love with you?" *Would his lust ever turn to love?* Right now he was willing to protect what he believed was his.

She laughed. "I told him I'm a witch."

Ethan finally turned his attention to Alasdair, who shot him a sympathetic look.

Ethan's concern turned to ire. Still suspect of the wounded warrior, he continued to probe. "That still does nae explain why he's here with you in the captain's private cabin."

"It was an accident," Alasdair said. Then he took a few steps toward Ethan. "Put away your sword. There is no need to defend her."

"I do nae need protecting," Ursula said defiantly.

"She denies our bound, but in my heart she is mine," Ethan pledged as he advanced quickly toward the Highlander. "That I will defend." He lurched forward to strike.

The Scot stepped back, and Ethan found himself stumbling and slicing at air instead.

"Do nae do that again," Alasdair said flatly.

That was all Ethan needed to spur him to try again. But he didn't expect Alasdair to meet his blade.

The two wrestled with their swords. Higher and higher the blades rose until by sheer force they split apart and both men jumped back.

"Stop at once. Drop your weapons," commanded a voice Ethan did not recognize.

He glared at Alasdair who had the advantage of knowing who was behind him, while Ethan's back was to the door.

Alasdair inched forward with his sword pointed toward the ceiling and his other hand raised to match. Then he put his weapon on the navigation table.

"Be gone. You are in my quarters," a gravelly female voice said. Ethan lowered his sword and turned around.

He gasped when he spied Princess Margret standing in the doorway, bejeweled from head to toe. Ethan gave her a curt nod and sheathed his sword.

When he strode toward the door, he called over his shoulder, "Ursula."

Once on the deck, Ethan walked to the railing and waited. When Ursula did not appear after a few moments, he returned to the captain's cabin, wondering why he was the only one who'd followed orders.

When he reached the cabin, he found the door shut and a hulky knight guarding it.

"Where did the man and woman go after they left the captain's quarters?" Ethan asked the knight.

The soldier gave Ethan a blank stare and responded, "What man and woman?"

"She is beautiful, with long hair as black as night and eyes to match. He is ugly, oversized, and walks with a limp."

The guard shook his head. "The door was closed when I arrived, and it has stayed that way. 'Tis her majesty's wish."

Where would they have gone? Were they still inside? Could Ursula have done something to upset the royal guest? He considered the possibilities as he walked to the wardroom. No one else was there.

He took a stool at one of the barrel tables, picked up an empty tankard, and banged it on the wooden surface.

A young lad careened around the corner from the kitchen and slid to the table where Ethan sat. The boy yanked up breeches too big for his bum.

"Hello, mate, what you havin'?"

Ethan set the heavy pewter tankard down on the table. "Fill her up with the strongest brew. One that will bend nails."

The lad eyed him up and down, as if measuring his pluck.

Ethan growled, and the lad jumped.

"Aye, aye, sir," the lad squeaked, turning on his heel and scurrying back to the kitchen with Ethan's tankard in hand.

Scratching his head, Ethan began to piece together the scene he'd left in the captain's quarters. Even though he'd found Ursula and Alasdair together, he could only imagine he'd interrupted a tryst before they'd begun.

The lad soon returned with the strong brew.

"What is it, lad?" Ethan asked, peering into the top of the tankard.

Captain's favorite. He put his finger to his lips and let out a "*shhh*" sound. "This will be our secret," the lad promised, hiking up his drooping drawers again.

Ethan eyed the mug suspiciously, but then took a deep swig.

The boy stood patiently by the table and waited for a reaction. Ethan gagged first, then spit the liquid onto the floor.

"Is this horse's piss?" Ethan cried as he wiped his lips with his sleeve. "Are you trying to kill me?"

The boy looked sheepish and shook his head. "Like I said, 'tis the captain's favorite."

Drinking seawater would have been better than the captain's favorite," Ethan said. "Perhaps that's what Quinn drank before this concoction."

The lad lingered, and Ethan asked him to take a seat. When the boy hesitated, Ethan promised, "I won't bite."

Hiking up his drooping drawers, the boy inched a butt cheek onto the stool across from Ethan.

"So what of Moaning Molly?"

The boy's mood lightened. "You have met her?"

"She is hard to miss when she hangs over your bed and moans like a cow in heat," Ethan said.

The lad chuckled.

"What's your name?"

"Corky," the boy said, perking up and looking less like he wanted to run from the wardroom and never look back.

"Corky, what's Molly's story? You must know it."

The boy looked at him a bit sheepishly. "We young lads call her Meddling Molly. She cannae leave well enough alone."

Ethan laughed. "Does she spank you?"

Corky's eyes went wide. "Nay, she is always rearranging things in the kitchen. Or hiding things from us," the boy said as he scrunched up his face. "She's a menace. I wish she would leave us, but the captain said they are married and she brings us good luck."

Ethan laughed heartily. "She's the captain's wife? Did she die at sea?"

"Nay, she came with the ship," the boy said.

That was possible. Castles came with ghosts. His castle in Somerset had a family of them. But Moaning Molly was loud and obnoxious.

"I know what you are thinking," the boy said, "but the captain won't have of it. Molly saved his life."

"How so? She has no arms."

"Do nae underestimate her. She does nae need arms," Corky said, then leaned in as if to share a secret. "She has ears."

Ethan laughed again. "Go on."

"Well, like I said, she has ears," Corky said. "And a few years back she heard the captain's crew planning a mutiny."

Ethan raised a skeptical brow, but the boy forged on. "Aye, she heard six or more of his men plotting to throw him overboard, and she told him about it."

"You mean she doesn't just moan, she can speak?" Ethan asked.

The boy raised a brow. "Ghosts can do almost everything we do but eat and sleep."

"And take a crap."

Corky gave Ethan a screwy look before he went on. "No matter. Molly warned the captain that night," Corky said. "Told him what they were plotting. So Captain hid in the storage closet outside his cabin until the renegades burst through his door. He told me he'd created a decoy of himself made of meal sacks he'd hidden under his blankets. When the renegades thought they were running their swords through his hide, they were only putting holes in the burlap.

"Then, while the men were stabbing the meal sacks, the captain locked the cabin door, trapping them inside. Once the *Merry Maiden* reached port the next morn, he invited the sheriff and his men to haul the traitors away."

Ethan clapped after the entertaining tale. "Thank you, Corky. I have a higher regard now for Moaning Molly."

"You shall think she's a saint if she tells you where the Skye Isle Viking treasure is buried."

The lad hopped off the stool and scooted out of the wardroom.

Treasure? Ethan liked the sound of that. Perhaps the next time Molly came a calling, he'd need to spend a little more time with the captain's wife.

Chapter 15

One moment Ursula was in the midst of a sword fight, and the next, she was pouring tea for Princess Margret.

She was unprepared to be a royal roommate, her current status. Ursula had not expected Princess Margret to treat her like a servant once the captain left the room with the other men, but that was the current state of affairs.

"Girl, are you listening, girl?"

Ursula's head snapped up from her ruminations. She'd been called a lot of things in her adult life, but girl was not one of them.

"Mi lady," she said respectfully and with a short curtsy.

"I asked you if you had any healing skills," the princess said, looking very perturbed at Ursula's lack of attention.

"Aye, mi lady, royal healing skills. Berwick upon Tweed for Lord Hailes and his family." She bowed her head slightly. "May I be of service?"

"I'm in need of a love potion."

The grand dame said it with such seriousness, Ursula had to choke on her own amusement. "A love potion, mi lady?"

Ursula's expression must have given away her surprise, for the princess frowned immediately and shook her finger at her. "Not for myself. 'Tis for my son."

Ursula bristled under her calm demeanor. As much as she was called to healing, she was opposed to charms for love. Even though Ethan's potion was altering, it wasn't designed for him to fall in love with her.

The princess tsked before she went on. "I can already tell you do not approve, but let me explain why I need it."

Ursula nodded. Being on the wrong side of a royal had brought many a witch to hanging, so Ursula agreed to hear her out.

"The potion is for my son," the princess said, wringing her hands. "My son loves . . . he does not love women."

Ursula's right eyebrow twitched. Men who practiced sodomy were burned like witches. An injustice. Her heart softened. Perhaps she could make an exception.

"Tell me more," Ursula encouraged her.

"He has always been artistic. Plays the harpsicord like an angel. Sid can even embroider. I never wanted to discourage him. But when I caught him with one of the stable boys in his bed, well . . ." She fanned herself with her lace-gloved hand. "Like any mother, I want to help him."

As she patted the princess's hand, she struggled with the potential consequences of her response.

As a royal heir, Sid's actions would always be scrutinized. Rarely did the scandalous movements of a royal escape the gossips. If Sid were accused by a prominent citizen, he could face the court and be tried.

Ursula squeezed the princess's hand, "I would like to help him, too. There are binding potions, and I think that is best. They are designed to bring two people together in agreement. Like a business contract. You do nae want a love potion."

The princess appeared skeptical as she turned up her chin and stared down her nostrils at Ursula. "If Sid is not in love with a woman, how will that keep him from humping a man?"

Ursula swallowed her snicker. "Love and commitment can coexist but are nae the same. Love can fade. 'Tis nae long-lasting. Commitment, on the other hand, is about duty. That's much of what being noble is about."

"What do you know about being noble?" the princess snapped.

As much as Ursula wanted to hold her tongue, she did not. Perhaps she had been around Rosalyn too much. "Being noble and being royal are nae the same."

The princess twittered and relaxed. "Right you are."

The royal woman's answer surprised Ursula. Instead of defending herself, she could put her energy into the reasoning behind her recommendation.

"By giving Sid a binding potion it will allow him to find acceptance in the required ritual." Ursula shrugged. "You know yourself most marriages are arranged for land acquisition, monetary gain, or advancing one's status."

"True."

"Why don't you let me talk to him about it. I had a brother like Sid, but he wasnae so lucky to have someone like you to protect him."

The princess's lower lip trembled a little. "Was he taken to court?"

"Burned, along with my mother who was found guilty of witchcraft."

The princess shuddered. "Will the binding potion last?"

"Does love last?"

The royal heiress soured. "How long will it last then?"

Ursula tossed both hands up. "No two people are the same. But if Sid understands the purpose of the potion, that it will get him past his squeamishness, then the herbs will have served their purpose no matter how long they last."

When the princess appeared defeated, Ursula amended, "But be assured, maintaining a binding relationship with someone is much easier than sustaining a loving infatuation through a love potion. You don't want to drug your son indefinitely. That would be cruel." In saying that, Ursula was reminded she needed to extend the same consideration to Ethan. As soon as they returned to Fyvie, she'd need to restore him to his natural, unnatural state.

The princess cast her gaze to the floor. "No, I love my son, and I want him to be himself. We need this marriage only for appearances."

Ursula was happy she'd steered the princess away from the love potion. A binding spell was more appropriate but used many of the same ingredients, just in lighter doses.

"Neither is absolute nor foolproof. Any spell has its risks. With binding spells, there are fewer consequences."

"Consequences?"

"Let's say challenges," Ursula amended, "in getting everything to align correctly."

The princess had a strange look on her face before she asked, "Are you married?"

It only took a moment for Ursula to figure out where her question was leading. "Aye," she lied, but was certain Ethan would corroborate. "I am newly married, and my husband is one of the men you ordered out."

The princess appeared crestfallen. "The Highlander, of course." She gazed at Ursula whimsically. "You would have been the perfect match." But then the princess perked up and asked, "Are there any available women aboard?"

Ursula was flattered by the consideration and decided not to correct the princess on her assumption that Alasdair was her husband. She answered the question instead.

"Nay, I was the only one until you and your handmaidens arrived," Ursula said. "But Inverness is one of the larger ports in Scotland. No doubt there will be a family willing to advance their standing by participating in a royal wedding."

Her thoughts were interrupted when she felt a slight jolt as if the ship had weighed anchor. Ursula glanced to the portside window to see if they were underway.

When the princess cleared her throat, Ursula turned back to give the royal her full attention again and said with assurance, “There are many a Highland lass who would love to be married into a wealthy family such as yours. Especially a girl with a humble dowry.”

The princess’s spirts seemed to drop, prompting Ursula to ask what she feared, “Must the bride be of royal blood?”

The royal hesitated for a moment before she answered. “It would be preferred, but Sid is three seats removed from the throne. And he must be married no later than tomorrow.” The princess paused and wrung her hands again. “Or he will be disowned by the royal family. With my son’s legacy at stake, when is more important than who.”

Ursula brightened with a plausible solution. “If his bride comes from a remote enough village in the Highlands, chances are no one will know if her father was titled or nae.”

Princess Margret’s expression changed as she rubbed her hands together and let out a villainous laugh. “We shall invent her history.”

Ursula was beginning to admire this royal who wanted only the best for her son, and she was more willing than before to make an exception to her rules.

“I accept your request to make a potion that will pair Sid with a worthy Highland lass. However, we need to convince Alasdair and Ethan to stay in Inverness for the day once we dock.” Ursula frowned. “But we must also persuade the captain to host the wedding on his ship the same day.”

This was becoming more complicated than Ursula initially thought. They had to locate a willing bride in a hurry and coordinate the ceremony, all in a few hours shortly after they arrived at Inverness.

The princess clapped her hands together, snapping Ursula out of her negative thoughts. “As the second in line to the Scottish throne, I can demand a ceremony be held in my honor. By the time the captain realizes it’s a wedding ceremony for Sid, we’ll be too far gone for him to object.”

"That could work," Ursula agreed, "but how do I convince Alasdair and Ethan to delay our journey to Eilean Donan Castle when they are traveling with me on an urgent matter?"

The older woman pointed to an ornate chest Ursula hadn't noticed until now. "Inside the chest are pieces of gold. I shall promise five to each of the passengers on board to entice them to stay."

Ursula coughed politely before she told the princess why that would not work. "Mi lady, five pieces of gold would be enticing for a healer like me, but nae for the other two passengers. One is a lord and the other a laird. Each have their own massive landholdings and armies."

Ursula did nae mind exaggerating Ethan's standing. And although she had yet to see it, Ursula believed Alasdair had the army he promised.

The princess narrowed her gaze. "Well, we shall need to dig deep into the chest for the fanciful swords."

Swords? That sounded promising.

The princess snapped her fingers, and two of the handmaidens rushed to the ornately carved wooden chest. Another waited for the princess to hand over the key strung around her neck.

"Fanciful swords are like candy for grown men," the princess said as she dangled the heavy key above the maid's hand. With all that wealth in one place, Ursula wasn't surprised this royal had to keep her valuables under lock and key.

The maid took the key, then unlocked the chest. The heavy brass latches creaked when the lid was lifted. Once the woman had her hands inside, Ursula could hear the sounds of clinking coins until a heavily jeweled scabbard was withdrawn.

"*Aah*, there's one," the princess squawked, clearly

excited about the find. "Bring it here, dear." She reached out for the elaborate weapon.

But instead of taking it from the girl, she directed the weapon to Ursula. Once she studied the sword in her hands, Ursula was certain a gift like this would detain Alasdair and Ethan for a day, maybe two. She just had to make sure they didn't try to kill each other with them.

But then a wave of sanity washed over Ursula, and she handed the sheathed sword back to the servant. "'Tis too extravagant," she said, shaking her head. "Perhaps they would stay because I asked." She waved her hand at the sword in the maid's hand. "You should not have to part with family heirlooms."

The princess let out an abrupt cackle. "These are not family heirlooms, my dear, I can assure you. They are spoils of war. I will part with these as easily as I would part with a bad lover."

Ursula admired the princess. Not only for her unroyal-like behavior, but also for her directness.

In no time, the other servant girls had unearthed three more swords just as opulent as the first. Now all four were displayed on the navigation table.

"You may nae need to give all these away," Ursula said. "Who else needs one outside of Alasdair, Ethan, and the captain?"

"You forget, the father of the bride may need some convincing," the princess said, followed by a smirk and a raised brow.

Ursula laughed. "I'm sure the father will be a willing participant with or without the sword when he finds out his daughter is marrying royalty."

"His daughter will be marrying Sid," the princess said. "He will need the sword."

Chapter 16

Moaning Molly had a secret. Assuming what Corky had told Ethan was true, his venture to Skye Isle might prove more profitable than he'd imagined. If he could uncover a lost Viking treasure, he'd forget about storming Eilean Donan Castle and return to England to command one closer to civilization, and bring Ursula with him.

Sitting alone in the wardroom, Ethan took another swig of ale and contemplated his next move. Typically, he'd spend his time plotting how to best his twin. Although Lachlan had allowed Ethan to make Fyvie his residence of late, he never felt at ease there.

That was one reason why he was willing to accompany Ursula and learn if Eilean Donan Castle was worth the mettle or was a grand hoax designed by Lachlan. At least he'd be able to spend more time with the dark-haired sorceress. She seemed to be as much an outcast as he was, and he found her more desirable than any woman he'd ever met. And the vision of his mother in the church had urged him to help her. Why couldn't he help himself to her in the process?

No doubt he'd put Ursula off by calling her a witch, but she wasn't the type of woman you could give compliments to. Some women you had to keep off-balance and show them who was in charge.

On that note, he'd waited in the wardroom long enough for Ursula. He was ready to seek her out now that the ship was underway and rolling gently with the tide.

Once he was above deck, Ethan scanned the main expanse and found her right away, surrounded by the new passengers. He was about to call out to her, but she spotted him and walked toward him instead.

"Ethan, I was looking for you," she said, a bit out of breath. "I'm in need of your help."

What was the minx up to? Ursula was never in need of his help, and she was acting much too friendly.

She grabbed his arm. "Ethan, I must have your agreement on a slight delay in our travels." She glanced back toward the princess and her entourage of women servants. Her son blended in with them as colorful as he was, and his gestures were just as similar.

"It's Sid," Ursula said in a hushed tone. "He is to be married, and we are to be a part of the celebration."

What could she be talking about? "You jest."

"'Tis true. Princess Margret has employed the *Merry Maiden* to serve as chapel and great hall for Sid's nuptials after we dock at Inverness. Nae right away. Late afternoon," she said as if she'd just asked him to pass the butter.

"Have you gone mad?" Ethan asked her as he yanked his arm from her grasp. "What happened in the captain's quarters? One minute you are flirting with the Highlander, and the next, you are begging me to attend a wedding of a spoiled royal I do not care to know."

Ursula gave him a perturbed look and a huff, then she put her hands on her hips.

Thank God. That's the Ursula I know.

"Listen, Ethan. I'm better at demands than requests. Let me be clear. We are staying for Sid's wedding." She turned to leave him, but then spun back around. "There's a royal sword in it for you." Then she sauntered off to join Princess Margret again.

A sword? Well, it was Ursula who was in a hurry to get to Skye and back to Fyvie with the flower for Rosalyn. If she wanted to dally in Inverness to fawn over a royal union, then he deserved a sword for his trouble.

"She suckered you with a sword, too?"

"There you are," Ethan said, turning to face the Highlander. "We have some unfinished business," Ethan claimed, standing toe-to-toe with the chieftain.

The Highlander was about a half-foot taller than Ethan, but he was bent over, as if he'd carried sheep from the field to the barn on his back all day.

"What business would that be," Alasdair asked, closing the gap between them even farther. The spit from his words splattered against Ethan's cheek.

Wiping the offense off with the back of his sleeve, Ethan glared back at the Highlander. "My wife. She is none of your business. Keep your distance."

"What wife? I've been told you are traveling with your sister."

Ethan spat. His spray hitting Alasdair's broad forehead. "She's not even from the same clan. She's a witch and a liar," Ethan claimed.

"Matrimonial bliss?"

"Not your concern," Ethan said. "The business I speak of is gaining control of Eilean Donan." Ethan did not budge from his spot just inches from the Highlander. Every muscle in Alasdair's face was magnified.

But Ethan continued, "Surely, you will not raise your army and storm Eilean Donan as a humanitarian gesture toward me and my wife."

The only thing that moved on the Highlander was his cheek. It started twitching, so Ethan kept talking. "But I recall you told us you wanted the castle and clan to stay out of the hands of the MacDonalds." Ethan clapped a brotherly hand on Alasdair's shoulder. "Therein lies our like-mindedness."

The Highlander raised his arm. For a moment, Ethan wondered if the man would strike him. But Alasdair relaxed and mimicked Ethan's actions, gripping his right shoulder and saying, "One thing we will always share is our hatred of the MacDonalds, but I will only promise what I can deliver, and that is my clan."

Ethan considered the promise and calculated it was more than he would offer a stranger. He suspected Alasdair wanted to storm Eilean Donan with or without him, but doing it on Ethan's behalf was a better excuse.

With some skepticism on both sides, Alasdair and Ethan parted ways on the deck that afternoon, and Ethan spent the rest of it with the captain in the wardroom talking about Moaning Molly.

Ethan wasn't certain if what the captain told him could be counted as fact or fiction. The old sea dog spoke with a convincing flair, but with a gleam in his eye and specific details that belied common sense.

But the captain corroborated Corky's story about the mutiny. As much as Ethan wanted to get the specifics regarding the supposed Viking treasure, the captain was fuzzy when it came to the details. Instead of giving Ethan an assurance that a buried bounty could be found near the faerie pools, he chalked the talk up to Molly's vivid imagination.

Ethan paused, though, when the captain spoke of Molly as if she were human. But a man alone at sea, for days at a time with no companionship, might imagine anything was possible.

As Ethan took to the lower deck to bunk, he recounted the events of the day. Ocean travel allowed for more interaction than road travel, but he had only one other encounter with Ursula after the late day meal, when she told him to get his own pleasure.

She needed to be wooed. He'd never done anything of the sort and would have to figure out how to accomplish it.

His thoughts jumbled with imagines of her long, black hair entwined in his fingers just as the moaning started.

Ethan opened his eyes and scanned the cramped space. He'd been given private quarters, but to do so, he'd had to agree he'd bunk with sheepskins in the part of the ship where the horses were stalled.

There could be worse places to sleep, and he could attest to it. If he could only get Ursula to bed with him, he'd have the privacy they'd need. But as much as he had fantasized about traveling alone with the Highland beauty, he'd not been persuasive enough.

When Molly moaned again, almost in his ear, he sat upright in his bunk.

"Ye are a handsome lad," the floating aberration said.

"Thank you," he replied, not sure what else would have been appropriate.

"Lonely?"

What an odd question to ask, but he nodded his head in agreement.

"I can fix that," said Molly as a chill like a winter wind swept over him. Then a white, ghostly figure settled between his right side and the ship's wall.

"I'm right here."

The words made his skin crawl, and a bolt of fear raced down his spine.

Molly asked, "Now, is this not better?"

It would be if only he could pry the secret to the Viking treasure from her. And with a reluctant sigh, he decided that would be reason enough.

Chapter 17

Ursula had trouble keeping her eyes open as she lay on a makeshift bed made of straw on the floor of the captain's quarters. Most of the female royal servants, along with Princess Margret, were snoring like piglets.

At least the barnyard noises had served a purpose other than annoyance. They kept her awake until it was time to prepare the herbs and concoct the potions she'd need for Sid and Ethan.

Making her way quietly from the cabin and across the main deck, Ursula carried a candle with the hope there would be enough hot embers in the hearth to ignite the wick. In the meantime, the moon lit her path.

Once through the swinging galley doors, Ursula silently walked toward the counter where the vegetables were chopped and set her basket down. Kitchen tools hung from chains at the wooden table, no doubt to keep them from sliding around during rough waters.

When her gaze settled on the hearth, she was delighted to find enough fire to stoke, not only for her candle, but also to set the water to boil in one of the ship's kettles.

Ursula removed the silk satchel from her basket and unwrapped the bundle. She always carried a good amount of herbs wherever she went. Being a healer meant thoughtful preparedness.

Damiana, mandrake root, henbane, rose petals, and beetle wings. She laid them out on the worktable, as well as the tiny vials she'd need for storage. Eventually, each potion would be discretely dispensed in a goblet of wine on the morrow before the ceremony.

Although timing was critical, Ursula had experience with these herbs and was confident in her abilities as she went to work chopping mandrake.

"Hungry, too?"

Ursula bobbled the paring knife. When it slipped out of her hands, she shrieked. Peering down, she was relieved to find the knife dangling from the iron chain.

"I could have hurt myself." Livid, she spun around and did not care who caught her wrath.

"As skittish as a feral cat, you are," Alasdair mumbled as he met her at the worktable. Reaching for the small knife, he grinned at her as he stooped to retrieve it. "You've spent too much time in a castle, getting soft. You can nae survive in the Highlands. You spook too easily."

If his brogue and demeanor had not been so endearing, she would have sounded off on him. Instead, she softened her hard lip line into a smug smile.

"Mayhap it is because I do nae sail often and am not attuned to my surroundings." She shrugged her shoulders.

Alasdair scoffed. "'Tis mental strength that produces a steady hand whether you are on land or sea, not your surroundings."

He made a good point, and she'd appear petty if she argued with him, so she changed the subject. "Late yesterday you were telling me about Titania when Ethan interrupted us."

"A jealous man he is. Although you say you are nae married, 'tis clear he wishes to be."

"Ethan?" It was her turn to scoff.

"I do nae know why a man would claim be to be married unless he was hiding from the law."

Ursula chuckled. This Scotsman wasn't like the unkempt clan members she'd encountered in the Highlands. She was reminded of what Quinn had said to her earlier.

"Tell me about your great-great-great-grandmother."

"You may be easily spooked, but you are nae forgetful," he said.

"Are you hungry?" Ursula asked, knowing she would have better luck keeping him in the kitchen if she fed him.

He perked up at the question, and before he'd even answered, she was at the cupboard, taking out dried meat and figs.

She felt his eyes on her as she set the food next to her herbs, and again as she turned to stoke the fire in the hearth.

"I've been away from Dunvegan for a fortnight," he said softly.

"Then you've been away from high table eating," she said, turning to face him. "'Twill take more magic than I have to replicate that here in the galley, but I'll do what I can with the dry figs and beef.

"No better time than when a cook's at the hearth to fill her head with stories of the Fae," she said with a wink as she walked to the table. Taking some fennel and sage from her basket, Ursula began chopping it with the figs.

"Just payment for a meal, I suppose," Alasdair said, taking a stool on the other side of the table.

Witch and laird made for unusual tablemates, she thought as she took to slicing the dried beef into bite-sized pieces.

She walked back to the kettle, then carefully dropped the meat into the rolling boiling water. Before she covered it, she took a swig from the ceramic jug by the stove, happy to find the wine suitable enough for her taste. Then she added it to the water before clapping the lid on the pot to simmer the beef.

"You can talk while I work," she prompted, surprised Alasdair had not started with his tale as payment for the meal she was preparing.

When she turned to look his way, she half expected to find him either gone from the table or asleep upon it. Instead, she found his gaze lingering on her and a curious grin on his face.

He blinked quickly and cleared his throat. Then his cheeks reddened, and she sensed some embarrassment before he began.

"Titania was a famous Fae. One who's been revered and remembered for her compassion and love of humans. That's what was passed down from my great-great-great-grandfather."

Ursula scooted back on her stool and propped her elbows on the worktable, her chin cradled in her hands. "A mortal and Fae marriage?"

"Aye, against the wishes of the faerie's father. As the legend goes, she convinced him to allow her to marry my mortal great-great-great-grandfather. Her father only agreed to the marriage for a year and a day, as long as she promised to return to the Fae world."

The captain had given her a similar version of the lore already. Yet, Ursula was anxious to see if Alasdair's depiction would vary. She also wanted to find out if she could pick up on his thoughts while she was this close to him.

Because she couldn't read someone when they were looking directly at her, she'd need a distraction.

"Here," she said, pushing a bundle of herbs toward him, "you chop up the rest, and I'll remove the excess liquid."

As she began to pour the water from the kettle into a drain on the floor, she prompted, "A year and a day?"

"Aye," he concurred. "A son was born within that time, my great-great-grandfather, Uilleam Cleireach MacLeod, the Fifth Laird of Dunvegan."

"Then the faerie's father must have changed his mind," Ursula piped in from the hearth, adding more wine to the stew.

"Nay, that is where the flag comes in. Because the faerie wife was forced to return to her world, she left an object designed for protection."

"How do you know the flag ever existed?"

"Because we have it under guard."

Ursula let out a gasp. She'd thought it was guarded by the faeries in Glenbrittle. "The Faery Flag was left as a safeguard?"

"Aye, for her son and husband. She told them, 'Whenever you are attacked by your enemies, the flag should be unfurled and flown to protect you.'"

"Have you ever unfurled the flag?"

He huffed and, in a moment, was next to her.

She almost let out a shriek again, but this time she controlled her response. Ursula refused to act in a way that would undermine her composure.

He had joined her at the kettle with the chopped herbs and had even found some potatoes to add. Scraping the board clean, he filled the space where the water had been.

"Thank you," she mumbled, as some of Alasdair's thoughts began to form in muddled images.

"As you said, I'll be able to eat sooner, and I am hungry now."

She stirred the pot vigorously, as if the stew would cook faster. "Now that we have potatoes, this will need more wine and extra cooking time," she said with her eyes on the kettle. "Plenty of time for you to complete your tale," she suggested as she poured the wine over the concoction and pushed the potatoes under the meat, so they would cook faster.

No doubt impatient for the food, Alasdair grumbled under his breath before he started again. "The flag has many properties, and most are nae shared outside the family, but we can count at least one time it was unfurled in battle." Then he paused.

Pain. Ursula was sensing extreme pain. Images of fallen bodies. A flag flapping violently aboard a ship. She glanced over her shoulder to find him taking a stool behind the worktable again.

"'Twas the Battle at Bloody Bay," he said with a touch of pain in his voice. Or did she feel it? "Over seven years hence. But it started before then." He heaved a sigh. "The MacDonalds were always a riotous lot. Not only with other clans, but between themselves. Sometimes sons oppose their fathers, and this was the case with John MacDonald, the Earl of Ross and Lord of the Isles."

"Son defied father? I thought clan loyalty was stronger than that." She pushed the meat around on top of the potatoes, wanting them to heat quickly, then shutting it all under the lid again.

"Aye, most oft 'tis, but I should amend this was John's bastard son, Angus, that started the trouble. Wanting John dead."

Ursula cringed. This was the same story line Quinn had followed. She would never understand violence between family members. Even what she'd witnessed between Ethan and Lachlan had shocked her. What also surprised her was the pain she could sense radiating from Alasdair's right shoulder, and she turned to see if he was all right.

Like her, he appeared to control his emotions. If he was in pain, his face didn't show it. But the connection to his thoughts was lost now that she faced him.

"Bastards are never treated as family, so therein lies the problem," she said, deciding it would be safer not to follow his thoughts. She enjoyed gazing at him instead.

"Aye, 'tis so," he concurred, "and at that time, the MacDonald clan was fractured, with some supporting Angus and some supporting John. Beyond the immediate family, other clans took sides, too.

"Angus and his followers did everything they could over many months to undermine his father's supporters, including plans to lay waste to our land and Dunvegan castle. To thwart those efforts, my father led our clan, as well as the MacLeans and the McNeils, to Angus's encampment. The bastard son of John, and his men, had come ashore to restock their galley ships.

"Based on a scouting report, my father felt it would be the perfect time to strike and keep them from making their way to the MacLeod territory.

"During the battle I was injured in the back." Alasdair grabbed under his right armpit. "An Angus supporter laid his battle-ax into my shoulder, but as I went down, I killed the bastard with my own."

He grimaced when he reached for it, as if the wound was fresh. "That rallied my father and his troops until we defeated the Angus-supporting MacDonalds. Lost most of his men, Angus did, and we destroyed ten of their ships by setting them afire."

"So the Faery Flag saved the day?"

Alasdair gave her a thin smile. "Nay, but food would save the day now, and perhaps I'll get to that part in the story," he said, nodding toward the stove.

Her cheeks heated. She'd been so engrossed in his story, his pain palpable, she'd forgotten all about the stew.

Getting back to the kettle, Ursula quickly ladled out a big serving for Alasdair in a coarse wooden bowl. His stomach growled as she set the food before him. Next, she carved a big slice of bread from the stale loaf on the table.

He'd watched her in silence as if a bargain had been made and he'd not divulge her prize until he received his payment.

Instead of taking the slice, he tore a huge chunk of bread from the loaf, scooped out the soft innards, then stuffed it in his mouth.

Grinning awkwardly while he gobbled down the first morsels, he shoveled a healthy portion of the meat and potatoes onto the bread's crusty hull and devoured it in a few bites. After a dribble of the wine gravy ran down the side of his mouth, he gathered it up with his tongue. Giving her a naughty grin, Alasdair let out a satisfied sigh.

Ursula took that as a signal he'd receive his payment. She busied herself ladling up a meager portion for herself, then joined him at the table.

The silence was not awkward, but pleasant. If they hadn't been on a ship, nor Alasdair a powerful clan leader, the scene could have been between a husband and wife in a cozy, Highland cottage.

After licking his lips, Alasdair produced the widest, most charming smile. "You said you were a witch," he chuckled. "You made magic of that stew. I could swear it was better than what I've eaten at Edinburgh Castle with the King of Scots himself at the table."

She turned her head away from him slightly, hoping to hide the blush burning her checks. She'd only taken a few bites as the stew had been quite hot and had come from the very bottom of the kettle.

His eyes glazed over, and he grinned even more at her as if a wee bit drunk.

She raised a brow. Perhaps he was sleepy now that his stomach was full. Probably best to start up again where they'd finished. "So the Faery Flag saved the day?"

Alasdair continued to stare at her with a lovesick look on his face. He placed his hand over hers. "You are even more beautiful than Titania."

Was he joking or too tired to think clearly? No matter. She was certainly not going to be deprived of what was promised. She jerked her hand out from under his and asked, "How would you know? You've never met her."

He gazed into her eyes with a passionate purpose and grasped her hand again. "I know." He said the words with such confidence it spooked her. Blinking hard, she left her hand underneath his. Even if she held him spellbound, she still wanted the rest of the story. "Honor her by telling me the rest."

Alasdair continued to gaze at her with devotion that hadn't been there moments before. It was as if she'd become an object of his desire. She tried to sit still, but she squirmed in her seat until he squeezed her hand lightly as if to settle her down.

"The Faery Flag was not needed when I was injured by Evan MacKail. Our troop had the upper hand that day from the start. And even though I was violently attacked, I got my revenge on that bastard. Nay, it was not until the Battle at Bloody Bay when the flag was needed."

Now that Alasdair was busy in his head, recalling the painful memories that led to his injury and a battle that scarred not only him, but also his clan for all eternity, she was able to get out from under his worship-like attention while he continued to talk.

She glanced about the worktable. The damiana and mandrake root were gone. All of it. Ursula sucked in a shaky breath as Alasdair explained how the division between the MacDonalds had spread to the division of the MacLeods. How the clansmen of Lewis opposed the MacLeods of Harris and Dunvegan. The men his father led, and who had supported John.

Her mind spun from the mishmash of clan allegiances and deceptions. But she was thinking clearly enough to realize she had concocted a love potion stew for Alasdair MacLeod. He had taken some of the herbs for Ethan and the others for Sid, chopping them up with the common ingredients when she'd put him to work.

Luckily, she had only taken a few bites. And thankfully, she carried an antidote for almost everything with her.

Her herb basket sat perched at the end of the worktable. Ursula slowly made her way there, keeping her eyes on the Highlander.

Without too much fuss, and nodding at Alasdair as he explained more about the battle, she was able to locate the vial with the antidote in her basket. But her sense of relief was short-lived when she noticed there was only enough for one dose.

Although this potion was more of a countermeasure than a cure, she'd rather play it safe and take what she had. Now she'd need to pray Alasdair's condition would fizzle out in a day or two.

She repeated that again in her head, and it sunk in. Even one day of him acting like a lovesick puppy would be one day too long.

As she tried to settle her spinning thoughts, she was drawn back to what Alasdair had said when she'd heard the words 'Faery Flag.'

"Up until this point, our troops were dwindling and my father was dead. We'd waited too long before it was unfurled. And because we had no experience with it, we expected the flag to miraculously turn the tide of the battle in our favor.

"It was Murcha Breac, our family priest, who called for it to be unfurled. What was miraculous about the flag was it united the MacLeods together as one . . . the Lewis MacLeods joining our Dunvegan and Harris clans once again. But unfortunately, the battle had progressed too far, and there were too few of the clan left to win against Angus MacDonald. Sadly, the priest and the twelve flag guardians were lost."

His eyes met hers again, and this time, they were filled with pain. She was surprised by Alasdair's final account of the battle. Had she misread his intentions earlier?

No, that was wishful thinking. The herbs were gone, and she'd better make sure she wasn't influenced by them. Ursula drank the last of the antidote while Alasdair's attention was on the last of the bread.

"The flag had guardians?" she asked, putting her herbs and the empty vial back in her basket.

He did not answer right away, and she expected he was still eating, but when his breath was in her ear, she was sorely mistaken.

Ursula turned. Alasdair's lips were only a whisper away from claiming her mouth. His gaze held her captive. And although he'd yet to touch her, in a wild, wanton kind of way, she wanted him to kiss her.

She closed her eyes and held her breath, waiting for a Highland invasion, but instead, she heard a soft apology.

Opening her eyes and releasing her breath, Ursula found Alasdair's mouth within kissing distance, but his expression had gone from affectionate to troubled.

She'd swear he'd just bitten his tongue to keep from growling. But it was clear, either the effects of the herbs had miraculously worn off, or he was in excruciating pain and did not want to show it.

He nodded politely, thanking her for the food, explaining he'd let his appreciation go a too far, and finally left as quickly as he'd come.

Now how could she sleep after all that?

Chapter 18

Ursula was in the wardroom the next morn, still groggy from the lack of sleep, both relieved and disappointed Alasdair hadn't taken her in his arms and kissed her senseless. She could justify his actions under the influence of a love potion, but not her own urges. She'd taken the antidote and had no excuse other than her own lust.

She chided herself under her breath as she discretely dropped the cooperation mixture into Ethan's wine, instructing Corky to reserve the tankard and the freshly baked bread beside it for Ethan.

Walking past the captain's cabin on her way to the main deck, Ursula was reminded of her promise to Princess Margret. Thankfully, she'd managed to have a heart-to-heart talk with Sid yesterday.

At first she'd been worried he'd tell her he didn't care whether he was disowned by the royal family and refuse to marry a woman for political protocol.

Instead, Sid had surprised her by saying he didn't understand why his mother had waited so long on the proposed solution. Sid promised to provide his new wife with a perfect paramour and trusted Ursula would produce a bride who would agree to the terms Sid wanted in the marriage.

Even though she had been distracted by Alasdair's love sickness, she'd finished her potion-making and delivered the promised concoction to Sid late last night. He drank the attraction potion with Ursula as witness, right before he and one of the ship's mates slipped off into the shadows. Sid would do what he wanted, and she could only hope he fulfilled his mother's wishes when the time came.

Later that morn, she was able to signal the princess on deck, letting her know it was time to find a bride, and to execute the plan they'd concocted. With the help of the fancy swords, Alasdair and Ethan were ready to fulfill their accepted assignments.

Certain Alasdair was still under the potion's influence, Ursula decided he would be sent off with the royal knights to find a suitable bride. And she would accompany Ethan on the search for a priest.

No matter the reason, Ursula was content to be back in the saddle again after their horses were brought out of the holding pens. As much as she'd enjoyed the reprieve from traveling by horse, it was confining to be at sea.

Ethan had led the way to a chapel she'd spotted from the ship, and they were just tethering the horses when she was surprised by another rider.

"I caught you. Praise the saints," Alasdair said with more exasperation than revelation. "We need a woman."

"Aye," Ursula responded, hoping her voice sounded firm and not as shaky as she felt. "Of course, Sid is to marry a woman," she confirmed. Dismounting as Ethan did, she wondered if Sid had found a way to convince the knights and Alasdair he was in need of a suitable man instead.

After Alasdair dismounted, he walked to her as if under a spell. Without warning, he swept her back into his arms and planted a sweet, wet kiss on her unsuspecting open lips. She pushed against his chest, struggling to get her breath and her balance back. When he did not release her, she bit his lip.

He growled as if he liked it, but before she thought of another ploy, Ethan had taken up the matter.

"Release my wife," he lashed out.

No words were returned, but Ursula was gently set on her feet. Then in the time it takes for thunder to roll, Alasdair had his sword drawn.

Ethan followed suit.

Ursula gasped and stepped between them. “You shall nae fight over me, nor will I be bullied into choosing between one of you.” She took turns glaring at each of them before she said, “Put away your swords. I will nae have one of you dead before we’ve begun.”

When they both hesitated, she stomped her foot. “Listen, I have lives to save in Aberdeen. My pregnant sister of the heart needs the guelder rose from Skye Isle, and you two have interests there as well.” She stiffened her spine and put her nose in the air. “We do nae have time for this petty fighting. Both of you have admitted you want to conquer the MacDonalds and secure Eilean Donan, as well as the lands of Skye near Dunvegan. Until I have the flower, neither of you are of interest to me.”

Ursula turned to Ethan. “Stop calling me your wife when I am nae,” she snapped, her head swiveling like an owl’s, giving each an impertinent glare. She waited, tapping her boot.

Finally, and simultaneously, each bowed his head and sheathed his sword.

Ursula sighed inwardly and looked to Alasdair, waiting for a better explanation than when she’d dismounted.

He peered at her sheepishly. “We need a woman for Sid, and neither I nor the knights have had success.”

“’Tis probably because you are either ordering her to comply or threatening her with swords.”

Alasdair shrugged his shoulders. “We did not threaten any lass with swords.”

“But I bet you looked intimidating. Armored knights and a Highlander covered in bear fur? I would run the other way,” Ursula confessed as she sized up the Highlander. His brawny legs were thick and muscular. Hairy, too. And she blushed after her eyes traveled from the edge of his kilt to meet his gaze.

Ethan grunted, and she turned to address him.

"Clearly we do nae have much time but much to do. We must set aside our differences to get what we want." She paused, looking for a nod of compliance. Instead she heard grumblings, but she kept going regardless.

"Ethan, you secure the priest, and I will go with Alasdair. We must find a willing woman soon." She gazed upward and took note of how high the sun was already, then handed Ethan one of the satchels filled with gold coins the princess had provided, hoping he'd not run off with it. Now it was time to see if the cooperation potion had taken hold.

Instead of waiting for agreement or an argument, Ursula mounted her palfrey and turned onto the main path, assuming Ethan would be vocal if not compliant.

As she rode farther away from Ethan without an outburst or objection, she relaxed into her saddle. Alasdair's horse fell in step with hers, and soon the knight contingent followed her and Alasdair out of the village.

As they traveled southwest of Inverness, the seaside village cottages became smaller and the plots of land bigger. Most farming done here was for the wool trade, and sheep dotted the landscape in every direction. She was certain if she found the daughter of the poorest farmer in the area, she'd have her willing bride.

Ursula wasn't looking at Alasdair as the contingent neared a farmhouse, but this time, the visons come through more vividly than she expected.

Who was the woman beneath Alasdair's naked form, spanking his muscular arse?

The woman had long dark hair. She screeched and turned to look at him just a few paces ahead, hoping to stop her intrusion on his thoughts.

Her shout must have alarmed the knights, for no sooner had she let out the scream than two officers were by her side. "Are you all right?" one of the knights asked.

She laughed like an innocent. "Dear knights, I meant no alarm. I was just overjoyed to spy a lovely lass by the farmhouse gate."

The knights spun in their saddles to confirm what she had said, but there was no lass at the gate.

"We may have scared her off," Ursula said. Then she had an idea. "I propose your group wait for us here. Alasdair and I will approach the farmer and assure him there is nothing to fear."

After the Highlander steered his horse in line with hers, Ursula blushed, remembering his thoughts of the two of them entwined. But his expression was full of mischief, not lust, when he turned to her.

"Never send a knight to do a laird's work," Alasdair suggested.

"Never send a knight unless the damsel is in distress," she countered.

He laughed. "No one would answer the door when we came knocking."

"No doubt the villagers thought you were calling to collect taxes or arrest them."

He sobered. "I apologize for my actions earlier." He paused as if searching for the right words.

She found them for him. "You were going to say a powerful urge came over you. One you couldnae control."

His mouth gaped for a moment, then he said, "How did you know?"

"I've seen it before."

"Your beauty, your radiance. Men must fall at your feet."

Her cheeks heated, but her words didn't. "That is nae what I meant. You mixed some of my herbs in with your stew. It may take a few days for it to wear off."

She glanced at him out of the corner of her eye as he cocked his head her way. "God's teeth, at least you did nae poison me."

"Poisonings are deliberate, nae accidental." After she said it, she clapped a hand over her mouth.

"You speak with some authority," he said.

"Witch. You've heard me called that name. I prefer healer."

"And you deserve that respect."

She smiled broadly and gave him a sideways glance.

"Let me understand what has happened." Alasdair brought his horse to a stop. Not because of what he'd learned, but because they'd arrived at the farmer's gate.

She followed suit and waited while the Highlander gathered his thoughts. His face scrunched up, brows knotted and lips twisted, before he asked, "You put a spell on me?"

"That is petty and ridiculous. You happened upon me in the galley, and you added the herbs to your stew. The herbs will weaken your inhibitions."

"Then you should be trying to kiss me and get under my kilt."

Her face heated again, but this time her words did, too. "I do nae want to do any such thing and am repulsed by the idea of it. You, sir, should clean up your thoughts and know the effects of the herbs will wear off soon." She huffed, frustrated she had to explain herself. "I did nae eat much of the stew, so do nae expect any lovesickness from me."

"You could have offered me an antidote," he accused her, "but instead you let me make a fool of myself."

"You were a fool to start with. I had nothing to do with it."

"Excuse me," came a timid voice from beyond their squabbling. There, standing behind the gate, was a young lass with hair as golden as the sun and a disposition just as bright.

"Are you a witch?" the young lass asked.

Ursula grinned sweetly at the girl before asking, "What would make you think such a thing?"

Chapter 19

"Aye, she is, lass. She's threatened to turn me into a sheep and have me follow her blindly about the land, but I have begged her not to. Can you help me?" Alasdair implored.

The girl giggled but looked a bit uncertain about who was telling the truth. Ursula slid off her horse and, in a few shakes of a horse's tail, was arm in arm with the Highland lass as they walked up to the farmhouse.

Alasdair was glad for the interruption. They had a task to complete, and he was overly distracted by the healer. At least he had some explanation. Although the urge to find a secluded place to seduce her ebbed and waned, he had found it difficult to not be infatuated by her.

But the more he pondered his obsession for her, the more confused he became. For he'd felt an attraction to this lass before he'd supped with her in the kitchen. As if he'd known her before he was born. There was a knowing he could not explain.

Thankfully, he kept his thoughts to himself. No, he'd not even confided in the captain, for there was no benefit in making himself appear weak or admit he'd been taken in by a woman who was a witch.

No matter what they called her, she was different from any woman he'd ever met. The clan was clamoring for an heir, but Alasdair didnae want to marry just to provide a son for his followers. Ursula appeared to be a woman who would consider bartering for what she wanted. Most healers preferred not to marry. Alasdair himself was of the same mind. Although he was a descendent of faerie blood, he rarely considered his skills magical.

Aye, the lass, Ursula, would be his goal. Even without her magic, he wanted her. The prophecy might be true after all, but it was too early to tell. She would have to return to the faerie pools with him to be certain.

"There you are." Her voice cut through his thoughts.

"Aye, right where you left me," he responded.

She was on her way toward him, still arm in arm with the young farmer's daughter.

"She is willing and able," Ursula gushed, then grinned at him.

Even in the short time he'd known her, this was out of character. But then he considered she had taken on the task of finding the bride. She might feel like he did on the battlefield after a trouncing of the MacDonalds. He'd give her that.

"Good, the knights have an extra horse." Better get the lass on her way before she changed her mind was what he wanted to say.

When they returned to the ship with a bride, no one was more surprised than the princess, who had her turn at gushing and fawning over the girl.

As much as Alasdair had been opposed to the idea of holding a wedding on a ship, the crew and handmaidens proved him wrong, transforming the deck into a respectable outdoor chapel.

Once the priest was in place, and the bride and groom ready, the mishmash of guests filed in and stood before the flowered canopy that had been raised for the occasion.

When Ursula walked from the captain's quarters to confer with the priest, Alasdair's jaw dropped. If she'd stood next to the bride, she'd have overshadowed the young girl for Ursula looked stunning. Unfortunately for him, she disappeared from his sight as magically as she had appeared.

Why did she find it necessary he attend? He'd prefer to be riding his horse in the fields outside the town, helping the destrier get his land legs back before they started on the journey to Skye.

Alasdair sighed begrudgingly, then took a seat on a barrel, and was just getting settled when a jabbing finger poked his scarred shoulder.

He almost jumped out of his seat in agony but ground his hands together to manage the discomfort before he looked up, ready to knock out the person who'd provoked his pain.

"Why were you staring at me earlier?"

Ursula.

"Was I?" he asked, still reeling from the throbbing in his shoulder. His vison swam for a moment until the pain subsided a bit and he could see her clearly.

Of course, he'd been staring at her. She'd changed into a green and gold velvet dress that reminded him of the Titania tapestry at Dunvegan. The hair. The eyes. The gown. She was only missing the crown.

"You remind me of someone special." He struggled to gather his thoughts. "The herbs. 'Tis your fault after all. I cannot control my adoration." He was stretching the truth, but it pleased him when she covered a gasp. Gazing at her face made the pain almost disappear.

She sputtered as if he'd left her speechless, then she huffed and stomped away. That had not been his intention, but until the effects of her concoction wore off, he'd best stay away from her, lest he forget how to be civil. Although Highlanders were not known for their civility.

That acknowledgment made him chuckle, but also drew the displeasure of the priest, who was standing under the pavilion ready to start the proceedings.

Ethan had brought him onto the ship just moments ago. Alasdair watched the man closely. The holy man appeared to be swaying back and forth. Was he drunk or in need of sea legs beneath him? No doubt a little of both.

Once the priest had everyone's attention, the groom entered and stood by his side.

When the bagpipes began to play, Alasdair almost bolted out of his seat. Although clearly a Scottish tradition, he had not expected it when the bride and the priest had been hard to come by. If he'd had his pipes with him, he would have joined in the revelry.

Not long after the first wailing of the pipes, the farmer's daughter appeared near the gangplank. If he was a betting man, he'd have put money on her running down the plank rather than down the aisle.

The lovely witch, though, escorted the bonnie bride down the aisle instead of the girl's father. But the lass looked almost as green as Ursula's dress.

Alasdair felt some sympathy for the girl, having learned from Ursula on the trip back to the ship that the bride was one of ten daughters. The youngest and last to marry. Da had said good riddance when he'd received the gold and the sword Ursula had brought for barter. Ursula had insisted she be the one to give the bride away.

Now the two progressed down the makeshift aisle between crewmen and handmaidens. Ursula looking fetching, and the bride, ready to be fetched. And Princess Margret was at the center of the proceedings, bawling her eyes out.

After the bride was handed off to the groom and Ursula stepped back next to the princess, the priest did his best to guide the vows.

By God's grace, it was a ceremony filled with only a few short promises. To stay together in sickness and health. Love and honor. Although Sid was in the traditional short coat, kilt, and sporran, the handfasting ceremony was skipped.

Word was the captain had to set sail soon and had insisted the ceremony be short but legal.

Traditions aside, Alasdair did not believe the marriage would last more than a week considering the circumstances, a farmer's daughter and an effeminate nobleman. But then his family was filled with unions of unusual circumstances, and many had lasted.

All he needed was an heir and uncomplicated circumstances. Time spent with Ursula would dictate her compliance. Now, how to rid himself of Ethan?

~ ~ ~

Ursula took in a deep breath and released it slowly as the couple walked down the aisle toward the gangplank. Thank goodness she'd found a willing bride. Even though the priest was tipsy, at least he'd made it through the legally binding ceremony.

And the herbs Sid had taken last night allowed for the completion of a union of unusual circumstances. Both the bride and groom appeared happy after the ceremony was complete. She was certain they would make it work. The young lass had been more than agreeable to Sid's terms and anxious to leave the tattered clothes and farm life for a castle to serve as a duchess.

Ursula blew out a sigh and tried to smooth back the locks the wind had tossed about. The sea was becoming choppy, and the ship rolled a little side to side. At least the weather had held through the nuptials, and her job here was done.

Now, to change into her traveling clothes and say her goodbyes. She'd heard the captain announce before the ceremony he was anxious to sail before the weather turned. With the exception of Ethan, Alasdair, and herself, most would sail back to Aberdeen with the new stock of raw wool gathered at Inverness.

After crossing the deck, Ursula ducked into the captain's quarters to prepare for the next part of her journey, to Skye Isle. Before her eyes adjusted to the light, she was swept off her feet. "There you are," a familiar voice whispered in her ear.

"Put me down," she insisted. "There's much to do, and you should nae be here."

"These are the captain's quarters," Alasdair said again in a stubborn tone, refusing her order as if the Highlander's answer made his actions right.

"These are my quarters at the moment, and you are nae welcome," she huffed, squirming.

"There's little time," Alasdair insisted, then his lips came down hard on hers, his tongue probing right after. She did not expect the assault and began pounding on his chest in protest.

When that did nothing to deter him, she kicked her legs with a vengeance. The action must have thrown off his balance for he walked backward as his lips released their hold.

She was about to scream when she felt herself falling forward as he stumbled backward, losing his balance. As his back hit the surface of the navigation table, instruments and rolls of parchment went flying in all directions.

"That went bloody wrong," he blurted out.

She wanted to respond with indignation, but before she could utter a word, the table beneath them collapsed.

Ursula went straight down, landing on top of Alasdair.

The scream that filled the air was not her own.

Chapter 20

A catastrophic mistake. Alasdair had hoped to surprise Ursula, but instead he was writhing in pain under her. This was not the vision he'd had earlier in the day when he'd lain naked above her, taking his pleasure and giving it in return.

His battle scar throbbed, and his howl had brought the knights to the cabin. Luckily, the shutters were drawn, and the fire was only embers. By the time the guards' eyes had adjusted to the light, both he and Ursula were on their feet.

"Everything is all right. No harm done," Alasdair said first. "When the lady cried out, I was outside the captain's quarters and rushed in to provide assistance."

"Luckily, I caught my one hand on the edge of the navigation table, softening my fall," Ursula explained.

The story seemed to placate Princess Margret's knights enough that they filed out quickly and left the two of them alone.

Ursula opened one of the shutters, then turned to him. She appeared to be unharmed.

"'Tis your potion that made me do it," he said bashfully.

She wrung her hands.

"How long will I be tortured by this?" he asked.

She shrugged her shoulders. "I could try to mix together an antidote, but we must leave the ship soon. I will not have the time," she said with an agitated tone as she looked about the quarters. "I shall gather my things now, and we must be off."

"And leave me in misery. Wanting you, but not having you?"

She winced. "'Tis not fair, and I apologize. As soon as we make camp for the night, I will do my best to make a concoction to help you," she promised.

He rubbed his shoulder gingerly, and she moved to his side in an instant. "'Tis a wound from the fall?"

He contemplated his answer but decided to be honest about it. "'Tis a battle wound that causes some pain." He shifted his weight, uncomfortable talking about the scar now that he'd started.

She showed compassion in her gaze. "I have some herbs for this, too," she offered.

"I will be prepared for both," he replied, sporting a smug smile. "As long as you swear neither will be poisonous."

She returned the smug smile. "Why would I kill you now when you must guide us through the Highlands and help me find the faerie pools?"

He laughed heartily at that. "My good friend George Gordon, the Second Earl of Huntley, will give us a land berth and a comfortable bed at Urquhart Castle. If we get started now, we can reach it by nightfall."

He leaned toward her like he had a secret to share. "But you shall need to convince your husband that 'tis a good idea."

She spat before she answered him. "I promise to poison you if you call Ethan my husband one more time." With her hands on her hips, she tossed her head. "Out! Or we'll get Ethan's ire up before we've even started."

~ ~ ~

With the motivation of sleeping in a castle, Ursula quickly packed her satchel with the few personal items she'd left by her straw bed, then went to find the captain.

Rosalyn's uncle was in the galley talking to the cook and scullery boy. She curtsied when he turned to address her. "Good Uncle, you've been more than generous to provide an ocean passage for me and Ethan here to Inverness. You have spared us at least two travel days."

The captain grinned. His two front teeth covered in gold did not make him any less charming. "Anything for my sweet Rosalyn and you, Ursula. 'Tis no secret among family you are traveling to Skye Isle to help my niece." He reached into his pocket. "You are a brave lass to consort with the likes of Ethan and Alasdair," he said soberly and gently shoved a leather pouch into her hand.

Ursula suspected what it was, and she handed it back, shaking her head. But he did not relent.

"You took care of Rosalyn when my brother, Angus, was sick. Consider this a token of my appreciation." He withdrew a folded piece of tattered parchment from his pocket. "I almost forgot to give you this." He grinned again, and the two gold teeth glistened in the firelight of the kitchen.

When she started to unfold it, he shook his head. "You will know what to do with it." His expression changed from warm to crotchety, and he turned his back to her. "Now off with you before I get sentimental."

Ursula did nae need to be told twice. After she spun on her heel and headed to the stairs to go above board, she stuffed the tattered note between her breasts.

It was nae long before she, Ethan, and Alasdair were trotting their horses along the western side of Loch Ness with the sun still high in the sky. She took in a deep breath and marveled how the lavender-colored heather smelled as wonderful as it looked.

The flower was a mainstay in her herb collection. The dried variety she used often was almost gone. Replenishing her supply would be a top priority at their first stop.

Aye, it would be tempting to empty her satchel of clothing and stuff it full of wildflowers. Not only had the heather flower aided in easing some of the aches and pains in her older patients, it was a must when treating anything to do with gout or problems with the gut. Even her patients' sleeping disorders and breathing issues had been solved with a regular supply of her heather tea.

As they traveled the path beside the massive Loch Ness, they rode in single file, with Alasdair in the lead and Ethan in the rear. Her position between the men gave Ursula some peace of mind, but it also restricted her from any unusual movements. Not that she needed to make any, but Ethan had the best view of her actions.

At least she'd been able to get a fresh dose of the cooperation concoction into Ethan's ale before they'd left the ship that day. A workstation and an ample supply of ale would be hard to come by while they traveled.

As Ursula studied the surface of Loch Ness, she gave credit to Alasdair for suggesting they travel the road rather than the water. She had little experience with fishing boats and that would have been their only other option.

Without much swimming experience, Ursula had been wary of the water while on the *Merry Maiden*, but she'd trusted Rosalyn and Quinn. And although she'd been in water over her head, a cousin of hers had drowned in the Loch Duich when Ursula had not been quite five and ten years old.

Ursula came from a world where herbs could fix just about any ailment. But if someone went under the water and couldn't swim, there was no potion that could bring them back.

While she was fixated on the water, Alasdair's shout made her docile palfrey step sideways in an awkward trot. After a few soothing strokes to her neck, Tempest settled back into a normal canter.

Ursula was about to chastise Alasdair, but when she looked up, he was pointing toward the loch. "There, do you see it?"

She scanned the surface of the water. "What am I looking for?" she asked, loud enough for him to hear.

"'Tis gone," he said with a frustrated sigh. "No point offering an explanation of what can nae be explained."

She shrugged her shoulders, then turned to look back at Ethan, who rolled his eyes and twisted his lips in a disgusted manner.

When Ursula turned back around in her saddle, Alasdair was dismounting. Ethan and Ursula followed suit, then the three tethered their horses to a tree by the path in silence.

After Alasdair headed for the water, Ethan came to her side and stood as close as a husband would a wife. She took a step back. "I am nae afraid of whatever Alasdair thought he saw," she offered. If he'd come to comfort her, she did not need his help.

"You look lovely today," Ethan said.

The compliment was so simple, and he appeared genuine. She couldn't help but grin back at him, but she offered him nothing more. If anything, she'd learned when Ethan was under the influence of her potion, he was more honest than not.

What was he thinking? Although she'd given up on trying, she wished the potion's effects would let her in. She'd never even been able to pick up even the murkiest of images.

"These flowers are truly lovely," Ursula said to him and turned away. "I shan't waste a moment of this reprieve," she called over her shoulder as she walked toward the loch, hoping she would have time to pick the heather that was plentiful on this side of the trail, and get away from his attention.

She busied herself selecting the largest, most vibrant blooms, expecting Ethan would find his own distraction as had Alasdair.

As she plucked the blossoms, she concentrated on

catching Ethan's thoughts. Perhaps the potion would give her an assist.

Once Ursula cleared her own mind, it was never long before images would form. Some were vivid. If no images came, a voice would speak to her. As if she could hear what someone was thinking. Sometimes she had both sight and sound, like with Rosalyn. The closer she was to someone, the stronger the signals.

She bent low, finding a particularly fragrant batch of heather, and inhaled the seductively sweet smell, hoping the scent might assist her, but instead of Ethan, an image of Rosalyn appeared . . . sitting on a bench in her garden.

Oh, poor, poor, Rosalyn. The lass was so much bigger than when Ursula had left a few days ago. She counted on her fingers. Four weeks to her predicted delivery date with a normal birth. With twins, Rosalyn could go in less.

Ursula shouldn't have been surprised a vision of her friend came through just then. Although Ursula had found it difficult to read someone at a significant distance before, she'd never been as close to anyone as she was to Rosalyn. Perhaps that was the reason Ursula could make a connection now.

Ursula closed her eyes and took another deep inhale of the heather at her feet. *Could the flowers be aiding her?*

She squeezed her eyes together tightly.

Aye, Rosalyn was sitting in the garden and . . . *She was singing!*

Ursula could not discern the words, but Rosalyn was clearly singing and looked happy. She even rubbed her belly while she sang. As much as Ursula wanted to let this vision make her feel at ease about being away, it still worried her that she was away from the castle.

Pregnancies were unpredictable, and with twins, even more so.

When Alasdair shouted it was time to leave, the vision shattered. Seeing Rosalyn reminded Ursula she had much to accomplish in a very short time.

After the three had gathered at their horses, readying to ride again, Ethan asked Alasdair what he was looking for.

"Nothing, really," he said with some hesitation. "There are legends about this loch. Most, I can tell are exaggerated stories. One as old as the crusades," Alasdair told them as he stared off across the large expanse of water. "I thought I saw something." He shook his head. "Most likely, it was only the sun shining off the surface of the water, playing tricks on my eyes."

Ursula's gaze went out over the water again. The liquid churned and rose in waves, even out in the distant middle. Whatever Alasdair thought he saw, Ursula did not want to see.

"This is no hunting expedition, Alasdair," Ursula prompted. "We must make haste. Three days of travel to find the guelder rose."

Alasdair gave her a love-drunk smile. "As you wish." Then turned his horse and coaxed him into a canter.

The heather had reinvigorated her, and she couldn't wait to let her head hit a comfortable pillow again. Ursula gave her palfrey the commands, and in short order, both she and Ethan were galloping at Alasdair's heels.

Chapter 21

It wasn't long after they'd turned off the Loch Ness trail that Alasdair guided his horse and the others over the drawbridge and up to the grand entrance to Urquhart. When he waved his gauntlet at the sentry, the clanking chains ground loudly and the latticed-grill gate disappeared into the grooved opening above.

The lord of Urquhart Castle had been a longtime ally of Alasdair's. As far back as he could remember, George had shared his hatred of the MacDonald clan.

Alasdair had been out of his element on the northern coast at Inverness and was more at home in the Highlands. But even though he felt at ease here, he'd never let his guard down unless he was in a fortified castle like Urquhart.

Once they'd been welcomed inside the keep by the castle's steward, Alasdair tugged his bearskin cloak off his shoulders and tossed it into the arms of a young lad. The boy took a few steps back after he caught the cloak, looking overwhelmed by the weight of it, as if a bear had gobbled him up. Alasdair chuckled.

George's bellowing laughter, however, made Alasdair peer down the corridor for him. It echoed through the high ceiling and bounced down the keep's grand entry walls.

Alasdair's friend strode briskly toward them, George's silver hair shining like polished armor in the glow of the sconces he passed on his way to greet them.

The color of his hair, however, wasn't indicative of his age. The slender face, high cheek bones, and icy-blue eyes belonged to a man closer to Alasdair's own years.

Once George reached them, he grasped Alasdair's arm above the elbow, and he did the same. It was a handshake they'd developed after Alasdair's injury. George was well aware a slap on the back, with the customary embrace, could cause Alasdair much pain.

"Lord Gordon."

"Good to see you, Laird MacLeod."

They both tipped forward in a formal bow. When rising, George grinned at him like a boy. "Make yourself at home in my humble castle, Crotach."

Alasdair warmed to the nickname he'd inherited after the Battle at Bloody Bay. He turned and gestured to Ethan and Ursula. "I trust your hospitality will extend to my two traveling companions as well, Lord Ethan Luttrell of Clan MacKenzie and Lady Ursula of Clan Fraser."

"Any ally of yours is welcome," George declared, then he made a grand sweeping motion. "Come, we are just about to sup, and the tables will be laden with all your favorites."

His friend pointed to the staff waiting for instructions. "Leave your satchels with my servants, and your chambers will be ready after you've had your fill of mead and more."

Alasdair grinned broadly and followed his host into the great hall. After navigating through the trestle tables, they all took their seats at the head table on the dais.

Castle Urquhart was no Dunvegan, but it was still a substantial stronghold, and George profited from being the only fortified castle on Loch Ness, the gateway from Inverness to the Highlands.

George raised his chalice and introduced their contingent to those in service and to the local nobles there. After a toast to the food and the company, trenchers of peacock and salmon were served. Alasdair filled his own trencher with generous portions of both. When the bread was offered, he did not hesitate and took a Highlander's portion of that and the potatoes as well.

When one of the serving lassies flirted with him as she filled his chalice with mead, he gave her tight arse a quick spank.

The aghast look from Ursula was worth the gesture, and he had trouble controlling his chuckling over it. As much as he enjoyed teasing her, the idea of having her was more prevalent than before. He wondered if she would remember the offer of an antidote and the healing herbs she'd promised earlier.

When he raised his chalice to take a long guzzle of George's hospitality, he stole a sideways glance her way. Ursula's content expression glowed in the light from the tapered candles. She looked like a satisfied, royal cat after a bowl of rich cream. For a moment, he wanted to ask her what she was thinking about, but his host interrupted.

"Crotach, 'tis good to share a table with you, my old friend."

"Am I old, or an old friend?" Alasdair postured, propping his elbow on the table and placing his hand under his chin.

"How about my friend of old?"

He winced. "What about longtime friend?"

"The best of friends." George paused as if trying to remember something, then his face lit up. "Aristotle calls that 'a friend of the good.'"

Alasdair narrowed his gaze on George. "You have a friend named Aristotle?"

His host slapped the table, making some heads turn. But George did not seem to care when he answered, "The Greek philosopher." George looked in both directions and softened his voice, "I read Latin. The classics."

Alasdair let out a hoot. "You are a Highlander. There is nothing classic about us."

George eyed him up and down. "Speak for yourself. The Skyelanders are much more like the pillaging Vikings of old."

"Are you calling me old again?" He leaned both hands on the table as if he was about to get up and fight. "Do nae speak ill of my late ancestors," Alasdair threatened. After a long pause, he winked. "You may need our protection one day."

His friend clasped Alasdair's forearm, just as he had in their greeting, but this time his expression darkened. "Speaking of protection. We should talk privately." Once again, George glanced about, and that made Alasdair take stock of his position, too. Checking to see how Ursula was faring, he found her in a heated conversation with Ethan.

The bastard was nothing but trouble.

If it were not for Ursula, he would have abandoned Ethan in Inverness and made his way back to Dunvegan with her. Instead, he was relegated to navigating the trip home with the twit.

Now he was conflicted. Clearly, the information George had would be relevant to their travels, but it was apparent Ursula needed rescuing. And she had a promise to keep.

The squeeze on his forearm reminded Alasdair his host was waiting for a response. Turning his attention back to George, he clasped his free hand on top. "My friend, you are a fine host, and the meal is the best I've had outside of Skye"—he gestured with a head nod toward Ursula—"but my fair lady needs rescuing. Can it wait til morn?"

George spun around in his seat and swore. "I'll call my guards to settle this," he offered when he turned back to Alasdair.

"I must take care of this now," Alasdair said through gritted teeth, squeezing his friend's shoulder as he walked past him to promptly join the arguing couple.

"Take your hands off her," Alasdair said, confronting Ethan at the great hall entrance.

Ethan cut him a look. "You have no authority here," he snipped back at Alasdair, eyeing him up and down.

George was at his elbow. "I give him all the authority he needs," his friend promised.

Ethan dropped Ursula's arm and backed away as Alasdair put a protective arm around her shoulders. "If Ursula does not give you permission, then you do not touch her, understand?"

Ethan glared at him for a long time while George's men filed in around behind Alasdair. A mini army had assembled, ready to move forward to support his efforts.

"Ethan," George said, breaking the silence and the standoff, "my castle steward would like to give you a tour of the armory."

With a sharp nod of his head, Ethan sulked off to follow the servant. Ursula's deep sigh prompted Alasdair to turn toward her and deliver a chivalrous grin.

She returned the gesture with a subtle smile, reminding him of a rare flower.

George snapped his fingers and summoned four servants. After a few words of instruction, he turned to Ursula. "Alasdair has told me about your love of plants and herbs. We have one of the most vibrant gardens in the Highlands. I hope you'll be my guest and let my servants show you around before you retire for the evening."

Without another word, she curtseyed and was off, almost skipping as if she were a child on her way to play with her favorite toy.

George turned to Alasdair. "We can have that talk in my study," he offered, crossing his arms over his chest in a satisfied way. "Ethan will be in the armory for at least an hour, and Ursula will be visiting our indoor gardens. Afterward, she'll be taken to a special chamber where you two will reunite."

Then George struck his hands together lightly back and forth, as if dusting them off from manual chores. "Leaving us time to discuss the state of the clans."

If it were not for the promise of a rendezvous with Ursula, Alasdair may have dreaded the necessary clan briefing, but keeping up with the latest developments would be critical to his success as he returned to Skye. The meeting with King James had been the reason for his journey from home, but he couldn't discuss that with his good friend.

After they settled in George's massive solar, with Alasdair's chalice filled, his friend suggested they sit at the circular table in the middle of the high-ceilinged chamber.

Alasdair stretched out his legs and crossed them as George unrolled a large parchment in the center of the table and anchored each end with an empty goblet.

His host pointed to Urquhart Castle on the map and made an arc with his finger to Kyle of Lochalsh. "From Urquhart to Glengarry, you will be well-protected by Clan Cameron. But once you cross this range and move into the Glen Shiel, you must be on your guard."

Alasdair rose and braced himself on the table, leaning over the map to get a better look, his eyes following the arc George had traced.

"I have at least six men I can spare who will travel with you from here to Dunvegan. They wear my coat of arms, which is neutral to even the MacDonalds. You must wear it as well, Crotach."

Alasdair's head whipped up. He'd never been asked to hide who he was.

"Crotach, I know it goes against everything you stand for, but 'twill be a guaranteed passage."

Alasdair considered his friend's offer. He was never quick to make a judgment and had learned the hard way that calculated movements, even on the battlefield, merited greater success than impatient action.

"You are right my friend of the good," Alasdair finally said after the long contemplation. "I've proudly worn my family's colors since I was a swaddled babe." He turned to pace in front of the massive fireplace that burned as hotly has he felt. If it weren't for Ursula and Ethan, Alasdair could travel without Gordon's protection.

"I'm no use to my clansmen if I'm dead, so I shall accept your offer and wear your colors."

George met him at the fireplace. "Our colors are different, but our hearts are the same. We share the same hatred for the MacDonalds. And in that unity you will find peace."

Alasdair nodded. "Aye. Now what of Eilean Donan? What can you tell me of her laird?"

"Clan MacDonald ousted the MacKenzies. A brute named Ian is her laird."

When Alasdair fisted his hands, George said, "The clan has nae had a strong hold there for much time. The ownership you know has been debated."

Alasdair nodded and knew as much.

"Aye, after the death of Colleen MacKenzie, her English husband took control as I recall," his host offered and gestured to the chairs.

Alasdair stood steadfast at the hearth.

George touched his fist to his forehead. "Of course, the rendezvous," his friend said, chuckling. Then with a curt nod, he led Alasdair to the door, but turned back with a smug smile. "It's clear she's bewitched by you."

Alasdair snorted before he barked out a laugh. "My friend, 'tis the other way around. She's bewitched me."

Chapter 22

Not only rare flowers but exotic herbs permeated the Urquhart Castle gardens. As Ursula strolled the grounds, enjoying the flora, she wished for Rosalyn as fine a display for Fyvie. Given the time and resources, she'd like nothing more than to build a bountiful private haven for her sister of the heart.

There were many rare varieties scattered among the common perennials. Her eyes lit on a particular rose, and for a moment, there was a flicker of hope that she'd found the guelder. But that would have been too convenient.

Solitude had been a rare commodity, so Ursula basked in the quiet. Thanks to Alasdair, she was enjoying this reprieve as he'd had a hand in saving her from Ethan's beratement. He'd been suggesting they share a room. Of course, she'd refused, and Alasdair had handily put Ethan in his place by coming to her rescue.

The two men barely tolerated each other. They were complete opposites. Ethan full of angst and lust. Alasdair playful and amorous. She did enjoy the attention from both. One more than most. And thanks to their pursuits, her pain of Joshua's loss was fading.

Over the last few days, especially aboard the ship and with a change in her routine, Ursula had thought long and hard about Joshua. Although she had cared for him, she had not truly been in love. She'd settled.

Long ago, her virginity had been stolen from her. Most men would consider her soiled. But her mother had said purity was of spirit not body. They were witches after all and were not expected to adhere to the social norms of the royals or upper class.

She'd understood the faerie code but had never abused the freedom her spirit allowed. Only with Joshua had she explored those urges. He had helped her appreciate her body in ways she may never have discovered without a lover like him.

She shivered a little as if his spirit had just touched her cheek. Although she was a seer, she could not see the dead, unless they were stuck between worlds like Moaning Molly.

Taking a seat by an ornate table near the hearth, Ursula unpacked the herbs from her silk bag. After the garden visit, Lord Gordon's servant had led her to this private solar at the end of a long hallway, explaining she would be needed for healing services before bed.

She was happy to oblige. As a guest in his household, she was willing to repay the laird for the generosity of providing his hospitality. Of course, she carried most of the herbs needed for common ailments.

Although she was pleased to provide a service to her host, she was concerned she would no longer be able to fulfill the promise she'd made to Alasdair to provide an antidote for her potion and to take a look at his battle wound.

The door opened abruptly with no knock. When Ursula turned to see who had entered, her mouth flopped open and shut like a fish. She had no words.

"You look surprised." Alasdair's brow rose. "We had an appointment."

"You startled me," she confessed. The last time she'd been alone with him was in the captain's quarters when his kissing had gone wrong.

She had been disappointed their intimate moment together had ended so abruptly, before she could explore the possibilities. But the time and location had been a poor choice. But the memory of them laying on the floor together in a tumble made her smile at him.

Alasdair swept into a low bow. "My apologies, my lady."

When he rose, he was wearing a mischievous grin. And as she studied the laird more closely, she noticed he was wearing different clothes than before, a rust-colored linen shirt with a wide open ruffled collar. And instead of a kilt, he was sporting snug leather breeches and soft slippers.

Alasdair caught her staring at him.

His face reddened when he glanced down. "*Och!* You do nae recognize me in George's clothes." He captured her gaze on the way back up with his own sheepish one. "Our host insisted his servants wash my clothes."

She had to admit she was shocked to find Alasdair transformed from a rugged warrior to a refined gentleman. He looked more like a spoiled Englishman who'd never dirtied a hand in the Highlands or waged a war with an enemy.

"I suppose an annual washing is preferred by some," he said, crossing the room. He took a seat on the other side of the table. "For me, that is still too often."

She stifled a laugh, still off-balance by the two of them unchaperoned. She was not naïve, but it was a bold move to have her meet him alone in a bedchamber after dinner.

"If you cannae fix my obsession for you, I will have no course of action other than to remove your clothes and take you to bed." He'd declared his intentions as if he'd just asked for more mead at the head table.

Ursula blinked hard. She'd yet to have a word, and she did not need to read Alasdair's thoughts, because he was speaking them aloud.

He rose and approached her slowly. "You must be considering my offer. Otherwise, I'd have a black eye by now."

Was she considering his offer? She was smitten. Captain Quinn had called it. Aye, this man who'd tugged at her heartstrings aboard the *Merry Maid* was stirring wanton feelings in her now.

Had the antidote worked, or was she affected by the herbs in her stew? But aside from her feelings of lust and confusion, Ursula was overridden with guilt. His infatuation was her fault.

She reached for her silk satchel by her feet, but by the time she'd raised her head and brought the bundle to her lap, Alasdair was down on one knee before her. He reached for her hand and helped her rise to her feet.

Towering over her, he said, "On second thought, I am nae sure any antidote would work."

Ursula swooned a little, and Alasdair's hand was behind her back in moments, keeping her from toppling over. His other arm wrapped around her waist. This close to him, she marveled at how tall he was.

"I promised you relief from your injuries," she said, holding her silk pouch between their faces as if it were a shield she could use to protect herself from his flirtatious gaze.

He gently pushed her hand down and grinned at her when he could see her face again. "That 'twas not what I had in mind," he told her as he turned her toward the massive chamber bed covered in a dark-blue velvet that matched the canopy above. Both were richly appointed with golden ropes and tassels.

She resisted his progression toward the bed. "Nay, Alasdair, I did not promise a rendezvous in this secluded Highland castle."

He chuckled at her feeble attempt to refuse him. She tugged harder at his hand and stopped in her tracks.

His solution was to sweep her off her feet. It was her turn to chuckle. "You are persistent. I'll shall give you that."

Alasdair closed his eyes.

She sucked in a sharp breath before his mouth claimed hers. What could she do but kiss him back? This was no time for an argument. She relaxed and let herself be swept up in the moment.

Alasdair's lips were gentle and aggressive at the same time. A lot like how he was when she was with him.

Maybe the sheer size of him intimidated her when she stood close to him. Yet every time they'd been alone, even in the captain's quarters when he'd kissed her after Sid's wedding, he moved like he was taking her prisoner, attacking her with a subtle seduction, leaving her wanting more.

His groan brought her back to the chamber, back to her senses when she broke the bond of their entwined lips.

"What was that?" she asked, surprised her breathing was labored.

"A kiss." His lips cocked up on one side.

How could she be perturbed by this man and his gentle humor? She sputtered before she answered, "Your intention?"

He looked at her as if he felt sorry for her. She likened it to an idiot asking a scholar a question.

"You promised me relief from my injuries?"

"Aye, I did promise, but I had an herbal remedy in mind."

"You and I do not see eye to eye. I had a physical remedy in mind."

"How will we come to a truce on this?"

"You agree to try my way first, and if that does not work, then we'll try your way."

She was taken by the Highlander in more ways than she could count and wasn't opposed to time in his company. It had been too long since she had experienced this kind of pleasure.

When she closed her eyes to contemplate her options, Alasdair's lips locked with hers. She wanted to argue with him about his proposal, but she groaned into his kiss before she could control her response.

He growled back, quickly conquering her mouth with a surprise invasion, his tongue probing about like a brave soldier ready to take her emotions hostage.

She was not afraid. She was not uncertain as he laid her on the bed, climbing in next to her.

Of course, Ursula had been kissed before by Alasdair, but not like this. Even his attempt on the *Merry Maiden* seemed self-indulgent compared to the intensity of his adoration for her in this moment.

If anything, she'd have expected the herbs' effects to have faded. But instead, Alasdair's complete infatuation with her had only intensified.

And she did not mind at all. No, she could not control the sensations of pure lust coursing through her.

Even when he stopped to catch his breath, the short distance between them seemed too great.

"'Tis all your fault," he said with a wicked glint in his eyes after he rose to brace himself on one arm and gaze at her adoringly. "I cannae keep myself from wanting to worship your soft curves, your pouty mouth, your face that reminds me of another time and place."

"Do nae apologize, for it is I who have put this curse on you," she said, reaching up to run her finger across his swollen lips.

If she remembered what her mother had told her about the herbs he'd taken, Alasdair's memory of their time together tonight would fade as the herbs' potency faded. This would serve her well as she'd not have to explain her actions to him later.

He touched the space between her brows. "Do not be concerned. We will be discreet. No one will think less of you if they find out you're sleeping in my quarters tonight," he promised.

Ursula grinned wickedly at Alasdair, and the knot in her brows relaxed, for public opinion was furthest from her mind.

Public opinion be dammed. Because the public damned witches. But she was more of a shaman, more of a faerie, more of the otherworld than a witch.

If Alasdair worshiped the ground she walked on for tonight, no one else's opinion mattered.

His devotion liberated her. From the moment they'd first met, he'd treated her with respect and dignity. A spark of attraction had ignited on the parapet at Fyvie Castle. Nothing but raw emotion guided their feelings then and now.

We'll start slow," Alasdair said, rubbing the back of his hand across the rise of her breasts, which were straining against the bondage of her traveling dress.

But that's not what Ursula wanted, and she wasn't going to wait. Pushing him down on the bed beside her, she boldly reached for the buttons on his breeches.

"Then we'll go fast," she promised as her hand pressed against his hardened shaft, willing to give him pleasure instead of taking her own.

Alasdair swore softly in Gaelic before he rolled her over on top of him. He simply gazed at her for a long moment before he said, "We have nae been together long, but I cannae shake the feeling I've known you from afore. How can that be?"

She had the same sense, too, as if their history had been written by scribes and whispered in her ear as a babe. She sensed a connection to Alasdair that scared her, but fear would not stop her from exploring his body and freeing his spirit.

"Your birthing faerie should have determined your fate, perhaps our time together is predestined."

Her words deepened his grin. "My mother spoke of a Norse fate, our Nornir, who was in charge of our future."

"Only time will tell," she said as he gathered her in his arms. His lip twitched in the most appealing way, and he moved his hand over one of her taut nipples straining against her dress.

"Modesty will rule the night, but you will choose where we go," he promised, kissing down her neck and poking his tongue between her cleavage.

Ursula sucked in a shaking breath, trying to calm her rioting emotions. As much as she wanted to behave as if she would have no regrets, she was happy Alasdair would not rush her, or force her into an intimacy that would not serve her right now, but she could allow his provocative exploration to surprise her.

"Will you stay with me tonight?" His words came slow and thick with longing.

Silence stretched between them. Their breathing shallow and labored. When she finally kissed him with her passion unleased, Alasdair had his answer.

Chapter 23

Alasdair studied his profile in the long mirror as he stood in George's chamber, smiling slyly at his reflection, the memory of his body tangled with Ursula's still fresh in his mind. But those moments had ended too soon, and he could remember very little.

He straighten up. Stood taller. But then the pain in his scar flared again.

"God's teeth, you are ugly," he swore to himself, crumbling back to his hunched position but relived to be dressed in his kilt and sporran again.

"Crotach, I am ugly, but I do nae expect you tell me so."

Alasdair doubled over laughing, happy to have his good friend to distract him from his frustration. George walked to the mirror and stood next to him.

"Here," his host said, offering the House of Gordon's blue-and-purple tartan.

"You think this disguise will hide me from the MacDonalds?" Alasdair asked him through the mirror's reflection.

"I shall need to provide a larger piece of plaid if you plan to hide from them," George replied in a logical tone and serious face.

"God's nails," Alasdair swore again, but this time he laughed. "'Tis true. The fabric is too small, but I would never hide from the MacDonalds."

"You will be less of a target without the MacLeod colors and the Faery Flag."

Alasdair turned to look directly at George.

"I do believe in its powers and the legend," his friend responded as if challenged.

Alasdair sighed. "It has not been unfurled since my father's death, and according to the legend, there is only one unfurling left."

"What if a new faerie and mortal marriage were to take place?" his friend suggested. "Do you think the flag could be regenerated by Faery magic?"

The idea was intriguing, and it had Alasdair daydreaming for a moment about Ursula. She called herself a witch. But most likely she was trying to hide her skills with herbs behind a veil of witchcraft, instead of revealing her roots in Faery magic.

Alasdair shook his head. "The Fae are fickle and can be evil, too. Most are," he preached. "More men have gone to the faerie pools or glen than have returned."

George shrugged his shoulders. "Depends on what you ask of the faerie, I've been told. Trick them before they trick you."

"Wise words from experience?"

"I stand before you, do I not?"

"In breeches and nae a kilt. That is the problem."

"The kilt is practical for your Highland life, not mine," George said as if a kilt was barbaric.

"A kilt is impractical for the way you live? Is that what you are saying?" Alasdair shot back.

George burst out laughing. "If you stay a few days rather than march off, you will see how preferable breeches can be. I packed a pair in your bag," George confessed with a superior tone.

Alasdair raised a brow, then waved away any concerns with his hand. "I'll tear them up and use them for bandages if we run into trouble."

"Well, Clan MacDonald spells trouble to me. So keep them at the ready if you need to patch yourself up." Then he pointed to Alasdair's shoulder. "Crotach, you do nae want another injury like that."

He straightened, tall again in the mirror at George's challenge. *There it was again. The pain.*

Alasdair relaxed back into his normal stance with a taunt grin. *Humpback* was the name his enemies used when they called out to him. He'd replied to them with his sword and silenced them for good.

George rolled up his fine linen shirt to bare a horizontal mark across his chest. "Scars are reminders of the sacrifices we've made for others," he said, then let his shirt fall back into place. "Some can be hidden, but all must be worn with pride."

"We are both full of pride, brother," Alasdair said, grabbing his friend's arm below the elbow in their customary salutation.

George took hold of Alasdair's arm. "If you do nae want to see how we live here at Urquhart and enjoy the civilized way of life in breeches, I will reluctantly take you to the armory for supplies before you depart."

Alasdair released his grip and followed his friend out of the solar, until George stopped abruptly and said, "You did not tell me how last evening fared."

Alasdair gave George a friendly shove. "That was my intention."

~ ~ ~

Ursula wrung her hands and stared at Ethan, hoping what he'd said to her was a mistake. Her night with Alasdair was still fresh in her mind, and she'd yet to decide how it would color their future together.

She stalled. "We should nae leave this place without thanking our host, nor should we abandon the plan to travel with the Highlander. I made a promise."

"Break it."

She stomped her foot. "You made a promise, too."

Ethan crossed his arms over his chest and stared down at her. But she refused to be intimated or bullied by him.

"I break promises," he said, raising his head defiantly.

She stood her ground. "He has offered to help you with a battalion of men. To assist in negotiating Eilean Donan Castle."

He squinted his eyes. "You are a fool, Ursula. Why would he bring his army to Eilean Donan, secure the fortress, and then hand it over to me?"

She opened her mouth to answer, and then stopped. For the first time this journey, Ethan made a good point. As much has she was taken by Alasdair's charms, the idea the Highlander would provide support without reward was far-fetched.

Ethan pushed further. "He never revealed why he was in Petershead without a troop of soldiers. Perhaps he is estranged from his clan. Men rarely travel alone. Unless they're on the run."

Her further hesitation gave Ethan fuel for his argument. "You are a smart lass, Ursula. You must admit his actions are suspicious, regardless of his connections here." He swept his arms out where they stood in the lower bailey near the horse stalls.

She baulked. Evan though his arguments were surprisingly convincing, abandoning Alasdair seemed irresponsible. "'Tis no reason to separate ourselves from his company yet," she insisted. "He is familiar with the local roads through the Highlands. You told me yourself you had nae been to Eilean Donan in ten years.

"We can hire a local guide, Ursula." He said it with such practicality she almost agreed, until she remembered last night, being in Alasdair's arms. He had transported her somewhere else.

She shook her head vehemently. “We will honor our promise. If we do nae find his story consistent with his actions, we can part company. We can be straightforward with him.”

Ethan did not appear convinced and scrunched up his face, showing his displeasure.

She retaliated with a sweet smile, hoping the herb potion she’d added in his breakfast ale would start to take effect and she would have compliant Ethan again.

As she waited to see what he would do or say, she remembered the map Quinn had given her, packed safely in her satchel. It could prove helpful if Alasdair was left behind.

Ursula needed to figure out, once the rare flower was found, who would join her on the return trip to Fyvie. It might be neither man, for both had clans and castles to contend with, and having a woman underfoot might not be a welcome distraction.

“Did you hear me?”

Coming out of her mental fog, Ursula finally realized Ethan had given her his answer.

“Nay, I was contemplating what you’ve suggested,” she admitted.

“Good because it is our plan.” He glanced hurriedly over his shoulder. “You want to return to Fyvie as quickly as you can. A march to Dunvegan, before Eilean Donan, will add two days to our journey.”

Of course. Time was the enemy for Ursula. Not Ethan or Alasdair. She sighed deeply.

Chapter 24

Hills and sky were inseparable by nightfall that evening when Ursula turned her horse up the castle path behind Ethan.

She wasn't sure how he'd convinced her to leave Alasdair behind. Perhaps it was the fear of trusting a man she did not know. Other than Joshua, few men had stripped her bare of all but her emotions.

Alasdair had been infatuated with her last night. No doubt the herbs had influenced him, but while it had been glorious to be worshipped by him, she was certain his feelings toward her would be short-lived. Once the final effects of the herbs wore off, in a day or more, she'd be nothing more to him than a means to his pleasure. They had shared an evening filled with touching, kissing, and passion, but nae love.

She'd taken no risks with her future, and if they were destined to meet again, she'd have to trust in the power of fate.

Ethan was at least controllable, and they both had similar goals. As Ethan had pointed out, Alasdair's reasons for assisting them were questionable at best, and adding more days to their journey would be gambling with Rosalyn's future.

So it was with much regret that Ursula agreed to Ethan's insistence. Although she could control him to some degree, even with extra herbs that morning, she couldn't convince him to include Alasdair in their plans any longer. She could only hope his common sense would override his jealousy when she agreed to this new arrangement.

Her mood lighted after they passed through the portcullis. Glengarry was one of her favorite places in the Highlands, and Invergarry Castle was home to friends and Clan MacDonnell.

After they'd been welcomed, and she'd unpacked, Ursula was greeted by Conn outside the great hall.

"You know, Ursula, I've always considered you a daughter of my heart," her host told her while giving her a generous hug and a kiss on the cheek.

"Conn, you have always been a thorn in my side," she said affectionately, returning the hug and then stepping back.

He chuckled at her aside. Ursula held on to his hands and studied the elder clansman while their arms formed a friendly bridge.

Conn MacDonnell was taller than most Scots, and he commanded a room better than anyone she knew. His bright-red, shoulder-length hair did not show his true age, nor did his agility. As far as she knew, he would have been the same age as her uncle, but he looked more like a brother.

After Ethan suggested they journey on without Alasdair, she agreed as long as they stopped at Invergarry. With Conn's help, they could approach Eilean Donan with some of his men. She hoped he'd spare them.

"My, my, Ursula, you are just as witty but more beautiful than I remember," he said smoothly with a short bow.

"Conn, you flatter me." She batted her eyelashes. "That's hard to do."

He swept his arm out for her taking, and she hooked her hand around it as he escorted her through the crowded hall and to the dais. She was giddy with delight to see Conn again. With Ethan taking his meal in his chamber, she'd have the freedom to visit with her old friend privately.

Once he'd finished with a welcome to guests and her introduction, the food began to fill the table. Venison, wild boar, swan.

It wasn't until she finished her food that Ursula raised her head from her meal to take in the surroundings. The great hall was well appointed, and Conn had some of the finest trappings of any castle in the Highlands.

Riding all day, with only breaks to relieve themselves, had only offered time to eat the last of the hard meats Captain Quinn had given her, but that hadn't been enough. She'd been famished when she'd taken a seat beside Conn at the head table and had yet to say much to her host.

"'Tis a good thing you wandered by my castle this evening, or you may have eaten a squirrel for dinner."

Ursula turned to her host and smirked. "Squirrel meat is tender," she chirped. "You should try it."

The disgusted look on Conn's face was worthy payment for her response, and she returned it with a satisfied grin. Because Ursula could let her guard down when she was with Conn, she was able to free herself from the burdens of others she'd been carrying. Even though he'd promised to be a father to her if she needed one, what she needed right now was an ally.

The high table was empty except for the two of them, and she finally had all of his attention.

"You must have made a major decision. Your expression just clouded over." He touched her check gently. "What troubles you?"

Ursula sighed first, gathering up in her mind the information he needed to know. Then she collapsed onto the table for dramatic effect, bowing her head over her folded arms as she pleaded, "I need your help, Conn."

He laid a hand gently atop of her head. "Of course. If you wish it. It will be done."

Inwardly, she leaped with glee. The ploy had worked for her many times, and she was certain she could sucker Conn with her antics. But she couldn't rush the lamenting, so she added, “I will need a good number of your men to travel with us to Skye.”

“Done,” he said, stroking her hair. “I am sure you have a sufficient need.”

Her head nodded under his hand.

“Where are you going on Skye?”

“First, Eilean Donan,” she told him. The words were a bit muffled with her face against her arm.

“The MacDonald stronghold?”

She bolted upright. “Is it held by the MacDonalds?”

“Now, I cannot swear to it, but ’tis the rumor. My men usually travel between here and Loch Ness. We rarely cross the sea to Skye.”

She kept her gaze on him as she sat erect and explained further. “Eilean is on a tidal island in Kyle of Lochalsh, across from the Isle.”

“So you plan to march with my men to knock on their porticus gate?”

“They have no quarrel with me,” she defended.

“They do nae need to have a quarrel to do what they want. They are heathens, Ursula. Do you nae know what you propose?”

She sighed again. “I only need to deliver Ethan to Donan, and then be escorted to the faerie pools at Glenbrittle on Skye Isle.”

“The faerie pools?” He said it with such shock in his voice it cracked. He looked at her as if she’d gone mad. “Eilean Donan was bad enough, but my men will go nowhere near the pools even if I order them to, and they are loyal men.”

Ursula collapsed on the table again and began to sob. Now, would her dramatic acting be convincing enough to get what she needed?

~ ~ ~

Beyond heinous. Treasonous. Ursula's actions against Alasdair cut to the heart. Just when he was falling in love with her, letting himself be vulnerable, she'd abandoned him.

Although he suspected Ethan to be the culprit, convincing her to leave without him, Alasdair would like to think she only agreed because the bastard had threatened her.

He hoped to find more resolution when George met him in the baily, but his good friend was just as shocked by their unannounced departure.

No matter if they were both guilty of rebellion, Alasdair had told his friend Ethan would be putting Ursula at great risk. They had both agreed the MacDonalds were a bloodthirsty clan.

Although Alasdair had originally planned to gather his own troops before approaching Eilean Donan Castle, Ethan forced him into accepting half of George Gordon's men. His captain, Douglas Stewart, was a great companion, suggesting a shorter route to Glengarry first before their contingent made the longer march on the MacDonalds.

As Alasdair became comfortable with his new plan, he thought more about his night with Ursula. The memories were no longer clear, yet he was left with a desire to find her, help her, and love her again.

As his contingent neared Glengarry at nightfall, he wondered if his old friend Conn MacDonnell would welcome his company. Even though Gordon's men were capable of camping on the ground, he'd learned from the captain that the men routinely returned to Urquhart after a day of service.

He would not call them a pampered battalion, but they were no match for the Highland outdoor weather. It was raining heavily now, and there would be no place dry to sleep except inside the walls of Invergarry Castle.

Once he'd conferred with Douglas and secured his approval, the group of servant knights joined Alasdair late that evening in the castle with the promise of finding their host and some food.

Walking into the great hall, Alasdair was reminded of his own at Dunvegan. A bit of homesickness made his heart ache for the castle that had been the stronghold of his family for eight generations.

Like his gathering room, Conn's white stone walls were covered with dark tapestries, most depicting MacDonnell clan victories.

More spoils of conquests were displayed on the ornately carved sideboards behind the head table.

As he approached the dais, Alasdair recognized his friend. Then he froze in his tracks and his gaze riveted to the woman beside him, holding his friend's attention.

At the same time, Gordon's men rushed past him like he was a logjam in the river and they were the waters. But once the path was clear of Gordon's foot soldiers and Alasdair could see the head table clearly again, she was gone.

Where was she? Even if the woman wasn't Ursula, how could she have been there one moment and gone the next?

Conn sat alone on the dais. The red-haired MacDonnell raised a pewter goblet and waved it in earnest for Alasdair to join him.

Conn was grinning when Alasdair took a seat beside him. "Good to see you, Crotach. You did nae dress for dinner."

Alasdair glanced down at his soggy kilt. He'd removed his damp bearskin cape, but his leather vest and wool tartan were dry. His mane of hair was another story. He shook it in response to Conn's comment.

"A Scottish hound would have better manners," Conn declared and laughed heartily. He raised a hand to slap Alasdair's right shoulder, but his slight flinch must have reminded Conn not to.

Instead, Conn reached across and grabbed Alasdair's forearm in greeting as George had. "You do appear more wolfhound than man tonight. How fare thee, my good friend?"

"I fare better than the brethren I bring with me. Your good man, Luther, took us in."

"He will shelter dogs and men from friendly clans," he joked, then grew serious and flicked at the plaid that stretched across Alasdair's chest. "What are these colors?"

"I'm in disguise," Alasdair said proudly.

"Who do you think you'll be fooling?" Conn asked sarcastically.

Alasdair wanted to say the MacDonalds but resisted. "From a distance, I won't be recognized as Alasdair MacLeod," he said, pointing to the only men at the trestle tables. "I wear the House of Gordon's colors. This way I blend in."

Conn waved him closer and said, "You never blend in." Then he leaned back and slapped the table. "Why must you hide who you are? Is there a price on your head?"

Alasdair crossed his arms against his chest. "Nay, Conn, 'tis a precautionary measure too complicated to explain." It was best not to admit he planned to knock on the MacDonald's portcullis and ask to be admitted as if he were one of the clan. With Ethan and Ursula at his side nonetheless.

Ursula? Conn had distracted him.

He waved Conn closer. "Who was that beautiful woman by your side when I came in?" Alasdair looked around the great hall. "It was as if she disappeared in a puff of smoke."

"That was my lady friend," Conn replied, then one of his eyebrows rose. "You are my guest, but you may not feast on all that is at my table," he warned, leaning in within a breath of Alasdair face.

He backed away. "Never mind," Alasdair said, his cheeks heating. "I thought she looked like someone . . ." But he would have seen Ethan at the table as well. Perhaps the resemblance between the two women was just a coincidence or due to his fatigue. Maybe his eyes had played tricks on him.

"There are many women in the castle. Let me send one to your chambers." Conn's offer woke Alasdair from his musings. As much as that would distract him from thinking about Ursula, he did not want any other than her in his bed.

"Your hospitality is beyond my expectations, good friend, but I need to depart at sunrise with my pampered party."

Conn glanced over at the trestle tables still full of Lord George Gordon's men. They were boisterous and blatantly drunk.

"You have a daunting task," Conn agreed, nodding toward the tables. "Gordon's guards appear to be muddled in their mead already."

Alasdair shook his head. "My clansmen would never be that disrespectful. Not at Dunvegan and especially not here at Invergarry."

Conn turned his attention back to Alasdair. "How fares Dunvegan?"

Alasdair grasped his chin in contemplation. *What to share?* His hesitation wasn't lost on Conn.

"You fear the MacDonalds will rule all of Skye?"

Alasdair started to boil inside, his defensive response innate. He waited for the rising ire to pass. He did nae want to go off on his good friend.

"The MacLeods and the MacDonalds will forever be mortal enemies." Alasdair got up to pace on the dais. This wasn't a subject he could discuss sitting down. "Our clans have too much hate. Too much history. Too much angst between us. A truce will never be." Alasdair stopped and faced his host.

Conn pursed his lips as if he wanted to say something but remained silent. Alasdair took it as a cue to continue. "If the MacDonald clan gains dominance one day, you can bet your family fortune we will be fighting to gain it back the same day. The score is never settled."

Conn chuckled lightly and smacked the seat Alasdair had vacated. "Come, friend. I want to discuss a rumor and have you put it to rest. I cannot talk to you as you pace."

It was Alasdair's turn to chuckle as he took up his place next to Conn. "'Tis not true. Not my fault. I'm not guilty."

His friend burst out laughing. "You sound like my stable boy."

Alasdair grinned, but Conn grew serious.

"There is trouble between here and Skye, my friend, and it is not all coming from the MacDonalds." Conn leaned in. "I've heard Volar is back."

"The Viking?" Alasdair had heard of a man who had come to Skye from the Shetland Isles. He'd been told this Viking and his men had patrolled the wharfs of Inverness, pillaging and causing general havoc until they were forced back to their long boats.

"My course has been east to west, Conn. I am nae coming from Dunvegan but returning. I was just two days from Inverness where I learned King James had dispatched several battalions of soldiers to assist ridding his Scotland of the Norwegian barbarians."

"My friend, they may have decided on a new port to pillage, for there are rumors of Viking mayhem from Portree to Bernisdale. I do nae want to alarm you, but Dunvegan may be their next target."

Alasdair pushed back into the regal chair and crossed his arms. "The Vikings make a yearly sport of attacking Dunvegan. 'Tis nothing new in our world."

Conn made a *harrumph* sound, then pointed to Gordon's men at the trestle table. Many of them had their heads on the table, out cold.

Alasdair shook his head. "I should send the whole lot of them back tomorrow and travel on my own," he said with disgust.

Conn brightened and leaned forward. "You may be in luck. I am lending a large contingent of my soldiers to aid a friend on a journey to Skye in the morn. Why not join their group? When they reach their destination, my men will escort you to Dunvegan."

When Alasdair started to object, his friend stood. "This is settled." Then he turned to his servant who'd been waiting patiently off the end of the dais and waved him over. "Get these pieces of shite out of my hall," he told the man, pointing at Gordon's men.

Alasdair laughed as he followed Conn out into the corridor and gave his good friend's shoulder a friendly squeeze. "Loyalty and competency are not the same thing."

"Remember, Crotach, these men are not Highlanders. I'd hate to even count them as Scotsmen."

Alasdair agreed, "They act more like Englishmen, weak and pompous."

They both laughed as they said goodnight.

Making his way up a narrow, winding, stone staircase, Alasdair almost tumbled backward when a rush of skirts and a dark-haired lass threatened to knock him down.

After she grumbled an awkward apology and struggled to regain her footing, Alasdair grabbed the lass by the shoulders and set her upright. "Slow down or you be causing a calamity of major proportions."

When she did not look up to address him, he shook her gently.

"Yes, mi lord," she finally mumbled.

Alasdair was about to release her when he took a second look. Although the staircase was dimly lit from a sconce around the next turn, the weak glow gave out enough light for him to recognize her.

His heart leapt. "Ursula?" Alasdair's voice was thick from the shock. It had been her at the head table after all.

Chapter 25

What could Ursula tell him? Ethan had forced her to leave? That he'd threatened her? Some of that she could claim true. But it would be hard for Alasdair to forgive her for bolting from the great hall when he'd appeared, after begging Conn not to give her away.

He released her as if he'd grabbed a hot poker. "'Tis you," Alasdair said, his frown fierce and his glare deadly.

"Walk," he ordered as if he'd take no arguments, pointing down the corridor from which she'd come.

Ursula stayed mute and spun on her heel, shocked at the coincidence they'd arrived at the same place at the same time. Good luck or back luck, she'd soon find out as they walked in silence, Alasdair behind her.

After a slow tortuous journey down multiple corridors, they finally reached his guest chamber, where he told her to stop. He marched up to the entrance and shoved open the door. It banged against the wall inside.

She shivered, wanting to scream and run, but she was certain he'd catch her and drag her back to his room to . . . *Would he harm her?*

The room was lit by the glow of the hearth. As she stumbled in, he pointed to a chair and left her without entering. Once the door closed, her heart pounded like a rabbit caught in a fox's lair.

Although it seemed like an eternity, it wasn't long before he returned. She almost jumped out of her skin, her heart still pounding, when he opened the door without knocking.

Highlanders.

As if he'd forgotten she was there, he tossed his sporran, then his leather vest, on the bed and began to pace. Saying nothing. Giving her no idea what would happen next.

Ursula studied his profile in the amber glow. He stopped moving. Had he come to some decision, or was he ready to make an accusation?

Although the muscles covering his bare shoulders and arms glistened like bronzed armor, Alasdair hunched over as if suffering from a fresh wound.

His posture was more apparent to her now than in the past. Quinn had spoken of him being hunchbacked. He appeared that way to her now, and defeated.

Fearful as she was, her heart still went out to him. Ursula wanted to heal him. She had promised but not delivered on attending to him at Urquhart Castle. Because—she blushed—because he had needed something else. But he'd been a gentleman to her that night, and he had only sought his own pleasure. Pleasure she'd been willing to give.

Did he want her to touch him again? To heal him? Or did he wish to punish her?

When he turned to her, her gut wrenched. Filled with dread and uncertainly, she thought she'd vomit.

"I'm in need of an heir. What is your price?"

Ursula blinked hard. *What was that? What is my price?*

She'd been prepared for a lecture on responsibility. To be called a traitor. A witch. Untrustworthy. She finally gathered her wits and was surprised she didn't deliver harsh words with the fury that was building inside.

"You want an heir?"

"Aye. All my brothers are dead."

She coughed, using the gesture to sort through possible responses until she found the suitable one.

"I do nae want to appear callous, and I'm sorry you're the last of the MacLeods, but my purpose in this lifetime is nae to bring a babe into this world."

Alasdair stared at her. "God created women for that purpose. And to please men," he declared with absolute faith, as if those words had been written by the saints.

She coughed even louder this time. "That is blasphemous and irreverent." His ignorance and stupidity would not be tolerated. Ursula bounded up from the chair and strode to within inches of his chest. She began to poke it. Hard.

"You say you want an heir, but that happens only when two people consent to join hearts, minds, and spirits. To recreate their likeness in God's image." Her poking turned into a shove. "You cannot play God without dire consequences."

When she finished her rant, Alasdair was backed up against one of the canopy posts.

In the next moment, before Ursula could take a breath and start into another diatribe, his mouth was on hers. Grabbing her about the waist, he spun her around until they awkwardly toppled onto the soft velvet bedcover, his lips still locked to hers. Demanding.

Would he take what he wanted without her permission?

Could he?

Her heart beat frantically when he lifted her on top of his chest. She pushed against him, trying to separate herself from him, but his arms tightened. Exasperated, she bit his lip.

Yelping like a pup, he let her go and pushed her off.

She rolled over to her side, precariously close to the edge, but he grabbed her arm just before she would have tumbled to the floor. He tugged her back to his side.

Ursula breathed hard. Should she seek help from Conn or settle this herself? Her adoptive father would never condone Alasdair's actions. If she asked Conn, she was certain he'd boot Alasdair's arse out.

Turning to look at her and rubbing his lip he said, "You must have a price."

He'd ignored everything she'd said.

All right, if he was going to be pigheaded and obstinate, she could, too.

"The Faery Flag. That is my price." *Why had she said that?* She'd planned to tell him why she would never agree.

He was silent.

She closed her eyes and tried to focus in on his thoughts.

Was he considering her offer?

Ursula had always assumed she was barren and had given up on the idea of having children after watching too many women die in childbirth while helping her mother, where she'd learned her craft. For every birth she'd assisted, she'd felt the pain, but she'd never realized the joy. For the babes were never hers.

'Twould be sweet retribution if she was given the flag but could not produce an heir. Would he hold the flag hostage until he could see proof? She needed the flag for Fyvie.

"You ask for too much," he said softly. She was shocked he was even considering her request. His thoughts were not clear to her, but she could read the agitation on his face.

"You do nae believe what you asked of me is too much?"

Alasdair was quiet again. She opened her eyes and watched his chest rise and fall, wondering what it would be like to wake up with him every morning. She shook that idea out of her thoughts. That wasn't going to be, regardless of his decision.

"You are a fine woman, Ursula, and I do nae mean to dismiss your value when I ask you to consider joining with me to produce a legacy for my clan."

Ursula's heart softened, and she sighed inwardly. Creating a legacy for his clan was more palatable than producing an heir under his command.

"If you had put it that way first . . ." She paused.

"You would have said yes right away and told me the honor would be enough," he said, turning his head toward her with a hopeful look and eyebrows raised.

She burst out laughing. He was so incorrigible. She waited for him to speak again, but when he didn't, and all that returned was his steady breathing, she went on.

"'Tis nae that I want the Faery Flag for myself, or for the glory of the having captured the secret of Skye Isle. It is to protect those who have become my family." She choked on the emotion building in her throat. "Rival clans are uprising in Aberdeenshire." She took in a shaky breath. "My sister of the heart is pregnant with twins and trying to rule with her half-English husband."

When Alasdair's face twisted into a confused expression, she held up her hand. "'Tis another story that, but I have promised not only to bring back the flower to save my friend, I have also pledged to bring back the flag to save them all," she said with a confidence as if it was possible.

Alasdair bolted upright.

Was he angry with what she'd just confessed?

He was still in his kilt, his boots dangling over the edge of the bed. She stared at the maimed mass of muscle on his back and upper right shoulder. Until now, he'd kept it hidden from her. Even last night, he would not let her examine it when she'd asked.

Alasdair glanced at her over the scarred shoulder with a pained expression, as if her gaze upon him caused him discomfort.

When his eyes darted away, Ursula sat up and reached under her skirt for the pouch of healing ointments she always had tucked in the sewn-in compartment. She sensed a force more powerful than their own will guiding her.

With a vial of oil in one hand, Ursula moved closer and climbed over one of Alasdair thighs as he sat at the edge of the bed. She balanced herself there while she carefully removed the top of the container, spilled some of the oil into her palm, and then put the remedy aside.

"Close your eyes," Ursula instructed, releasing a ragged sigh. There was a familiarity from last night, but that had been different. He had guided her actions, and she had pleased him.

If it not for that time together, though, Ursula wouldn't have the courage to be this close to him now, gazing into his handsome face with his high, proud brow.

Taking a deep breath to stop herself from trembling, she said, "Let me do what I was born to do."

And with that, she leaned into his chest, resting her chin on his left shoulder, then reaching across the expanse of his broad back, she began to rub the light ointment onto Alasdair's scar.

With her eyes closed and all her focus on that spot, she went into a trance-like state.

Soon Ursula was in the pandemonium of the battlefield, Alasdair's enemies killing men he loved. Clansmen bloodied on the ground around him, childhood friends. She could stand witness to it.

Looking into the eyes of the man who had maimed him, Ursula cringed when the axe came down on his shoulder. The grimness and the gore.

But as she manipulated her fingers into the seam of Alasdair's mended wound, she massaged deeply, reaching beyond the severed muscles and skin that had healed on the outside to his emotional scars buried beneath.

As Ursula worked, she imagined she had found Alasdair's untreated insecurities and shame buried in the deeper recesses of his physical wound.

There, she began to stitch together the ragged edges of his feelings. To mend the emotional wound and give Alasdair a chance to redeem his pride.

Ursula had been so focused on her work she'd tuned out Alasdair's aggravated groans. But as she was finishing her healing treatment, she noticed the moaning had taken on a very different sound. Evidently, Alasdair was not only getting relief, he was getting aroused. She could not ignore his manhood rising next to her thigh, pushing up his kilt.

The image almost made her laugh, but it also made her realize how much she wanted Alasdair MacLeod. Her selfless nature had all but snuffed out any feelings brewing inside.

Ursula's massaging hand slowed to a stop when she leaned back and her gaze met his. She could almost feel the heat radiating from the center of his dark-hazel eyes.

Alasdair leaned into her, and his lips captured her breath, then stole it.

Her mind spun. She wanted more of him. Flag or heir, neither was important now. They had crossed into a new realm of understanding.

Alasdair groaned into the kiss. A passionate, prisoner-takes-all kiss. She abandoned her inhibitions as she gave in to his spellbinding touch.

Now it was her turn to groan. She stretched her neck and arched her back with a sweet sound of approval.

Alasdair lifted her up into his arms, cradling her like a babe. He turned around from where he stood and carefully laid her on the satin pillows before he climbed onto the bed beside her.

How was it she had brought this man to bed again so soon? This time he had not mentioned the herbs, nor their effect on him as an excuse for his actions, which made her wonder if they'd ever had any power over him at all.

But there was more to this man and this moment. She was certain. Call it her intuition that never failed. As much as Ursula wanted to gaze into a future, she could not. Right now, she wanted to look at him, not his thoughts.

No matter his scar, or his clan, she welcomed him to her body. He stroked her hair as he lay on his side. Words were not necessary now, for they had already decided why they would come together. 'Twas not for love, or lust. *Well, perhaps a little lust.* But for mutual respect and a commitment to a legacy. An heir.

Ursula had bristled at the suggestion at first, but now she was warming to the noble idea of being a part of his future.

Her rambling thoughts finally stopped when his hand slid under her skirt and he began to caress her between the thighs, making her lose her mind. But when his two fingers glided into her channel with a rotating motion, she lost control.

"You do nae need to pleasure me to bury your seed. Be on with it," she said through gritted teeth, trying not to sound ungrateful.

"That is the most unromantic thing I've ever heard," Alasdair said with a chuckle, still continuing with his method, not slowing or stopping.

She laughed along with him. "Aye, but you have to admit my words speak to your request."

"I want an heir?"

She nodded and smiled. A bit of the tension broke, but she was in need of some relief.

"No matter the goal, my wish is to make you feel as desired and special as possible," Alasdair promised. But then he interrupted his gentle, lascivious attention and moved his hand away from her heat.

"You have too many clothes on," he declared as if she had asked his opinion, but she agreed.

Rising to the side of the bed, Alasdair guided Ursula to stand before him, his chest at her eye level, muscles rippling with every breath.

Had the antidote she'd taken strengthened the potion's power instead of weakened it? And if she felt the pull of the spell, Alasdair would be even more under its influence.

Even though counterfeit love could not be trusted, Ursula did not care, because it felt so sinfully good.

A man as delectably desirable as Alasdair MacLeod would no doubt test the sensual boundaries of the most prudent woman. His gaze alone made Ursula feel she could burst into flames if he stared at her long enough.

But he did more than stare. With one swift movement, he tore apart her traveling dress from the neckline down to her toes as if swatting away a flimsy spider's web.

Standing before him in the warm glow of the hearth, her breath hitched when his gaze raked over her naked form as if he was seeing it for the first time. And before she had time to exhale, his lips began an exploratory assault.

With lavish kisses, he meandered his way from one ear, dragging his lips along her neckline, and then down to the middle of her breasts. A torturously slow, delicious seduction.

Deliberately holding her gaze, he sucked on one of her taught nipples, while he rubbed the other until it stood at attention. Her carnal reaction to this simple act made her want him more than ever. Without the need for commitment or promised marriage, Ursula felt free to satiate her desires in a wanton way.

If temptation had a name, it would be Alasdair MacLeod.

Ursula wanted to beg. To have him inside her. But she bit her tongue hard to keep from speaking the words. Fortunately, he stopped the gentle torture.

"As much as I adore worshiping you as you stand before me like the queen of the Fae, not of this world but of magic and myth, I must admit I do nae have the patience I'd hoped for." He gazed at her with a mix of passion and compassion. "Are you a virgin?"

When she denied it with a headshake, he responded with a wicked grin. And before she could blink or take in another shaky breath, she was cradled in his arms and laid back on the chamber bed.

Ursula heard his boots tumble to the floor, but before she

could worry about what was coming next, Alasdair was on the bed pushing her legs open.

And with one quick movement, his shaft was inside her, pumping the full length of her channel. She met him stroke for stoke, and they joined together as one, her body trembling from Alasdair's salacious movements.

This was what she'd wanted. What had been told to her by generations of women could be had, like a rare diamond, not discovered by many. And as much as being worshiped at the beginning was lovely, this manic, wicked lovemaking was what she craved.

Alasdair made no apologies for his shift from seducer to lover. And Ursula responded with wanton gasps and sighs and panting.

When she could bear the intensity of his movements no longer she said, "Please, I beg you, let it be done." And with one final effort, they rose to the highest heights and then, as if falling off a cliff, dropped back to earth with Alasdair collapsing gently on top of her.

The seed was planted.

Once their labored breaths subsided to sighs and soft moans, Alasdair gave her a big smack on the lips before he dropped to her side and draped a warm arm over her middle.

"My brother once described the act of mating as a chore," Alasdair admitted. "'Tis a pity he never experienced anything as heavenly as I have with you tonight."

Ursula beamed inside and out. Alasdair's compliment would have been the last thing she'd have expected to hear when they'd first discussed their business arrangement. Then, she had expected to be fulfilling a duty. Instead, he had worshiped her like a goddess.

Chapter 26

Conn's men met Alasdair in the lower baily just as the glorious sun rose over the Highland Mountains, signaling a promising day of travel. Alasdair took it as a good omen for the future as he prepared his horse and secured the saddle with the help of a stable boy.

He didn't look up when a rider approached. But when gravel and dust hit his face, that changed.

"*Och!* What bastard dares this?" he asked, standing to his full height, finding Ethan waiting for him with a smirk on his face.

"Remember this, bastard?"

He wasn't sure whether Ethan was referring to himself or calling Alasdair one, but he would clarify. "Any man who is nae of full Scottish blood is a bastard," Alasdair stated plainly.

Ethan did not bat an eye when he withdrew his longsword from its scabbard.

Alasdair let a beat go by before handing the reins to the stable boy. Then he asked Ethan, "What are we fighting over?"

"That should be obvious."

Alasdair shook his head and began to move to his right as Conn's men stopped what they'd been doing and gathered to watch.

As Ethan started circling in the opposite direction, Alasdair withdrew his sword, ready to defend himself. Clearly Ethan wanted to fight. And Alasdair did not have to wait long.

The intention was in Ethan's eyes before his limbs. With a slight rise in his sword, Ethan lunged toward Alasdair.

But Alasdair was ready and leapt out of the way.

Ethan almost stumbled when he'd rushed at Alasdair with such force, expecting to connect with his sword. But the bastard gained his footing quickly and spun around, sputtering under his breath.

"Are you fighting for England? For I am fighting for Scotland."

Ethan spat. "You should be fighting for your life."

"What quarrel do you have with me?" Alasdair asked, circling to his right. Letting Ethan be the aggressor, he'd fend off the poor louse until it was time to depart or someone called the farce off.

"You covet my wife."

"As far as I'm concerned, I do nae know your wife."

Ethan made another lunge forward, clanging with a mighty force into Alasdair's blade. Even though his back had been injured in battle, he overcame his pain when he fought.

Alasdair parried to the right. Then left. Right again. He exchanged multiple clashes with Ethan's sword as the two used their skills and muscle to deflect their weapons.

Soon Ethan was wielding his sword with both hands. The longsword was a mighty weapon, but a weighty one.

With an exaggerated shout, Ethan charged. He missed Alasdair's blade, swiping at air instead. That brought Ethan to his knees.

Alasdair strode forward and pointed his sword under the perpetrator's chin. "Had enough?"

Ethan spit on the sword.

"I shall take that as a yes. Sheath your weapon. You can join us or stay behind and wait for the House of Gordon's drunken contingent to lead you to Eilean Donan."

Ethan stayed on his knees, staring down at Alasdair's

sword. Not until he heard Ursula's shout did the imbecile scramble to his feet as Conn's men went back to the business of readying their horses.

Ursula's hair whipped around in the wind. Her eyes were filled with concern. After Ethan sheathed his sword, Alasdair followed suit.

"We were having a discussion," Alasdair offered.

"A difference of opinion," Ethan added.

Conn strode up to join them. "A battle to the death?"

That made them all laugh, even Ethan.

But then Conn added, "All battles are fought over women or land. Which was it today?"

Ethan's responded by turning his back and walking toward the stables.

Alasdair shrugged his shoulders, and Conn burst out laughing.

Ursula blushed, either from the realization of why they were fighting or because it was the first time their eyes met since last night.

"How fares my lady?" Conn asked.

His lady? Those words punched him in the gut. Frantically his mind whirled over what Conn had said last night. Had he committed a crime of passion? Conn had told him at dinner Ursula was his lady friend. What had he said? *You cannot feast on everything that is at my table?* How could he be such a fool?

Alasdair turned to face his friend, interrupting their conversation. "Conn . . ." Then he glanced at Ursula and grabbed her hand, bringing her to his side before he confessed, "We are now one."

Conn's eyes ticked back and forth between them a few times before they settled on Alasdair.

His friend's face was stoic. Unsympathetic. Perhaps even verging on anger.

Alasdair braced for a thrashing of words or fists, but

at the moment he thought Conn would strike him, his host reached for Alasdair's hand instead and said with a warm smile, "She's yours."

Ursula huffed. "As if I can be bartered."

"I'm your father of the heart and with that responsibility comes the opportunity to give you away."

She rolled her eyes.

Alasdair let out all the air he was holding and bent over at the waist with a sigh of relief.

When he raised back up, his friend's eyes were full of mischief. "Let's just say I was protecting Ursula until she could see what was right."

She looked back and forth between them with some alarm. "You may not marry me off now, Conn." She looked at Alasdair. "We have an arrangement, and that is all you need to know."

Conn grinned. "Name the date and the town, and I will be there for your nuptials."

Ursula let out an even bigger huff and crossed her arms over her chest, mumbling something under her breath.

Alasdair had been single-minded last night. At least he hadn't breached a friendship. Not once had what Conn said at dinner registered. Not until now. He thanked the Lord he did not have to choose between them, nor fight for her and lose a good friend.

Which reminded him of the battle he'd just had with Ethan. He was silent as Conn and Ursula continued their verbal sparring, giving Alasdair a moment to consider his options.

Should he refuse Ethan passage with their contingent and leave him to his own devices, which could include traveling to Donan with Gordon's men? Or should he ask the man for a truce until they arrive in Kyle of Lochalsh, when they could all know for certain what they were facing?

If Ursula held no loyalty to the bastard, they could bypass

the MacDonald stronghold and head directly to Dunvegan. He'd been gone too long from his home and needed to make sure what was his remained so.

By the time Alasdair had made up his mind, he'd arrived at the stable entry to retrieve his horse, just as Ethan and the boy appeared at the entrance.

Alasdair waved the half-Englishman over while the lad tended to Alasdair's horse and tightened the saddle.

When Ethan was within earshot, Alasdair called out, "A truce."

Meeting him halfway, Alasdair stuck out his hand, "I propose a truce during our trip to Donan. I will honor my original pledge and guide you, Ursula, and Conn's men through the Highlands to your castle. Conn's men have agreed to protect us and stay loyal until I release them. You can either accept that or make it on your own with Gordon's men."

Ethan studied him for a moment. No doubt sizing him up and his options. But Alasdair did not take Ethan for a fool. He was sure the man would have a counter.

Finally, after staring at Alasdair's outstretched hand for a few moments, Ethan said, "This is not your quarrel or your quest. You are inconsequential. You are not needed."

Ethan came a few steps closer. "She's mine. Do not defy me."

Alasdair dropped his hand by his side. He thought about what Ethan had said for a moment. The stakes were complicated. He needed to see to Ursula's safety. And as soon as Ethan became entangled with the MacDonalds, the bastard would nae be able to honor his promise to help Ursula find the Skye flower. Now it was Alasdair's turn to counter.

"You take Conn's men and Ursula to Donan. And I will make my way there with Gordon's contingent. We will meet at the ridge overlooking the castle. 'Twill be two days journey at most." He paused. "Then the lady will choose."

"Aye." Ethan nodded. "We shall let the lady choose."

Chapter 27

Ursula was confused. One moment she was readying her horse to leave with Alasdair for Eilean Donan Castle, and the next he was promising to meet her there with Gordon's men instead. He mumbled something about once they arrived at Eilean Donan, she would choose.

Choose what? Choose to rid herself of men who were fighting over her? Choose to take Conn's men to the faerie pools on Skye and have them escort her back to Rosalyn without delay? Choose what was right for herself? Aye, that was what she'd prefer.

As she mounted her palfrey to follow Ethan and Conn's men out the portcullis gate, she considered her priorities.

There was no need to dally at Donan. That was Ethan's quest. And if she could rid herself of him there, she would and make her way with Conn's men and the map Quinn gave her to the faerie pools. Ursula was weary of drugging Ethan and listening to his matrimony claims.

The Faery Flag and Alasdair were other matters. Once one goal was accomplished, she would tackle the other. Sadly, she'd thought both the flag and the flower could be had at the pools. If what Alasdair had said was true, did he have the flag at Dunvegan, and was it now hers?

After their lovemaking, neither had spoken of the promise again. Would proof of an heir be required before she could collect her prize?

It would be a strange twist of fate for Ursula to return to Fyvie bearing Alasdair's child. He seemed a man of his word, and she hoped he would help her honor the promises she'd made to both Rosalyn and Lachlan before she settled on where she would call home.

Home. That had been many places for Ursula, but eventually, the contingent would come close to her Highland home. It had been ten summers. Would her people remember her? Who would be there? Would her sister still be alive? Ever since she'd become a royal court healer, she'd left her past where it should be—in the past.

She shuddered for a moment, and her horse must have felt it, too, for Tempest slowed and tossed her mane. Her horse was not from these parts, but horses were sensitive creatures.

Ursula was thankful to be left to herself as the hours wore on and the day waned. Ethan led the troop and conferred with Conn's men as they traveled. But they finally stopped as nightfall approached. With her childhood home only a few miles ahead, she had an idea she hoped Ethan would consider.

"Are we close to Shiel Bridge?" she asked as he tethered his warhorse to a tree, knowing full well they were, but wanting to make Ethan feel important.

"Aye, we are near, but that is not on our itinerary."

Ursula frowned. "You can nae be thinking of camping outdoors," she said, already feeling the bite of wind as the sun was setting.

He studied her carefully as if he was calculating her response to his initial plans. But because he was still hesitating, she made her case even stronger. "The laird of Spurr Fhuaran manor is an uncle of mine. I am certain we'd have comfortable lodging for the night."

When Ethan opened his mouth to reply, she added, "And I know 'tis only a four-hour ride from Shiel Bridge to Kyle of Lochalsh."

He huffed out a breath, but she kept going, "Shiel Bridge

is protected by Clan Fraser. I used to make the trip to Skye with my mother when I was a wee child."

A bit of emotion caught in her throat. Remembering the trips to Skye with her mother brought back a flood of memories.

Ethan's expression turned sympathetic, giving her the resolve to push a little harder. "Consider this. By midday, you could be the new laird of Eilean Donan. Would you not want to look rested and well-groomed to meet your clan?"

Playing to Ethan's ego had helped Ursula sway his opinion in the past. She prayed while his lips twisted in concentration, but he finally nodded his head curtly and grunted. "I shall go tell the men."

Ursula's heart leaped with glee and trepidation. Her Uncle Cameron had always been kind to her. Even if he'd died and his scowling eldest son was laird, no Fraser clan member was ever turned away from Spurr Fhuaran manor.

After a few moments, Ethan returned with the rest of the troops, and they were off in the direction of Shiel Bridge as the sun was setting ahead of them.

The northwest journey toward Skye was one of the most beautiful parts of Scotland, and even in the dim light, the views of the mountains against the darkening sky took her breath away.

Ursula found it bittersweet that this journey could reunite her with some of her clan and her homeland. And as they approached Spurr Fhuaran manor, with the Fraser flag flying proudly, Ursula sat taller on her mount.

One of the castle's parapet sentries called out. "State your business. State your clan."

Ethan hesitated, but Ursula did not. "Lodging. Clan Fraser." *That should be enough to gain entrance.*

When her request was greeted by the sound of grinding gate chains, Ethan turned to her and raised a brow. She shrugged in response. "We're family."

Once the gate to the fortified outer wall was finally up, they were met by a regal-looking, silver-haired leader.

Ursula let out a squeal when she recognized her uncle. She forgot there was a courtyard full of clansmen when she threw her arms about his neck and gave him a big kiss on the cheek.

"Uncle Cameron," she said in a long breath.

"Ursy," he croaked, his voice full of emotion. She gazed into his crystal-blue eyes as she hung on to his neck, remembering days when he'd lift her up just as they were now and spin her in circles while she giggled hysterically.

He grinned at her. "Want to take a spin?"

She almost nodded her head, but a group of clansmen standing behind him reminded her it would be a difficult invitation to accept.

She winked at him instead. "Before we leave on the morrow."

He lifted her up by the waist a few inches to give her a generous hug, and then gently set her down. "I'll collect on that promise, or you will regret it."

She laughed at the threat, then sobered, realizing she must introduce the contingent behind her. She swept her arm toward them. "These are Lord Conn MacDonnell's men. Leading them is Lord Ethan Luttrell."

"Welcome," Uncle Cameron said warmly. "We will sup in the dining hall shortly." He turned to Ursula. "Your aunt will be thrilled to see you." Then he whispered in her ear, "Let's play a trick on her."

Ursula wasn't surprised at her uncle's suggestion. As long as she could remember, he'd pulled pranks on her aunt.

While the men dispersed in groups, following servants in different directions, Ursula walked with her uncle toward the main entrance as he gave her the details of his deception.

It seemed innocent enough, until she was finally in the dining hall a few hours later, balancing a heavy tray of quail.

As Ursula stepped gingerly up the dais steps, she kept her head bowed under the dark-blue servant's cap and prayed her arms would hold out until she could set the massive tray on the head table.

Catching a wink from her uncle, Ursula smiled shyly and turned her attention to the food in front of her. Selecting a trencher, she filled it with the freshly roasted quail, then made her way toward Aunt Sophie.

She was dressed in a gorgeous green velvet gown with emeralds about her neck, and her strawberry-red curls were piled on top of her head, secured with an emerald comb. To Ursula, she appeared not to have aged at all.

Following proper protocol, the lord and lady of the house would be served first. Ursula set the trencher in front of her aunt, then gave her a big kiss on the cheek. When her aunt sputtered in surprise, Ursula hightailed it behind her uncle as he got up to make a toast.

When Uncle Cameron raised his goblet in the grand, great hall before all the clansmen and women who'd gathered, Ursula heard her aunt complaining over the treatment she'd just received. While Ursula was hidden behind her uncle, she tugged off the servant's cap, then slid off the gray frock that hid her finer clothes and waited.

"Good men and women. I welcome you to Spurr Fhuaran manor, home of Clan Fraser in the heart of Glen Shiel." He lifted his pewter vessel higher. "'Tis my pleasure this evening to welcome back one of our own."

He turned to Ursula and put his arm around her, then stepped back so he was no longer blocking her from where her aunt sat.

A screech rang out before Uncle Cameron finished his introduction. He was shoved aside as Ursula was scooped up into her aunt's arms. The great hall erupted in applause and hazzahs.

Then one more shrieking female accosted her at the head table. Ursula's teary-eyed sister, Ella, threw her arms into the fray.

The pandemonium at the head table had Uncle Cameron roaring with laughter, and the rest of the guests joined in. After a few more moments of squealing from her aunt and sister, Uncle Cameron unwound them from each other and held up one of Ursula's hands.

"As you can see, this clan member was missed greatly by her aunt and sister. We welcome Ursula back to Spurr Fhuaran manor, where she belongs."

After Uncle Cameron finished a few additional introductions at the head table, one of the servants moved a chair so Ursula could sit between her aunt and sister.

When she dropped in between, they acted like two bees sucking nectar from her petals. Ursula smiled as they talked over each other, questions pouring out before she had answers.

Uncle Cameron must have noticed she was a bit flustered, for he came about to her side and placed his hand on the back of her chair. "Let her eat first, then she will answer all your questions."

"I only have one pressing question," her Aunt Sophie insisted before her husband could overrule her. "Are you home to stay?"

Ursula shoved a piece of shepherd's pie in her mouth to avoid answering the question.

"Come now, Sophie," he chided. "Cannae you see the girl is famished. Let her eat."

Uncle Cameron had always looked out for her. If it hadn't been Aunt Sophie or Ella wanting her attention, it was someone else in the castle. Ursula had been in demand for her healing skills at a young age and had sometimes worked long hours taking care of others.

Aye, her uncle had done much for Ursula, and now he was making sure she could enjoy her food before she visited with her family.

Of course, Ursula wasn't home to stay, but she would have to be ambiguous about her plans for the future. She didn't need to lie, for currently her plans *were* ambiguous.

The last thing she wanted was for Ethan to pick up on her aunt's urgency to marry her off to the first willing man, under the stipulation she live in Shiel Bridge forever.

Ursula took a long drink from her chalice, washing the last morsel of food down. Over the rim, she glanced left, then right. She could delay the interrogation no longer.

"Finally," her aunt huffed. "Are you fed and satiated enough to give me your undivided attention?"

"What about me?" her sister asked, sounding like a child.

"Ladies, there is enough of me to spare between the two of you," Ursula said.

"But not enough for me to spare her," came a provocative prompt from the man behind them.

Ursula shuddered. She didn't spin around in her seat like the other ladies, who twittered at the innuendo.

Both her aunt and sister sighed before they turned back her way. Ella elbowed her in the ribs, and Aunt Sophie raised her eyebrows as high as they could go.

Finally, to stop her aunt from nodding her head toward Ethan, she turned to him.

Ethan clicked his heels together and, with a bow, said, "My love, I must whisk you away for a respite. We've had such little private time together."

The twittering between the ladies began again, and Ursula shrugged her shoulders. But as much as she did not want to be interrogated by her family, Ursula wanted to be alone with Ethan even less.

"Ethan, you must understand, I've been away from my family for a verra long time. I can nae delay my reunion."

She turned to stand and laid a hand on his arm. "I am sure you will understand."

And with that, she stepped off the dais, expecting her aunt and sister to follow.

As she started across the great hall, she could hear her Aunt Sophie apologizing and gushing over a potential union.

Ursula rolled her eyes. She'd have to put an end to that notion.

It wasn't long though before all the three of them were settled in her aunt's solar in front of a roaring hearth, sipping blackberry heather tea.

"Ursula, I almost fainted when Cameron stepped back and there you stood." Her aunt put a hand over her heart. "I'm too old to be surprised like that."

She waved her laced kerchief at Ursula. "You went along with Cameron's prank. Kissing me on the check when I thought you were a serving girl."

Her aunt reach over and patted her hand. "I've missed you," she said with a tinge of sorrow in her voice. Glancing at Ella, she amended her words, "We miss you."

"I have missed you, too," Ursula admitted, her throat thick with emotion. "I did nae realize how much I've missed home until I walked through the manor gates and Uncle Cameron lifted me off my feet."

"Have you been happy?" her aunt asked, eyes full of concern. "As much as we've missed you, we would be less fretful about it if we knew you were living a blessed life."

"Is Ethan a lover?" her sister asked before she could answer her aunt.

"He's a scoundrel," Ursula said, crossing her arms protectively over her chest. She couldn't even begin to explain her relationship with Ethan. It was too complicated. Perhaps the ladies would move on to something more interesting if she asked the questions.

"What have I missed since I've been gone?" she asked, hoping to steer the conversation where she wanted it to go.

"Nae, you are not going to get away with that trick, lassie," her aunt chastised. "You have been gone ten years. You have changed, but nothing here ever does."

Ursula raised a brow. *How had she changed?*

"I see a self-assured woman. One who could lead an army if she wanted," her aunt said, answering Ursula's unspoken question.

"One who could live her life without a man, because she could take care of herself," her sister added.

"A woman who could make a little magic happen or even a miracle if one was needed," her Aunt Sophie finished with a wink.

Kind words from women she loved brought more tears to Ursula's eyes. And she never cried. No, the tears might well, but she quickly blinked them away, honoring the emotion that brought them to the surface, but not allowing the sentiment to drown her. She was different. It was true.

For hours they talked. They laughed. And when the day began to dawn, the three of them piled on her aunt's massive chamber bed in an exhausted pile of comradery.

Finally, she told them about Alasdair, but only how he'd promised to help her find the needed flower for Rosalyn on Skye Isle. She told them nothing about an heir or her feelings for him. Alasdair confused her so.

And just as Ursula was about to nod off, her aunt had a final thought. "Alasdair MacLeod. Your mother would be smiling down from heaven on you if you chose one as fine as the laird of Dunvegan."

Chapter 28

The closer Alasdair got to Skye Isle, the less he liked the terms Ethan had set. The rogue was no Scotsman, even though he claimed his mother was of the land and she'd had the title of Lady of Eilean Donan Castle for years before her death.

But a man was made by his father. And an English duke, even a dead one, still spoke to his kin from the grave. If anyone was a believer, it was Alasdair.

Although his da had been gone o'er three years, whenever Alasdair had a major decision to make, he would visit one of the many standing stones scattered across Scotland. The one near Dunvegan was his favorite, but this one at the western side of Loch Cluanie would do for now.

Alasdair had given Gordon's men an early respite from the trail. They had set up camp along the loch and were already well into their mead. This was a favorite stop in a journey across the Highlands, and he did his best to spend time here whenever he was traveling through this part of Glen Shiel.

Even though the stone was hidden from the trail, it was used frequently. Piles of scattered dry heather bouquets were strewn around the base like a well-tended grave.

Alasdair wished the soldiers' camp was a little farther from this resting place for he could hear their boisterous laughter from where he knelt. But if he hummed his favorite Scottish hymn under his breath, he'd drowned out most of the ruckus.

The sky was clear, and the stars were burning bright. Alasdair gazed up at the stone from his kneeling position on the sacred spot. He imagined many like him taking the journey to the stone and asking it for blessings, forgiveness, and miracles, any and all.

For standing stones were magical. Through them, other worlds could be reached. The dead could speak with the stones' aid. He could reach his father.

Alasdair did not care if the magic was real or imagined, for what did it matter as long as the ritual gave him peace and perspective?

It was the same, he assumed, for all who sought the standing stones. The energy around them was unmistakable, more so after sunset. Not a cloud in the sky, nor wind to disturb the trees around the sacred place.

Alasdair blinked rapidly, his eyes adjusting to the brightness of the full moon rising over the top of the stone. The alignment no accident.

Just as he finished the last verse of the hymn, Alasdair noticed the camp had gone silent. Either the men had run out of their mead, or they were passed out from it.

He shook his head and brought his concentration back to his purpose. "Uilleam Dubh MacLeod, Seventh Laird of Dunvegan, I seek your presence at this hour. Clan blood is thick. Family blood is thicker. A father and son's blood thicker still. The House of MacLeod stands strong on Skye Isle, but only you and I know its secret. Come great laird of MacLeod. Speak the truth. Only you and I can atone."

Alasdair closed his eyes and listened. The sounds of the night were vocal. But the nocturnal chorus was comforting. Nothing in the hums, hoots, or hollers was out of sync. The racket was rhythmic, harmonious.

"You pray for peace, my son, yet it eludes you."

"Father!" Alasdair stared at the stone. His father's voice was as clear as if he were standing beside him, but there was no vision. Not now, not ever. But it didn't matter, as long as they could communicate.

"Aye. What troubles you, Alasdair?"

He did not hesitate. "Father, the MacDonalds may have laid claim to Eilean Donan. I shall be able to confirm on the morrow. This is the closest to Skye their clan has taken hold since my great-great-great-grandfather ruled. We may nae have the numbers."

"You can never rely on the numbers, son. That's why we have the flag."

"The flag. Aye. 'Tis safe at Dunvegan, but I worry. Is there nae only one unfurling left?"

"That would be true, if the legend is true."

Alasdair paused, reviewing in his memory the tidbits that added up to the lore that was the Faery Flag. He'd seen it unfurled once in his lifetime.

"'Tis nae too soon? Over eight generations, and we've used it twice? Would I nae be failing the clan, the MacLeod name, if I were to use it for the last time, father?"

"You would nae be failing the clan if you saved them. A leader must use the resources he feels necessary at the time to protect the clan. Use it if you must."

Alasdair took in those words and weighed them. Getting permission from his father lightened the load of responsibility if he used the flag, but he was still not convinced.

"Why do you question my recommendation?" his father asked, surprising Alasdair. He was still in awe that he'd found a way for his father to communicate with him, but this was the first time he recalled his father picking up on his thoughts.

"Why should it be odd for me to hear what you are thinking, whether you are praying to me through a standing stone or from the hearth at Dunvegan? I hear you just the same."

"Well, that does surprise me for I can only hear you at a sacred stone."

His father chuckled. "You are nae listening closely enough. I am always giving you advice."

Now it was Alasdair's turn to chuckle. "Just as when you were alive, I wasn't always listening to you."

The laughter between them warmed Alasdair's heart, and although his father had never been openly affectionate around his men, he'd shown Alasdair, even as a grown man, his love for him.

"Remember, the legend promises three unfurlings, but this is not written down in any form. Perhaps the magic of the flag is never-ending," his father suggested.

"Then I will not be the one to give the flag any limitations," Alasdair said.

"Aye, my son. Belief is a powerful weapon. Trust it and yourself."

Alasdair was quiet for a moment. Even if his talk with his father were more the makings of a prayer to a higher spiritual power than a manifestation through belief, or an outright miracle, he had resolution.

"Goodbye, my son. Stay strong. Live strong. And continue the MacLeod legacy. Protect Dunvegan and Skye Isle."

And as Alasdair whispered his goodbye to his father, the natural hum of the forest changed. A wolf's howl fractured the rhythm of the woodland creatures.

Alasdair quickly got to his feet and walked briskly back toward camp with his sword drawn.

Walking through the woods wasn't difficult with the moon lighting the way, but when he arrived, the sight of Gordon's men on the ground had his blood turning cold.

Alasdair rushed to the first soldier, knelt down, and flipped the man over.

Blood. Blood everywhere. Cut through the chest with something more violent than a sword. *An axe?*

Alasdair clutched under his arm. The wound was burning. The memory of the axe strike in his back vivid now.

Whoever was responsible for this, this massacre of innocent men, would pay for what they had done.

Before he rose, however, Alasdair glanced warily over his shoulder and around the perimeter of the clearing. This part of the forest was still. Dead. As if the night creatures had been frightened away by the violence.

Waiting, listening. Alasdair was mortified by the actions of the men who were responsible. Gordon's soldiers had posed no threat to the clansmen who'd slaughtered them.

Alasdair rose slowly. The men who were responsible were gone. His feet resisted movement, but Alasdair dragged them reluctantly around the bodies, each step a painful reminder of a life lost.

When a groan came from his left, Alasdair spun around with hope in his heart. *Had one of Gordon's men survived?*

Racing to the spot where he'd heard the sound, Alasdair stood between four fallen bodies. Although it was almost pitch black in this part of the forest, some moonlight made its way through the branches, illuminating the fallen men.

He sheathed his sword, then crouched down in the middle of the morbid circle around him. One man was missing a head, but the one farthest from him moved.

Scuttling over to his side on all fours, Alasdair peered into the eyes of the man who'd moved.

When Gordon's soldier raised a sword, Alasdair jumped to his feet. Shuffling backward, he almost tripped over a body behind him as he tried to protect himself.

"I am friend, not foe," Alasdair said from a safe distance. "I'm your captain, Laird MacLeod."

The man dropped the sword immediately. "Sorry,

mate," the soldier said. "I took you for another one of the MacDonalds who'd come back to finish you off."

"Me?" Alasdair asked, not surprised to hear the bloody massacre was at the hands of his enemies but stunned they'd have known he was in Glen Shiel. The contingent had yet to come close to the MacDonald's protected lands. *Why were they so far south?*

"Aye," the solitary soldier replied. "The MacDonalds surprised us after our meal and ale. We were a wee bit tipsy when they arrived, and that compounded our inability to defend ourselves." Then the man leaned up on one elbow as if he was about to get up. "But even if we'd been sober, there were at least two of them to every one of us."

Alasdair rushed over and extended a hand to the man. "What be your name, lad?"

"Gavin," he said, accepting Alasdair's gesture with his left hand. Once he was on his feet, he sheathed his sword.

Alasdair had not gotten to know the men. Once the contingent had left Invergarry Castle, they'd ridden religiously from dawn to dusk on a trek toward Kyle of Lochalsh with little interaction. Alasdair knew very few of the men by their surnames.

"How do you know they were looking for me?"

"It was blatantly clear, my lord. When they burst into our camp with axes raised and war paint covering their faces, the only words the leader said were, 'Where's Alasdair MacLeod? He's a dead man.'"

Chapter 29

Ethan was his usual impatient self the next morn when Ursula's family and close friends met them at the manor gate to see them off. The weather was quite blustery, but that wasn't unusual for Scotland in the Highlands this time of year.

Ursula tugged her red traveling cape tighter around her neck to keep the whipping wind from stinging her skin, then gave each of her loved ones a generous hug.

She promised herself that morning when she'd dressed for the short half-day ride to Kyle of Lochalsh she wouldn't cry when she said her goodbyes. But leaving was more difficult than she'd ever imagined.

She bit on her lip to distract herself from her swirling emotions and to keep herself from snapping at Ethan, who was back to his old nasty self. She was out of the herbs that made his company bearable.

His behavior was a good reminder of why he'd never be a match for her. As charming as he'd been after he'd taken the concoction made of mandrake root and damiana, she could nae spend her life drugging her husband so she could tolerate his company and prevent him from poisoning her if she crossed him.

After she'd mounted Tempest and waved goodbye, she followed Ethan and Conn's soldiers out of the gate and into Glen Shiel's countryside, a piece of her heart breaking.

Although Ursula had been apprehensive about returning home, part of her was content with the visit, even though the questions posed by her family would haunt her thoughts in the days ahead.

As much as she fretted about her relationship with Alasdair, after she'd talked with her aunt about him further this morn at breakfast, she admired him all the more. Alasdair was a well-respected leader despite his handicap.

Ursula had a close look at the wound the other night. Healed on the outside, but not on the inside. She had worked to remedy that, but the pain was still there. She'd witnessed it. The pain that festered in his mind, where he imagined he was less worthy, less competent as a leader. As a laird. As a loving man.

She'd sensed the pain when she'd first met him. It had been as if he'd wanted to apologize for the slight stoop in his stature, as if he'd stand taller for her if he could.

It had continued when they'd been together cooking in the galley on the *Merry Maiden*, after he'd eaten the herb-spiked stew then had to excuse himself.

And the most pain of all—when he'd shown her the physical scar. As if revealing the wound had laid him more bare than exposing his naked form.

He'd cringed before she'd even touched his scar, as if she had somehow triggered the memory of the axe coming down on his back, making him relive the weapon tearing through his body.

Aye, as she rode in between Conn's clansmen through the heather-covered Highland hills, she thought more and more about Alasdair. What he stood for. What her aunt had said about his love of the arts. Ursula found herself missing him even as she was full of so many questions for him.

But when she remembered he wanted an heir, she almost lost her balance. She was a good rider, but the jolt of memory almost made her slip off her saddle.

Without thinking, she reached down to rub her belly. Could she be with child? She had lost track of her monthly rhythm. Had she been fertile then? Was the moon waxing or waning?

Och! It has only been three days. And even if she was with child, the telltale symptoms would not surface for some time.

Ursula sighed and blew out a shaky breath, keeping her eye on the back of the warhorse in front of her, working to steady herself inside and out. What if she was pregnant with a girl? There would be no heir, and she'd have a daughter to raise alone?

She shuddered at the possibilities of how her life could change. Just when the commitment she'd made was about to overwhelm her, a vision burst through her musings to scatter her worries away.

Rosalyn. Her heart warmed as she was reminded she would always have a home at Fyvie Castle with her sister of the heart. Beyond Aberdeen, she'd have her family in Shiel Bridge if she wanted to live at Spurr Fhuaran manor as her aunt had insisted.

A sly smile crossed her lips. If a child was in her future, she would welcome it as proof destiny can triumph over doubt.

Rosalyn was the woman she was striving to help, the gentle soul who trusted in Ursula. Trusted she would return with the guelder rose from Skye Isle to make sure not only did Rosalyn's twin babes enter this world safely, but that she would fare well, too.

In Ursula's vision, Rosalyn sat in the garden at Fyvie with two maids by her side. The sweet pregnant woman, her belly swollen with twins, was smiling as the handmaidens gathering flowers in a basket for her.

The scene made Ursula smile broadly, happy to find her friend in a state of grace and acceptance. She hoped Rosalyn's twins had become accustomed to the cramped space they shared and were no longer being disruptive, knowing they had a mother who would love them unconditionally.

The thought strengthened Ursula's resolve even as the vision of Rosalyn faded just as they reached the peak of the foothills.

When Ethan raised his hand, the horses slowed, then those in the party gathered by his side, forming a strong united line across the top of the hillside.

Ursula gazed down upon the glory of the three lochs. The waters reminded her of aquamarine velvet, with Eilean Donan Castle glittering like a jeweled broach in the center.

Her view from the foothills made the castle appear tiny, like a toy. As much as she had let faith guide her this far, she had to trust Ethan had a plan for approaching the castle. But it did occur to her, as she waited, the arrival would require a ceremonial approach.

Where was the MacLeod laird waiting?

As she glanced about the countryside from her high vantage point, her eyes strained for some movement. She had hoped to find Alasdair's white warhorse and dazzling smile close behind them. He'd plan to meet them here.

What had he said? *Then she could decide?*

*But with Gordon's men as a liability, did he even m*ake it this far? Or had he abandoned the mission and returned to his lairdship at Dunvegan, never to look back? Perhaps the cost of the Faery Flag was too high for an heir after all?

Ursula became so distracted by all the possibilities she didn't notice the contingent had begun their decent toward the tidal castle until one of Conn's men gave her horse a smack on the rear as he passed.

Eilean Donan not only resembled a shining broach among the sea lochs, it was the royal jewel of the Highlands. Tales of the legendary landmark had filled her childhood, but she'd never set foot before its grand entrance and looming parapets. She'd only dreamed of what it would be like inside, not sure she could believe the stories of its grandeur.

Ursula glanced over her shoulder and up the mountain to the pass from where they'd traveled, still hoping for some glimpse of Alasdair and Gordon's men. But nothing.

As Ursula scanned the countryside, she was surprised to find the distance they'd traveled so far was deceiving. It was taking much longer than she expected to get to the lip of the land where a boat waited to carry passengers to the sea gate.

Once they finally arrived, Ethan instructed most of Conn's men to set up camp in a large clearing secluded from the shore. After the work was done, six chosen clansmen and Ursula climbed into the longboat with him.

The soldiers found oars at the bottom of the craft, and in a few short moments, Conn's men were pushing the paddles deep into the dark waters as the boat surfed toward the tidal island.

Eilean Donan loomed before them like a fortress rising out of the sea. The stone walls shone golden in the bright rays of sun that peaked through a mostly gray sky.

The weather this close to the sea changed rapidly, rain and sun coexisting, producing rainbows as a result. For now, it appeared the sun would win the battle and triumph over the clouds. But the tall curtain wall that surrounded the castle appeared unyielding to weather or traveler.

Even up close, the parapets were foreboding. She imagined MacDonald warriors, faces painted, longbows in hand, ready to take aim at their party through the open spaces in the parapets.

But her neck could only crane so far, until they were directly in line with the castle's main gate off the seawall, where they'd docked the longboat.

After their party disembarked and made their way up the main path, Ursula's noticed on their approach a Gaelic phrase carved in stone panels above the main entrance. She read to herself: *Cho fad 's a bhios MacKenzie a stigh cha bhi Friselach a stigh.*

Ursula gasped and, unfortunately, drew the attention of the men. She shook her head to signal she was all right, but the translated words haunted her, for the sign said, *As long as there is a MacKenzie inside, there will never be a Fraser inside.*

And as much as she'd begged her mother to see Eilean Donan up close, even go inside, she now understood why she hadn't. The Frasers were not welcome here. Her mother had always promised it would be another day.

Her day had come.

Ursula shuddered from the shock of the warning above the Eilean Donan castle entrance. But there was no turning back. Whoever ruled, MacKenzie or MacDonald, she'd have to keep her identity secret. Yet, by now either clan would be preparing for their visit. No one approached a castle undetected or unexpected. Especially one so well fortified for Norse invasions from the sea.

She looked ahead through three gothic arches that lay in successive recesses. The last housed the barrier to their entry, a massive wooden gate, cross latticed with iron strips, held in place by giant, round iron nails.

Although the last recess held the visible door, Ursula was certain the other two would not be there if they did not hide additional doors capable of crushing unsuspecting visitors.

Unwilling to be deterred, Ursula squared her shoulders as the porticus gate began to grind open, the iron teeth rising up like a wolf opening its mouth to bare its fangs. Someone inside had to know there were visitors wanting to get in.

Chapter 30

Ursula must have entered Eilean Donan Castle without his protection. Alasdair cursed under his breath.

They were late. He assumed she was already inside as he waited for some sign of activity. If only he hadn't been hunting for game, he would've been able to cross over with the group in the longboat that was tethered to the tidal island's secluded wharf.

With his hands clenched together behind his back and his attention focused on the castle's entrance, Alasdair paced beside his warhorse, hoping for some movement in or out of the fortress.

Gavin swore. "God's teeth, man. You'll dig a ditch in the ground with your pacing."

Gordon's only surviving soldier had Alasdair laughing at himself. "Aye, 'tis time for action." And without another word, he mounted his warhorse and started down the hill toward the sea lochs, ready to talk with Conn's men.

He wasn't about to leave Ursula in the hands of the MacKenzies or the MacDonalds, and he was finished with letting Ethan have his way.

~ ~ ~

Although they'd made it this far into Eilean Donan under a civil reception, the largest of the Highlanders walked forward to greet them. The man's hands were as almost as large as Ursula's head, and he towered above the tallest of Conn's men.

"I am Ian MacDonald, laird of this castle, of this fiefdom"—then he pounded one of his enormous fists on top of his open palm—"of the Highlands."

Ethan behaved himself. She was sure he'd bit his tongue to resist saying the words that were on his lips, nodding his head instead.

"I am Ethan Luttrell, Duke of Somerset, and these are Lord Conn MacDonnell's clansmen from Glengarry."

When Ian's gaze moved to Ursula, she spoke up, "I am Lady Luttrell, your lairdship." Then she curtsied and bowed her head.

"Come"—Ian gestured with a sweeping arm—"let us talk in the great hall." He turned and started across the grand expanse, darting around empty trestle tables. Servants rushed in from behind the dais with pewter pitchers to fill the goblets.

Their group was invited to sit at the head table while golden mead was poured and freshly baked breads were served.

Once Ian was seated in the center in a throne fit for a king, Ethan took a regal, but less formal, seat next to his host. A MacDonald clansman sat beside Ethan and another sat on the end, putting Ursula in between two of Ian's clansmen.

The rest of Ian's men positioned themselves on the other side of their laird, and Conn's six soldiers filed in the front trestle table.

Ursula relaxed a little as she gulped the sweet golden liquid from her goblet, pleased Ethan had introduced himself as a Luttrell.

Until they found out more about why the MacDonalds had full reign of this castle, he'd have to tread carefully. The consequence of Ethan claiming lairdship as a MacKenzie clan member, through a gambling debt award, could be catastrophic.

As Ethan and the MacDonald laird began an intimate discussion, Ursula studied her surroundings.

Indeed, the reputation of the grandeur of Eilean Donan hadn't been exaggerated. The grand hall, breathtaking.

Vibrant tapestries in Jacquard weaves, no doubt stitched with thread made of gold, each as large as the castle entrance, were displayed on the walls without apology.

Just to her right, a stone hearth dominated the wall, no doubt the most magnificent she'd ever laid eyes on. It was capped by a white marble mantle decorated with black iron candelabras full of burning tapered candles.

Ursula marveled at the intricate hunting scene above the fireplace that was carved in the stone. It depicted a Scotsman on horseback chasing a fox. Underneath the mantle the carved motto spelled out the Gaelic phrase, *Nec Curo Nec Caro*. She murmured the translation. "I want not, I care not."

On the opposite end of the grand room, Ursula counted more than half a dozen landscapes of Skye Isle vistas gracing the stone wall. Oil paintings were rare in the day, but she was certain they were of that quality.

As they dined at a massive mahogany table covered in fine linens, one important item did not escape her attention, the MacDonald coat of arms.

Ursula rocked forward on her elbows and craned her neck to get a better look at the heraldry insignia hanging on the wall behind them as she reached for a thick slice of hearty bread from the trencher. The man sitting next to her, an older soldier, winked at her when he leaned out of her way.

With the great hall virtually empty of other guests, the acoustics in the room were conducive enough for her to listen in and catch most of the conversation between Ian and Ethan.

"The MacDonalds have no quarrel with your King Henry. 'Tis our Highland enemies, like the MacKenzies and the Frasers that prove the mettle." The Highland laird's admission was thick with distain.

Ethan forced a laugh. She knew him well, and he could fake just about anything. His lies were convincing, as she'd learned almost to her detriment.

"We have no quarrel with your MacDonald clan, as my meager group, with borrowed escort, means only to travel to Skye Isle on the morrow to collect some healing herbs. We are not on a hunting mission."

Ian burst out laughing and his men quickly join in. When the snorts finally subsided the leader asked, "English lords put aside the pursuits of hunting game to gather flowers instead?"

Ursula wasn't sure the Highlander intended to be so defaming in his question, but from the color of Ethan's face, she was certain he'd taken offense.

"I assure you 'tis a noble task," Ethan replied, his words sounding measured.

"Therein lies one of the major differences between the English and the Scots. We do nae give a sheep's crap about nobility." Ian pounded the table with his massive fist. "He who leads men earns the right by action, not by birth."

Ursula was uncertain whether Ethan would be able to manage the verbal abuse, so she rose from her seat, ready to defend him.

"The cause is more humanitarian than noble," Ursula said. She walked toward the two men. Even if it wasn't her place to meddle, letting the conversation carry on without her intervention could have disastrous consequences.

"To save my sister in Aberdeenshire," she explained.

Ian turned to give her audience.

"She is carrying twins, and I must find the guelder rose on Skye Isle and return with it to Aberdeenshire as soon as I can. 'Tis a matter of life and death."

Ian looked to Ethan. "Can you nae tame your shrew?"

At that, Ethan threw his head back. This time his laughter was genuine and Conn's men joined in. After he regained his composure, Ethan asked the laird, "How do Highlanders handle their women?"

"Without proper English manners," Ian said, his eyes narrowing on her. And before she could protest, he'd yanked her over his knee and, to her horror, began swatting her bottom.

Ursula did not hold back and yelped as loud as she could. The sting of Ian's hands on her arse was worse than she'd expected.

Thankfully, her full riding skirt provided some cushioning, but she'd already been frightened by the size of the man and was even more put out because his hands were touching her in such an inappropriate manner.

As she yelled, she cursed.

Ian's laughter grew louder than her cries.

But the torture broke her endurance. Finally, in pure agony, she blurted out something she hoped would stop him.

"Ethan's a MacKenzie. Your hands should be on him and not me."

Immediately the beating stopped, and in an instant, she was shoved off his lap and onto the floor. She rolled out of the way of his feet as he stood up.

"A MacKenzie?" Ian's accusation burned with the sound of hatred.

Ethan laughed a stilted laugh. "The shrew will lie to get her way. Spanking is appropriate given her outspokenness in your domain," Ethan said. "I have better results when I lock my shrews in the dungeon."

Ursula cringed under the table, remembering the horror of those days when Rosalyn had been the object of his desire and she'd almost died because of his treatment.

"The dungeon is yours if you deem it necessary," the Scottish laird offered. Ian's boisterous laugh echoed through the grand hall. "You could nae be a MacKenzie. You are too weak."

When silence followed the snub, Ursula braced for the worst, but Ethan finally replied, "Noble Englishmen do not draw swords for battle over ladies, only over land titles."

Ursula sighed softly. Ethan had decided not to argue, and that may have curtailed any additional probing for proof of the MacKenzie accusation. She hoped her outburst wouldn't be taken seriously, and she chided herself for losing her wits under the MacDonald laird's heavy hand.

"Now that you have had some refreshments, my men will escort you around the grounds. I have other matters to attend to," Ian told Ethan.

As Ursula huddled under the table, she was happy to see the laird's feet go out of her view. After a few moments, the sound of retreating footsteps stopped. Had they forgotten about her? The head table's thick linen covering concealed her completely.

Now that the threats against her had ended, Ursula ruminated on her circumstance, angry that she'd let Ethan have his way.

If they'd traveled with Alasdair, he'd have never allowed her to enter the castle without a plan or protection.

Men could be such idiots. If she'd been granted permission to travel alone, she wouldn't be in this predicament.

Ursula crawled under the table to the end, where she poked her head out to assess her options. She let out a sigh of relief when she found the great hall empty.

If the laird had higher priorities, and Ethan was being entertained, she would find a quiet, secluded spot to hide until she could figure out a plan to get out of Eilean Donan.

How odd it was that the place she'd dreamed of visiting had become a nightmare. Even though the great hall was one of the grandest she'd seen, the ugliness of the MacDonalds spoiled the gleam of the jewel that was Eilean Donan Castle.

As she walked out of the keep through the kitchen, hoping to blend in with the servants and handmaidens bustling about, she found her way through an entrance to a courtyard. It was a beautiful space with a lovely, intimate garden. And beyond the flora was a courtyard of stone that looked out over a short seawall.

By now the sun reigned over the sky, and the sea loch waters glittered from all the attention.

It wasn't until she heard shouting that her gaze traveled to the far right of the courtyard. There, Ethan stood surrounded by Ian's Highland soldiers.

She squinted against the sun, shading her eyes with one hand, hoping to see what the commotion was all about.

Ethan's back was to the seawall and his hands were tied in front of him. Ursula tried to keep her wits about her as her heart began to race. Clearly, Ethan wasn't taking a tour of the grounds. He had been taken prisoner.

With panic about to set in, Ursula quickly glanced around, getting her bearings. She had no idea where Conn's men had gone.

Who would protect her if Ethan was locked away?

Had Ian taken her word that Ethan was of Clan MacKenzie? And if he believed that, what were her chances of getting out of here alive?

She slumped down and snuck around the corner of the entrance to the keep's kitchen. Even though she was terrified about what was going on, she could not look away.

Ethan stood on top of the wall, hands bound, glancing over his shoulder at the ocean behind him, making agitated movements as if he was trying to break free of his bondage.

Then in an instant, he was gone from the ledge. One of the soldiers had shoved him off.

Ursula swallowed her fear. She would have to figure out a way to escape the same fate.

She leaped to her feet and spun around, ready to run. Run anywhere. Just run. And run she did, right into the arms of Ian, Laird of MacDonald. The man who had spanked her.

"There's the lassie," he said, firmly taking hold of her shoulders. "What did your husband suggest?" he asked, staring over her head. He looked down at her, his eyes feigning surprise. "The dungeon, was it not?"

Chapter 31

The waiting had taken its toll. Once it was confirmed by Conn's men that Ursula had entered Eilean Donan, Alasdair was even more agitated than before.

After some discussion with Conn's men, it was clear to him the soldiers had lost their respect for Ethan after they'd journeyed under his leadership to Eilean Donan.

Alasdair found Conn's clansmen loyal, having promised their laird to guard Ursula with their lives. It wasn't difficult to earn their trust when he explained his concerns about her safety and his plan to steal into the castle to rescue her from the MacDonalds and Ethan.

Once darkness was complete, Alasdair led the men to the banks of the sea loch. Crawling on their bellies under a moonless sky, they traveled the length of a furlong from the woods to the edge of the loch.

With the water only up to their waists, they stayed low, wading across the short distance. Once the last man was on the island, Alasdair guided them through the sea gate, then up a narrow stone stairwell to a walled courtyard.

Alasdair had visited Eilean Donan only a year ago with his own clan captain. They'd been guests of the MacKenzies. And the proud laird had provided a tour of his fiefdom, even its dungeon.

That knowledge had been helpful to Alasdair when he had laid out the plan to Conn's men earlier. Now that they were on the grounds, Alasdair led them through a servants' entrance. Finding the great hall in the middle of dinner service and the buttery empty, he and the men wended their way around wooden worktables, dodging butter churns, to the door on the opposite side.

Finally, when all six were gathered in the outer hall, Alasdair guided them to a dark open doorway and an alcove with a narrow loophole window. Enough light shone into the space that housed a stone bench. It appeared to be a religious sanctuary.

After leaving two of Conn's men there, and two at the door to the back courtyard around the corner, he led Gavin to the spiral staircase opening.

He peered down the circular path. The dungeon was at the end of it.

When the light disappeared around the first bend, Alasdair reached out both hands, touching the walls on either side, cautiously placing one foot after the other. Slowly, he and Gavin descended the angled steps.

With each turn, the air grew colder. More damp. And after his right foot could step down no farther, an awful stench assaulted him.

Only the dead could smell this rancid. He shuddered at the thought of Ursula being here. Taking a few steps forward and keeping his arms outstretched, it wasn't long before Alasdair's fingers swept cross cold iron bars.

Gavin followed with his hand on Alasdair's good shoulder. They moved down the narrow corridor in silence.

Then he heard it. A faint wail. Like a crying child, one who couldn't catch their breath between sobs.

Alasdair quickened his pace. Brushing his fingers along the bars helped him stay the course as he moved toward the sound.

The cry grew louder, then piercing. He stopped, but Gavin stumbled over him in the dark. In his clumsiness, Gordon's man clawed at Alasdair's scarred shoulder to keep from falling.

Alasdair bit his tongue. "God's teeth," he ground out.

The sobbing stopped abruptly.

He held his breath. After a few heartbeats, he let it out.

What was he afraid of?

Whoever was here had to be locked in a cell, a prisoner who the MacDonalds hated enough to put behind bars with lock and key.

When a sniffle broke the silence, Alasdair spoke out. "We are looking for a friend."

"Alasdair?"

"Ursula?" His heart stopped racing. "Praise the Almighty."

"Alasdair, you've come to save me?"

"Well, I've come this far. 'Twould be a waste not to save you." He laughed. The action caused some pain in his scar, fresh from Gavin's stumble, but he shook it off. "Keep talking so your voice will guide me," he directed.

"They killed Ethan," she blurted out. "I was afraid they'd kill me, too."

Praise the saints he'd found her in time. Ethan could rot in hell for all he cared.

"Stick your hand through the bars so I can find you," he instructed, continuing to make his way and running his hands along the cell bars on either side. The hallway was that narrow.

Gavin shuffled along behind him in silence.

When her fingers brushed against his, a jolt of heat surged through his veins, and he ground to a stop.

Without a second thought, he covered his hand over hers. "I'm here."

Ursula let out a little sob, not like the wailing ones he'd heard earlier, but one full of gratefulness. She squeezed his arm lightly. "I've tried to find a key." She made a sniffling sound. "I've crawled along the floors and felt about the walls as far as I can reach outside this chamber."

Alasdair was amused. "What would be the point of locking you up if they left a key for you?" He rubbed her hand to warm it. 'Twas cold as ice.

Ursula let out an embarrassed chuckle.

Alasdair squeezed her hand. "Gavin and I will search for a key, perhaps left for the guards. If not, we'll force the door open."

When she gasped, he was determined more than ever to find a way to set her free. But after a few moments of futile reaching, Alasdair returned and gave her hand another reassuring squeeze.

"Step back and to the side in case the door collapses to the floor," Alasdair advised, counting on breaking the hinges.

"Let's find the outer edges of the door." He spoke out into the darkness with instructions for Gavin. "Then we'll synchronize our efforts with one mighty kick. That should do some damage."

Alasdair walked forward, and even though there was no light in the dungeon, his eyes had become accustomed enough to see the faint edges of the cell bars in front of him. "When I count to three. Ready, Gavin?"

"Ready."

Alasdair counted, "One, two, three."

When they kicked, the metal groaned in response, but did not budge.

"Again."

They both gave the door the best of their boots. It gave way, but he could tell, even in the darkened corridor, not far enough for Ursula to squeeze through.

"We are close. Again!"

When their combined efforts met the door, it groaned even louder this time.

Alasdair stepped up to the bars and examined the hinges. He shook the door near the lock where it was nearly coming apart from the frame.

"One more time. She's almost free," he said with jubilation. "One, two . . ."

"Three," said a voice he didn't recognize.

Alasdair hung his head. Time had run out.

Chapter 32

Ursula strained to hear some movement. Anything. There was complete silence in the dungeon. Why hadn't they kicked the door again?

A dull light appeared at the far left near the underground entrance to the dungeons. Her heart pounded as if it were in her ears.

But as the glow of a torch approached, and Alasdair moved toward the light, Ursula's heart sank, even before she recognized the words of the MacDonald laird.

"You were nae invited MacLeod. You know what we do with uninvited guests?"

"Show them what cowards you are when you hold all the power?"

There was shuffling farther down the corridor out of her view, and a torch fell to the floor. Ursula rushed to the bars from the back of the cell where she'd been ordered to stay. By the time she could see what was going on, Ian MacDonald had Alasdair in a headlock.

She choked on her gasp.

Peering between the bars, Ursula counted eight men carrying iron axes and torches, looking like they'd kill with no regrets.

"Trespassers are dealt with accordingly," Ian MacDonald said in a foreboding tone. He released Alasdair to one of his men and walked up to where Ursula stood at the bars to examine the damage on the cell frame.

"Out," the laird ordered when he was finished with his

assessment, glaring at her. "In here," he shouted, clipping his words and pointing to the adjacent open cell.

This was no time for Ursula to show disobedience. She acquiesced silently, shuffling into the adjacent cell. When she looked over her shoulder to find out what plans Ian had for Alasdair, she found the castle's laird shoving the Highlander in behind her, slamming the door closed.

"You should be the prisoner," Alasdair shouted. "You're trespassing on MacKenzie property."

MacDonald erupted in an ugly laugh. "There's nae a Highlander who would have the courage to lock me up," the laird boasted.

"Unlock this cage and let us have a fair fight," Alasdair proposed, gripping the bars tightly, while Ursula clung to the shadows. Better not to be caught between these two dueling Highland warriors.

"On the morrow your fate will be decided," MacDonald promised, and then the leader spun away from the cell, his men dragging Gavin with them. As the footsteps echoed and the light receded, she heard Ian say, "We'll see what you are made of."

The footsteps faded, but the dropped torch remained dimly lit in the corridor. Ursula took solace in the momentary light. She shivered as if the torch brought warmth that was fading with the glow. Total darkness had been dreadful.

"Oh, God, please help me," she called out in desperation, collapsing to her knees, sobbing.

Alasdair's strong arms lifted her gently into a warm embrace. "Hush now. I'll help you," he said with tenderness. Her sobs subsided as he draped over her like a protective shield, his chin resting lightly on her head.

"Faery Queen, I've missed you," Alasdair whispered softly in her ear. Instantly, her belly did a flip, and her fear was replaced with hope.

She sighed. "I've missed you, too." She slid her head out from under his chin. "Why did you leave me to Ethan?"

He gazed at her lips as if he did not care what she'd said. She was about to light into him about what had happened, but he smothered her next query with a kiss full of passion and purpose.

He started with a gentle assault of her lips. Then he flicked his delicious tongue in and out of her mouth as if she were a dessert he wanted to take his time consuming.

After teasing with his kissing skills, he began to fondle her arse, squeezing each cheek, alternating back and forth, and she giggled against his lips.

And if that wasn't already exciting wanton feelings inside her, Alasdair began to bunch up her skirt under her bum, while he played a dueling game with her tongue, aiming to conquer her mouth and render her senseless in his arms.

She welcomed his touch, his caressing, his adoration of her, telling her how beautiful she was. How could she have allowed Ethan to undermine her trust in this man, who by all accounts had acted in her best interests? She'd been foolish to trust Ethan and leave Alasdair. She only hoped these were not their final hours together while Ian determined their fate.

The torch fizzled out, and darkness enveloped them, requiring her to feel her way about his body with exploratory intention. As much as she enjoyed the distraction he was providing, and how she succumbed to his charms, she could not read his expression or gaze into his eyes for the authenticity she sought.

Even as Alasdair took her breath away, she wondered what would become of them. Would this be the last time he held her in his arms? A future heir potentially grew inside her. Would they try again anyway? Tonight, in this darkness, with a hope for a future.

"You are mine," he said softly. "My fur will be our bed," he told her, releasing her for a moment.

She stepped back in the darkness, her body tingling with anticipation and also her need for his warmth in the dank dungeon. Somehow Alasdair's earthly scent had doused the dungeon's stench.

"Come," he coaxed and guided her down to the fur, then slid beside her.

"Alasdair, what—?" But before she could finish, he placed a finger against her lips.

"*Shh,*" he soothed. "Do you trust me?"

She nodded with his finger still pushing gently against her mouth.

"Good, for I will keep you safe and find a way to save us."

As much as she wanted to believe him and fall under his intoxicating lure, she needed to know his plans.

"I'm grateful you sought me out when you could have returned home to your clan and forgotten me." She paused when her lip trembled, but she needed to tell him how she felt. "Ethan is gone, and I know not what happened to Conn's men," she told him, her voice shaky. "You're my only hope."

Alasdair shifted slightly on his side and drew her close. "I'm pleased to be your only hope, for you are mine."

"How can that be?"

"My grandfather used to speak of my great-great-great-grandmother with awe and respect, promising one day I would meet a woman like her. Faerie born, full of folklore and magic. A woman who could steal my heart but keep it safe with a spirit equal to mine own. A soul mate for all time.

"For years I've searched for a woman like you. Assured, sensual, smart, and otherworldly. My soul mate."

Did she dare dream? What had begun as a flirtatious and almost disastrous start might blossom into something she could hold on to?

She'd learned the art of healing from her mother and grandmother, but she had expected to live out her years alone.

Not until she met Joshua and became his lover did she believe there was a match for her in this life. And when he died, her flickering hope for a life with a partner had died with him.

Was this Highlander from Skye the secret to her happiness? When she'd decided to devote her life to the care of others, she'd expected her own care would be sacrificed in return.

"You did nae hear my question?"

Ursula shook off her rambling thoughts like a dog shedding water. "What was the question?"

"Now my feelings are hurt. You were not listening to my adoration of you?"

"Nay," she said, letting out an embarrassed laugh, "I heard everything and am in awe. Speechless, actually." She paused, considering the right words, then they came to her. "You give me hope."

"Good, for you can nae give up." He ran the back of his hand gently down her cheek. "I'll repeat the question. Clearly, I stunned you senseless with my compliments. How did they kill Ethan?"

She shivered. Not from the cold, but from the cold-blooded nature of men like Ian MacDonald.

"He was shoved off a wall and into the sea loch," she replied flatly, not sure it mattered. Perhaps he wanted to know if the MacDonalds might torture them on the morrow.

"Do you know how to swim?"

Ursula's head spun, thinking back to the horror of seeing someone shoved off a wall, helpless, into the tremulous seawaters of the loch.

"His hands were tied," she said with exasperation.

"That did nae answer my question."

Ursula took in a long, deep breath and reflected back on her childhood. Aye, she had learned from her uncle before they'd gone fishing in a river where the waters ran rapid. He had taken her to a shallow lake before the excursion, and he'd shown her how to float on her back if she stiffened her body like a board. He'd held her head until she'd felt brave enough to go it alone.

"I know how to float," she said proudly.

"That is not swimming, but better than drowning."

She let out a tiny whimper, and her heart almost stopped beating at the thought of being pushed into the sea and trying to float like a board.

"Floating is almost swimming. You just need to kick your feet, and that will propel you," Alasdair said, squeezing her a little tighter.

She relaxed more in his arms.

"Do you nae think they'll hang us?"

"The history of hanging in the Highlands is a long one, lass, but I can tell you the practice is more popular in Edinburgh."

"That's not comforting. My mother and grandmother were hanged in the Highlands, so my history may be different than yours," she said with a huff.

He nuzzled her neck before he began kissing his way toward her breasts with tiny pecks of sweetness. "If my words do nae comfort you, let my actions."

It wasn't long before Ursula had forgotten what tomorrow held, for tonight was bright with promise. Promise of love. Promise of a future. She would set aside her doubts and fears and dream of a future with Alasdair.

In the darkness, without words, he began his subtle seduction. Her traveling clothes were loose enough that he had little trouble slipping the fabric from her body.

As Ursula lay in the darkness on the warm fur, tingling with anticipation, she wanted nothing more than Alasdair to give her hope. And she was grateful it did nae take long before nothing separated them but the breath between their sighs.

Alasdair moved about in the darkness, kissing and stroking her in all the right places. Aching for him, she offered sweet moans and groans of encouragement.

Ursula's heart skipped a beat when he straddled her and gently rubbed his chest over her breasts, tickling them with his soft hairs.

Gone was Alasdair's tentativeness, for his scar was invisible to her here as he moved about her like it never was. His hands treating her body like a master potter would a fresh lump of clay, with loving, generous strokes.

Alasdair made her feel regal, raunchy, and riotous, all at the same time, as he murmured lovely words of adoration. When he sank deep inside her, she gave a squeal of delight.

She was slick inside when he settled into her channel, and his manhood moved with a powerful force intent on providing her pleasure.

Just when she was certain Alasdair's thrusting hips and nipple licking had taken her to her limit, he coaxed her into wanting more.

He was the master of a dance, one with the promise of sweet rewards. Fast and slow rhythmic movements. Their bodies intertwined. Words of endearment lacing their lips.

Alasdair came to his climax, and convulsions of pleasure surged through her. Collapsing next to her, he snuggled her neck, and she sighed with a feeling of satisfaction.

After a few lovely, indulgent moments of rest, his heart beating with hers, Alasdair took her hand and gave it a sweet kiss on the back. "My Faery Queen, will you take my throne?"

"'Tis not likely I'll aspire to be Laird of Dunvegan," she replied in a teasing tone. "Nor would I dare take it from you, even though you've offered."

He chuckled into her neck, giving her a few sweet pecks after. "The throne beside me, wearing your Faery crown."

Dared she dream of a life with this clan laird when another held their future? She could only hope their fate lay in the loch not the noose. At least then, she might have a chance to answer Alasdair's question.

Chapter 33

Was it night or day?

Alasdair had never spent time in a dungeon as a prisoner until now, and he marveled at the simplicity of the torture. Not all underground lairs were constructed like this one. But stripping a person of light, of their perception of time, was one of the worst punishments Alasdair could imagine.

Fortunately, MacDonald had thrown them in the same cell. Yet, Alasdair didn't want to underestimate the laird. In his small-minded way, Ian MacDonald could have a more devious plan in place than Alasdair imagined.

He wrapped his bearskin cape around Ursula, then quickly dressed. When he sat back on the floor to pull on his boots, she let out a satisfied sigh. Disappointed he couldn't revel in her beauty has she slept, he settled on picturing a look of contentment on her face instead.

She'd sidestepped his proposal. But she'd been a willing lover, and he would cling to that because the future held only uncertainty.

Alasdair shuffled over to the cell bars in the dark. Although he'd been distracted by his feelings for Ursula, it was time to see if he could do anything to weaken the door like he had the adjacent one.

With both hands firmly in place, one on the door and the other on the frame, Alasdair took in a deep breath and shoved as hard as he could against them.

The metal whined against his weight, creaking with age, but the mechanism holding the cell door closed did not yield.

Undeterred, Alasdair put his good shoulder into a second shove, but the try delivered the same result even though the aging iron grumbled in response.

He was about to give it another go when the sound of footsteps echoed down the corridor. A dim, wobbly, golden glow made its way toward him.

Alasdair's stomach grumbled. It had been well over a day and a half since he'd eaten. Roasted rabbit meat at midday and a few wild berries. The last thing he expected, though, was to be served a meal.

He stepped back and reached down to wake Ursula. She had dressed before falling asleep after their lovemaking, but she'd best be awake for their visitors.

"Sweet one. On your feet. Quickly."

He gave her his hand and helped her up. And by the time she was at his side, the torchbearer was at the gate.

Two sentries peered in. They were dressed in the customary kilt, leather vest, and bearskin cape. One carried a torch and sword, the other a key.

With quick movements, the soldier at the gate unlocked the door, then shoved it open.

"You." He pointed at Alasdair. "Just you."

What? He'd assumed he and Ursula would face their fate together.

She spoke before he had a chance. "Where Alasdair goes, I go," she said with a clear voice and an arrogant resolve, as if she was a queen commanding an army.

"Orders are for us to take only him," the man with the sword told them, gesturing to Alasdair.

"Take me anyway. My fate and his are tied," she insisted.

"Are you husband and wife?"

"We are bound to each other," Ursula said with conviction.

The two soldiers looked at one another.

"We are not criminals," Alasdair said, sensing some compassion from the two men standing outside the cell. "We are all Highlanders, lovers of Scotland and loyal to King James. What quarrel do you have with us?"

"We have no quarrel, but we must follow orders," the one with the sword told them. "Let's go," he ordered, seemingly out of patience with Alasdair.

What hope Alasdair had for compassion was squelched by the demand. Even if he could take one of them down, he was outmanned, his hands his only weapons. And the last thing he wanted was Ursula to get hurt.

Instead of fighting, Alasdair turned and embraced Ursula. Under his breath he said, "Go along with this, love. The worst may be getting pushed off the seawall." When she stiffened, he held her tighter. "Remember, float and kick."

Then he brought his lips to hers, pressing into their softness with a hunger and passion for more. A kiss to remind her of the bond she'd spoken of moments before. A kiss that said more than words. A kiss to show her who she was to him now, and how they would never be the same again.

A bond was a promise. He refused to believe they wouldn't see each other again and was determined to fight for their future, even as he was led down the corridor without her.

Not long afterward, Alasdair was shading his eyes from the glaring sun as he was led from the buttery into the walled courtyard facing the sea.

After passing the two checkpoints where he'd left Conn's volunteers, he wondered what had become of the men. Most likely they'd been found before they could sneak out. But because they had no quarrel with the MacDonalds, he hoped they'd been set free.

Without fanfare, Alasdair was led to the center of the courtyard where close to twenty clansmen stood facing the ocean. The soldier with the sword told Alasdair to stop.

In a few short moments, the other tied Alasdair's hands in front, then he was led before the men with his back to the sea loch.

Ian Macdonald waited in the center of the line. "I should have killed you when I killed your father."

"You did nae have the skill," Alasdair shot back.

"You had that damn flag with you."

"You believe in faeries, do you?"

Alasdair's gaze roamed the clansmen, and he caught most of them holding back a laugh.

"Donnae have anything to do with faeries. 'Twas me men who were spooked by the legend, and they failed me." The MacDonald laird stepped forward and walked toward Alasdair.

"Those men did not live to fail me again." He turned and gestured to the soldiers behind him, all wearing the MacDonald tartan. "These men are different. They will nae be frightened by legends, faeries, or"—Ian got within a breath of his face—"a MacLeod."

A whooping and a hollering followed the declaration, and Ian's men looked ready for blood. Perhaps Alasdair had underestimated their plans for him. Two things were certain. He needed to leave this castle isle alive, and he had to save Ursula. No matter what the means, he was willing to make the sacrifice.

"You've taken this castle from the MacKenzies," Alasdair said. "Do you nae have more hate for them than the MacLeods?" He looked Ian in the eye and did not blink. "They are your true enemies."

Ian's right cheek flinched. Then he spun away from Alasdair and began to pace.

Just a little farther.

As Ian droned on about the MacKenzies in their ability to defend an important Highland outpost like Eilean Donan, he walked farther and farther from Alasdair, and his clansmen's gazes followed their leader.

A few more feet.

When Ian's back was completely turned, Alasdair made his move. In one great rush, bounding across the courtyard toward the seawall, he ran until he reached it. Heart racing, chest heaving, Alasdair hurled himself over the wall feet first toward the water.

He inhaled a big gulp of air and plunged through the rock-hard surface, dropping as deep as the distance he'd jumped. Holding his breath tightly, Alasdair kicked with all his might, looking up toward the sun through the waves.

When his breath waned and his lungs burned, he didn't panic. Thoughts of saving Ursula and concern over being discovered kept him focused while he kicked hard and steered himself toward the island's foundation.

Finally, he broke through the blue canopy, sucking in a huge breath. As his gaze traveled upward, he found himself hidden under the wall where he'd jumped.

As much as he wanted to start around the castle now and make his way back to camp, it would be safer to hide under the ledge until dark. No doubt MacDonald's men were armed and searching for him.

But, he'd never be free until Ursula was free.

Chapter 34

Gone.

What would become of Alasdair? Ursula's thoughts were as dark as the dungeon. Shivering, she wrapped her arms around herself and began stomping her feet to get warm.

While she marched about the cell, her mood lightened a bit until her stomach growled, reminding Ursula she hadn't eaten since the banquet when they'd arrived.

Would they starve her to death? Instead of pushing her off the wall, might Ian let her rot, then have the rats finish her off?

Night and day were the same. It had been at least a day since Alasdair had been ripped away from her. He was the MacLeod's clan chief. But the MacDonalds didn't take kindly to the MacLeods, nor to the MacKenzies, and especially not to the Frasers.

Unless Ethan had revealed her true identity, why would they want to hurt her? She carried no weapon. She was not a threat. She'd simply been at the wrong place at the wrong time. Her circumstances were beyond her control. If she'd been allowed to travel alone, she'd have been to Skye Isle and back to Fyvie with the guelder rose by now.

She sighed, frustrated that she'd worked herself into a frenzy of worry. But thinking about the rose must have triggered a vision, for a fuzzy image of Roslyn began to form in her mind's eye.

Ursula took a deep breath and worked to push all other thoughts away, so she could focus on her sister of the heart.

How she wanted to be by her side, soothing her forehead and helping calm the two babes inside her.

There was Lachlan, sitting on a short stool and holding her hand. A shaky sigh made its way through Ursula. They were both at peace.

But as Rosalyn lay on her side in the chamber bed, Ursula could tell the babies had grown even more since her last vision, and a flash of panic surged through her. She had to get out of this dungeon. Rosalyn was counting on her.

The vision disappeared like a bubble bursting when a golden glow appeared outside the cell. It grew brighter as her heart beat faster.

A soldier halted outside the gate and peered in at her through the old iron bars. "You are summoned," he announced as a key cranked open the lock.

In moments, she was led up the winding dungeon stairs to an alcove next to the entrance. She was directed to sit on a stone bench inside what appeared to be a sanctuary, then she was left alone.

She studied its interior. Why was she here? Her gaze traveled around the nave. A basin protruded out of the stone wall across from her. On either side hung a cross—one Celtic, one Christian.

For her, Celtic traditions ran deep. But she wasn't ready for Christianity. Yet, this alcove, with a narrow loophole window, appeared to be ready to serve any faith. In her mind, one powerful God ruled overall, and she began to pray that today would not be her last.

With eyes closed, Ursula started, "Dear holiest of the holy, Father of all fathers, hear my prayer. I ne'er ask for much, you know. A place for shelter. A kind word for a kind deed. A bit of stale bread when there's not much to eat."

She opened her eyes for a moment and glanced about to make sure she was still alone, then squeezed them shut again.

"Lord our Father, I pray for those I care about. Those I have made promises to." She hesitated for a moment. God was all-knowing, but she was not ashamed of her actions. "You know who they are."

Her voice caught as she choked up with emotion. "Please protect Alasdair from harm. I pray he is still alive and that I may join him again one day. If not here in the beautiful Highlands, then at your pearly white gates."

She squeezed her hands tightly and stretched her neck. With eyes still closed, she gazed toward the heavens.

"And Father, please help me help my sister of the heart, Rosalyn. I must travel to the faerie pools for the guelder rose, then return to help her twins come into this world with your grace. Amen."

"Faerie pools?"

Her eyes flew open. "What?" Ursula exclaimed, startled to find the Laird MacDonald standing in the alcove alone with her.

"Are you nae afraid of the faeries?" he asked.

She stared at him, not knowing what to say.

"One of my men tells me you saved his life."

What was he talking about? Moments ago, the last word from her lips to God's ears had been 'Amen.' Why was the laird asking about faeries?

She glanced heavenward for some reassurance, and finally she found the inspiration she sought. "Nay, the Fae are only to be feared if you are ignorant."

That had the laird busting his gut. "The ignorant do nae know that they are, so they are fearful."

She considered asking if he was fearful but then thought better of it.

"But you must not be ignorant," he concluded, "and you are also fearless, for most wouldn't have answered my question."

Fearless? She was merely thankful she hadn't been thrown over the seawall . . . yet.

"You have healing skills?"

She blinked hard and then remembered he'd mentioned she'd saved a life of one of his men. She'd been so distracted by the query on faeries, she'd let the comment go past her.

"Aye, I dedicate my life to healing others."

"You said that with no hesitation and without being a braggart. It must be true."

She waited, wondering about this line of questioning and his interest in her after she'd been in the dungeon.

"My brother, Edward, is gravely ill," he said. "We have nae a healer on the grounds, nor within a day's ride of this fortress."

She studied Laird MacDonald. On the surface he appeared genuinely concerned. She wanted her freedom but could not demand it. So she considered starting with the necessities.

"I will volunteer, but I'm weak from the lack of food and drink." Although at least she was free of the darkness. She welcomed the warmth of the sun on her shoulders through the loophole window and the fragrant breeze from the sea tantalizing her nostrils, but she would nae last long on those.

The laird clapped his hands, and six servants hurried in, three on either side. "Take this healer to my brother's room and make her comfortable," MacDonald said. "Bring her whatever she wants but have a guard at the door."

He clapped his hands again, and two women servants rushed forward, each grabbing one of her elbows. Once she was on her feet, the laird was gone.

Ursula teetered between the two women. The lack of food made her knees buckle now that she was upright. A servant wrapped one of Ursula's arms around her neck, and the other woman followed suit. She was strung between the two as they assisted her through the castle archway and down a corridor, until finally they paused outside a massive wooden chamber door.

After a male servant stopped to assist with an efficient rap on the ancient door, it opened and Ursula was unceremoniously dragged inside the bedchamber.

The floor-to-ceiling dark plum and gold brocade drapes were drawn, shutting out any natural light. Instead, the room was illuminated by more tapered candles than she could count and the glow of the fire in the hearth.

An ashen-faced man lay in the center of an elaborately carved canopy bed, propped up by too many pillows. He appeared lifeless, yet, the rich embroidered blankets covering his chest rose and fell with his breath.

Although she'd needed some assistance walking at first, movement in general had Ursula feeling more like herself. She unwound herself from the servants and whispered her thanks.

Stretching side to side with her arms above her head, Ursula stared at the laird's ailing brother. She'd seen that color of skin before. Most likely he had smallpox.

She spoke softly to the servants, explaining what she needed from the kitchen for a potion. Both of them appeared shocked at the ingredients. But she knew they could be found in the castle. Maybe not in the kitchen proper, but they could be found.

When they asked what she wanted to eat, she told them any food would do. This wasn't the time nor place to be treated as a guest.

Once the women were off and the room quiet, she pushed open the depressing brocade draperies, letting in air and sunlight. Then methodically she walked about the chamber, snuffing out candles with the ornate goblet she found empty on the bed table. It didn't take long to turn the room from looking like a mausoleum to an orderly bedchamber.

"Blasted bitch. Why did you do that?"

Ursula resisted the urge to scream. *The ailing brother?* Yet, the voice sounded strong . . . but he'd called her a bitch?

Instead of letting her fury out, she put a cork in it. "I have a grumpy patient on my hands."

He snorted. "I'm not your patient. You can get out."

As much as she wanted to leave, she wasn't going to let this MacDonald order her about. "If you want to die." She shrugged her shoulders. "I can leave."

"Who are you?"

"It doesnae matter, does it?"

A grunt was his response. And luckily for Ursula, the two servants returned with food and supplies.

Ursula briskly walked to a circular wooden table at the far end of the chamber. She assumed it was used for dealings of high importance. But it was uncluttered and the perfect spot for mixing her potion and nibbling on the tempting scones and cream the women carried in.

After the servants placed the trays on the table, she surveyed the items. Thankfully, the breakfast food and potion supplies were on separate trays. The items needed to make the concoction for Edward were nasty in many ways.

"Thank you, my ladies," she said loudly, motioning them to her side. In a hushed tone, she said, "I shall do my best for this man, but he appears to be a few steps from crossing to the other side."

They nodded solemnly.

"I'm charged with healing him, but it may be beyond my capabilities."

They appeared to understand.

"I have someone who is near and dear to me who must be saved, and each day I'm here is one day more she could be closer to danger."

One of the servants put her hand over her mouth, the

other let out a little gasp. Ursula was grateful to have an attentive audience.

"Are you willing to stay here in this chamber for a few moments while I tend to Edward?"

"Mi lady, we are prisoners here, too," muttered the taller of the two women. "The MacDonalds are tyrants, and when the remaining MacKenzies knew the fight for their castle was for naught, the ones who could escape did."

The other servant leaned in even closer. "Some of the servants escaped, too, but most of us are here against our will."

Ursula grabbed each of their hands and gave them a squeeze. "I have a plan, but I need your help."

Chapter 35

One might call it a miracle, another a fluke, but Alasdair considered his reuniting with Gavin good luck.

Perhaps it was all of those together, for it really was a fluke that Alasdair and Gavin met at the Kyle of Lochalsh ferry. It was also a miracle they'd happened on the ship at the same time. And they considered it a stroke of good luck they'd both escaped from the MacDonalds and lived to talk about it.

Because he'd traversed his homeland many times in peaceful and war times, Alasdair knew the best, quickest, and shortest paths from Eilean Donan to his castle on the cusp of the ocean. The two traveled the short distance to Dunvegan together and plotted their revenge the entire way.

Now, Gavin sat with Alasdair and his captain, John, at the head of the table in Dunvegan's armory. Here, he'd gathered his best men and was preparing his troops for a march on Eilean Donan to challenge the MacDonalds' claim. Alasdair didn't fear their wrath, or the danger of being the aggressor. What he feared was battling against time. The longer he was gone from Ursula, the less control he had over her fate.

Something in his heart, however, told him she was still alive. There was a connection to her, telling Alasdair she was still bound to him. This was the intuition he needed to guide his words and rally his troops.

"Men, I know we have nae had a skirmish with the MacDonalds since the Battle at Bloody Bay. We have kept them out of our clan territory, and we have stayed away from theirs. The land demarcations are known to us all, but as long as they are not challenged, we can abide by the laws of King James and to his success of maintaining freedom for all of Scotland.

"As many of you know, I've returned from my journey to Inverness. My plan was successful, and I made a treaty with the clans the MacLeods of Lewis, Southerland, MacKenzies, and Ross. Before that, I had traveled to the Orkney Isles to visit the MacLeans and McNeils. I promised them our support if the Norse Vikings break their agreement with King James for the Isles of the Hebrides.

"We now have agreements with all the clans but the MacDonalds and Mathesons. As you know, our MacLeod clan and associated armies are vital to Scotland's independence from England. King James considers our stronghold here at Dunvegan, and the alliances I've made, the secret to his success of maintaining that freedom for all of Scotland."

The men at the table cheered, and Alasdair beamed with pride.

"But what troubles me now are the MacDonalds. They've taken Eilean Donan from the MacKenzies, and they hold the future of Dunvegan hostage."

The men pounded their fists on the table and stomped their feet. As much as Alasdair wanted to explain Ursula, it would be easier for the men to assume any MacDonald advance outside their clan's territory was a threat to Dunvegan. And it was.

"Although I've just returned, I cannae rest until we right this injustice." It was his turn to pound a fist on the table. "Who's with me?"

As he had hoped, every officer around the table, and their lieutenants, raised their fists in the air and shouted almost in unison, "I am!"

Alasdair turned to his captain. "As we march toward Eilean Donan, we'll send scouts ahead to rally."

His loyal captain, John, eyed him closely and asked, "Are we to bring the flag?"

"Aye. We will use it only if we must."

The room went silent. His soldiers knew the importance and repercussions of unfurling the historic flag.

That, too, was a secret to most outside the walls of Dunvegan. How Ursula had come to know of its existence he was not certain, nor had he interrogated her when they'd first met. Legends and myths abounded in Scotland, and he had not taken her interest seriously then.

"We march," Alasdair said with conviction. "Gather supplies, extra horses, and weapons. Most of the distance can be covered by nightfall. We'll camp far enough away from Eilean Donan to plan our attack in the wee hours of the morning."

~ ~ ~

As much as Ursula wanted to eat the sumptuous scones with cream, she didn't want to trigger the wrath of Edward, who could bark about her being a bitch and order her out of the bedchamber before she'd had her fill.

She welcomed the assistance from the two serving women, Gladys and Eliza, MacKenzie supporters and haters of Clan MacDonald. She'd found out they were sisters when they had agreed to help her escape.

Ursula would make the potion to the best of her ability with the limited resources and pray the three would be far from the castle before the remedy proved its worth.

Smallpox was a disease that once it reached its advanced stages was hard to reverse. When she'd been called on occasions like this, it had been for comfort rather than cure.

Thankfully, Eliza had procured the rat tail. It was the most important part of the potion. Without it, the concoction would be just a mild tea.

Ursula only needed the skin of the tail, so with her dirk in hand, she carefully shaved off the scales into the mortar that had been provided. While she prepared the potion, Eliza worked on Edward, fluffing his pillows and feeding him some of Ursula's scones and cream. Eliza even flirted with him when he said something ribald to her.

Men.

She rarely preferred their company, but she'd gotten close to Lachlan and found him to be overly charming and quite tolerable.

Alasdair, well, he was the exception. And she still needed to figure out how he had captured her heart and caused her emotions to riot. No matter how hard she'd tried to rationalize her feelings and get them under control, she could not keep from believing she and Alasdair were meant for one another. She had to hold onto hope. They had a bond, and her instincts told her he was alive.

If only she could pick up his thoughts, get a vison, she could prove he was still alive. They'd connected before. Even though she'd not built a bond with him as strong as Rosalyn's, she expected something to come through.

Letting out a frustrated breath, she cleared her thoughts, digging deep into her heart for the feelings he'd stirred. She waited. And waited. But nothing happened.

She huffed and her hands dropped, smacking the sides of her skirt. How frustrating. But when she recalled what her mother had said years ago—*Men are more difficult to read, their thoughts and emotions more guarded*—she stopped trying to force it.

Instead, she pushed Alasdair out of her thoughts and began to concentrate on the potion. She measured carefully, adding the common Highland kitchen items, ginger, saffron, and cardamom. Then she reached under her skirt for her herbal pouch and the final ingredient she'd need. The Highland heather.

Ursula glanced over her shoulder at Eliza, and the servant tossed her an exasperated look. Clearly, the lass needed rescuing from the lecherous lord, so she quickened her pace, taking note she'd assembled all she needed in the mortar.

At a fervent pace, she began to grind the ingredients into a paste with the pestle. But she was startled by the sound of the heavy chamber door slamming shut and bobbled the mortar before setting it down on the worktable.

"Is he healed?"

She wheeled around to find Laird MacDonald glaring at her. Ursula swallowed hard. "The potion is just finished now, mi lord," she said with a groveling tone that disgusted her, but she thought necessary. She finished with a bouncy curtsy.

"Do nae dally with your own needs before my brother's," the laird said. She glanced back at the half-eaten food, tempted to admit she'd given it to his brother, but she saved her breath.

"I've eaten the food, brother," Edward said, defending her.

He'd called her a bitch, and now he was standing up for her?

Laird MacDonald ignored his brother's comment. "Let us not delay. He looks to be at death's door."

"I look death in the face and laugh," Edward bragged.

That made the laird relax a little, and he strode over to where Ursula was working. She wasn't interested in being interrogated, so she quickly spun around and dropped the concoction into a goblet that had come with the supplies. She poured in the wine that had been provided, filling the goblet halfway. By the time she felt Ian MacDonald's presence behind her, she was finished.

"It is ready," she offered, turning. "You may deliver it if you'd like."

The laird grunted. "He may be my brother, but I will not dote on him." He pointed toward the bed. "If he lives, you live."

She started across the room, the distance now overly long. Clearly, no matter her skill, the laird would blame his brother's impending death on her.

"You at least have a better chance of surviving than your paramour."

Ursula's back stiffened, and she almost stumbled, slowing to gather her wits. *Alasdair? Was he saying Alasdair is dead?*

Pride would rule her emotions, she decided, before finishing her walk to Edward's bedside. Ursula didn't want the innuendo to impact her actions. "That animal," she said coldly as she glided to a stop at the canopied bed. "I'm happy to be rid of him. You should have kept us in separate cells."

At that the laird let out a dastardly laugh. "His death was of no consequence to you?"

Her heart sank, but she needed to know more. Had he died from the wall or the sword?

"Nay, grateful to know the bastard was punished. His death will compensate for the improprieties he took. He was a MacLeod." She said it as if his name left a dirty taste in her mouth.

"Rest assured his death was at our will. His body has probably washed ashore already. Although as full of holes as he was from the swords and spears, it's more likely his body is at the bottom of the loch, being fed on by the creatures that frequent these waters."

Bile scalded the back of her throat. She couldn't heave now, even as her hopes and dreams cascaded down a treacherous cliff of despair.

Alasdair was dead, killed by these barbarians. Why? When she was just beginning to fall in love with him. To plan a future with him. Perhaps deliver an heir. Her heart was breaking, shattering into a thousand shards of disappointment. But she wouldn't let these blackguards cripple her.

"Well-deserved punishment," she said through gritted teeth as she stood at the bedside of his brother. Eliza was still there, looking at her with wide doe-like eyes. Ursula gave her a taut smile, "Hold the lord's head for me, will ye, lassie?"

Then she turned her attention to Edward. "Shall taste like wine, mi lord," Ursula promised, now wishing it was poison.

Edward downed the liquid quickly, as if he was thirsting for this very drink. Perhaps he had the inclination this was his last hope.

Ursula took the goblet back from him, and Eliza wiped his mouth. He closed his eyes and laid his head back on the pillows.

"Now we wait," the laird said.

A bit of panic washed over her. She hadn't expected the laird to stay and watch his brother live or die. She needed to escape. But she also needed to eat.

"The potion will take time, mi lord. Sir Edward will not benefit from the full effects until at least the morn."

She gathered her courage and met his gaze. She stared straight into the eyes of the man responsible for killing her love. Her dirk sat on the table behind him. How she wished she had it in her hand now and could stab his black heart repeatedly for what he'd done.

If not for Rosalynn and the babes, she would have done the deed then and there. But instead, she looked at him with what she hoped was reverence and respect.

The MacDonald laird scrutinized her as if dissecting her soul. Finally, he said, "I will be back in the morn. We shall have a batch of thrushes brought in for you."

As he turned to go, she said, "I shall need thrushes for the servant maids as well. Should Edward need anything in the night, they are the only ones who can retrieve it."

He stopped with his back to her and his hand on the door's lever. "So be it," he said, and was gone.

Both women gathered with her at the round table, taking seats and waiting for her next direction.

They wanted freedom as much as she did. And they patiently waited while she shoved pieces of the sweet scones, slathered with jam and cream, into her mouth. She offered the plate of remaining scones, but they refused.

Once she had her fill, Ursula pushed back from the tray and sighed. Now that she had a full belly, her mind was clearer.

"Ladies, we must plan our escape while Edward is sleeping peacefully and the laird is out of our way," Ursula whispered.

Gladys perked up and leaned forward, as did Eliza. "Here's what I think will work," Ursula said in a hushed voice. And she went about explaining a plan that allowed for a way to trick the guard. It called for disguising Ursula as a maid, then Eliza coordinating other maids to travel in and out with supplies for the laird's brother until the guard would lose count and Ursula could be smuggled out, as well as the sisters.

"I shall make sure the guard has plenty of wine. When I came in here with the tray, he already looked sleepy," Eliza told them.

Ursula laid her hand flat on the table, and the other women followed suit, each placing a hand on top of the other, until all six hands were alternately stacked together.

They smiled at each other across their unified stance. Ursula's shattered heart was mending thanks to the sisters' aid. They were becoming fast friends. Maybe more than friends. Perhaps she'd be a sister of the heart to them like she was to Rosalyn.

Ursula could not bring Alasdair back from the dead,

but neither would she allow this tyrannical MacDonald to influence her future.

As much as she wanted to kill the laird's brother now, cut out his heart and leave it on the bedsheets, she was a healer, and it was against her nature to kill anyone. Her escape alone would have to be her vengeance.

Chapter 36

The army had grown through the Highlands at every village stop. Clans MacKenzie, MacKinnon, and even the Mathesons had joined in the march. Alasdair estimated the group at two hundred strong.

As they traveled, the group gathered catapults and cannons. Fire power was new to the Highland tribes, but the Mathesons said they'd perfected the new weapons.

Although the cannons would be helpful, they wouldn't arrive with the rest of the contingent, as they moved at a wagon's pace, drawn by four large workhorses. Still, the cannons could be vital to their offense when the other resources were exhausted.

When the multi-clan army arrived at the foothill overlooking Eilean Donan Castle, the sky was pitch black. Late into the night, the men set up a hidden camp overlooking the descent to the castle.

Fortunately, the moon was shadowed by dense clouds. They were not far from the rise where they'd approached two days ago. Had it been that long since he'd loved Ursula like no other? The woman had haunted his dreams since he'd been forced to escape the MacDonalds.

Alasdair had walked away from many a lass in his life with no regrets. But with Ursula, his only regret was not meeting her sooner. He cringed, remembering his initial self-interest. She was to provide him with an heir? What a Scottish arse he was to start their relationship that way.

She had to be alive. He could feel it in his bones, in his gut, in his heart. She was worth sacrificing all he had for her.

Now that they were within striking distance of the dungeon where she sat, he was ready to risk all to save her.

With that resolve, Alasdair gathered his men and recited the instructions again. The leaders of each rank knew the castle from top to bottom. They carried intricate maps drawn on dried sheepskins. Each commander had a team and a purpose.

From the north, Alasdair would wade through the low tide with Gavin, John, Kenneth MacKenzie, and most of the MacLeod clansmen, then climb up the outside to the seawall.

From the south, McTavish Matheson would position his catapults and archers at the fringe of the woods. From there, the ammunition would reach the parapets easily and take out the garrisons who manned them. If the cannons arrived in time, they'd add them to the offense.

From the east, MacKinnon's clansmen would lie low in the tall grasses, watching the north and south attacks, preparing to join whichever contingent appeared to be the most in need.

And from the west, on the sea loch, Clan MacKenzie would support the cause from nimble longboats. These clansmen had not only lost their castle to the MacDonalds, they had witnessed their cruelty and were ready for revenge.

Alasdair's most trusted men guarded the Faery Flag in one of the longboats. It was unclear, even to him, which one carried the flag, but he was assured it would only be unfurled if needed.

The clansmen who had sworn allegiance to Alasdair were in position and ready to take on the MacDonalds. The soldiers, covered in mud, blended into the landscape.

Alasdair raised his sword to the heavens, the signal for the planned ambush to begin. He led his group to the loch bank, where he'd journeyed across with Conn's men days before.

Thankfully, it was low tide again, the moon guiding the cycle of the waters at night. The men traversed the short passage, bending low so only their heads stuck above the water.

Once on the other side, Alasdair quickly climbed the bank with his men at his heels. They passed through the break in the seawall, then crouched down in the darkest corner of the castle's courtyard.

According to Alasdair's plan, the fireball attack would start first, drawing all available MacDonald soldiers to the south side of the castle's parapets. Once MacTavish Matheson in the south was confident he'd taken out enough of MacDonald defense, he would shoot a blazing arrow into the water. After the signal, Clan McKinnon's leader would release a fire arrow straight up in the air. Alasdair needed only to train his gaze on the eastern sky for the signals. Once he had them, the land approach on the eastern castle entrance would begin.

Alasdair watched the glowing fireballs arching into the sky and then disappearing beyond the large walls of the keep. Time stood still while his heart raced, pumping him up for what was to come, direct combat with the MacDonalds and the laird whose plans he would crush.

Ursula had to be alive. He willed her to be. If the prophecy was true, then she had to be. Undeniably, it was critical to his mission and to King James's sovereignty for the MacKenzies to regain possession of their castle. Still, his ultimate purpose was to save her.

The place to start his search was where he'd seen her last. And once he rescued her from the dungeon, Alasdair would guide her to the longboats.

Finally, the arrow from the south blazed through the night sky into the water, followed closely by another into the sky.

Alasdair's contingent began to move, half of them following him toward the entry to the buttery and the other half to the parapets.

Snatching a burning torch from its wall mount, Alasdair retraced the steps he knew to the religious alcove and finally down the winding dungeon steps.

Gone?

The cell was empty, and the door propped open, as if the occupant had been hurried out.

Even though his heart told him she was still alive, he dreaded looking for her elsewhere in the castle. But tormenting himself with possibilities would only lead to misery.

Now it was time for truth. Time for Alasdair to follow his plan to gather the MacDonald clansmen and lock them up in this dungeon. Time to face Ursula's fate. And his own.

He pointed to the spiral staircase, and once they had gathered again in the alcove off the entrance, Alasdair drew out his map and dealt out the instructions.

Half the men would go to the great hall led by Alasdair. The rest would advance with Kenneth MacKenzie to join the first group at the parapets and take down any survivors.

Once the castle was secure and in the hands of his battalion, they would hand Eilean Donan back to Kenneth and let him decide how to punish the MacDonalds.

Even though a match with Ian would be sweet revenge, Alasdair wanted as little bloodshed as possible. While he promised his father retribution, he wouldn't allow a duel with the MacDonald laird get in the way of his search for Ursula.

Storming the great hall from three different entrances, Alasdair led his group into the vast, darkened receiving room. The hearth flames were nearly extinguished, causing long shadows of his men to be cast on the stately, whitewashed walls.

The room was empty. Or so it appeared until Gavin poked his sword under one of the trestle tables, routing out one of the MacDonald clan. Soon, Alasdair counted nine of Ian's men who'd hidden rather than fought. No doubt when these men heard cannon fire, the cowards had taken cover.

It wasn't long before Alasdair's group had corralled the nine MacDonald clansmen and locked them securely in the dungeon.

After all the contingents met back in the great hall, there was much celebrating among the men. But Alasdair wasn't one of them. It didn't take long for most of the soldiers to sober and the celebrating to subside, the men no doubt realizing there was still work to be done.

Alasdair was proud of the men, but certain the MacDonald laird had eluded capture. He asked the question they most likely dreaded, "What of Ian MacDonald?"

As he circled the room with little anticipation of proving otherwise, the men could not meet his gaze. Eyes downcast, they were silent.

After a long wait with no response, he asked, "Any noncombatants?" He didn't speak her name for fear his voice might crack, but it was on his lips. It would be obvious to the men who he was asking about.

There was more awkward silence until Gavin finally spoke. "Your lairdship, no sign of Ursula. But we've yet to check the solars on the second and third floors."

Alasdair's unspoken fears were returning. Had Ian made an escape with his closest men when the castle came under siege? Had he taken Ursula with him? The only thing left to do was to sweep the solars and any additional bedchambers.

"We shall find them," Captain John pledged. Turning to the group of mostly MacLeod clansmen, Alasdair's leader scanned the volunteers, then began ushering the clansmen into groups of three or four and assigning them to sections of the upper chambers.

With determination, but not the same fanfare as when they'd arrived in the great hall, the groups dispersed. After making his way with John, Kenneth, and Gavin to the master solar, Alasdair strode into the first room with his sword drawn. As much as he wanted to take the laird down by himself, he was no fool. There was strength in numbers.

The room was almost pitch black, except for a few embers glowing in the hearth. A man appeared to be asleep in the bed, propped up by many pillows.

Alasdair approached the bed. The man lying there was not the laird, although he bore a striking resemblance to Ian. As he stepped closer, so did his men behind him. Their swords were held ready to defend their advancements.

Alasdair paused at the edge of the bed. With one flick of his sword, the man would be dead. He called out instead. "On your feet. The MacLeods have taken Eilean Donan. You are a prisoner of this castle."

The man did not respond, and Alasdair repeated himself. But that only yielded the same result.

A bawdy, low laugh belted out from behind him. Wheeling around, Alasdair found the MacDonald laird standing in the chamber doorway with his sword drawn and three guards behind him.

"He's dead," the laird stated flatly. "Your woman killed him."

Alasdair backed up against the edge of the bed, giving his men room to spread out. He'd made a major mistake not guarding the door behind them, being too eager to sweep through the final rooms in search of Ursula. Now he'd have to fight defensively.

"She's dead, too," Ian MacDonald said with finality.

Alasdair almost dropped his sword.

"The task was simple," MacDonald said. "Save my brother or die trying."

Alasdair's jaw twitched before he dove at the laird. Sword clenched in both hands, he met Laird MacDonald's blade, driving him back with such force he knocked Ian backward into his own men. The three stumbled over each other, one falling to his knees.

Led by a fury he could not control, Alasdair leaped through the doorway, over the tangled clansmen, and met Laird MacDonald's blade on the other side.

Alasdair's men were at his heels without hesitation, and as they burst through the doorway after him, they met blade for blade with the other MacDonald clansmen, slaying one quickly.

Alasdair had the upper hand as he battled the laird, advancing forward a step at a time while his adversary retreated, closer and closer to the end of the corridor until he finally had him where he wanted him. In a corner.

Chapter 37

Ursula's plan had worked with the help of Eliza and Gladys, and later that night, the three entered the sisters' family home, a comfortable cottage in Kyle of Lochalsh.

Once inside the door, their father rushed forward, grabbing each girl around the waist and squeezing them into a trio embrace, the girls squealing with delight.

"My bonnie lassies, how is it now that I can look upon your beautiful faces?" Then his gaze moved to Ursula. "Is this woman an angel of mercy?"

Ursula smiled. Perhaps she should have given the girls some privacy for their reunion, but their father opened his arms and motioned with his hands for her to join in the circle.

She blushed. As much as she was uncomfortable hugging anyone she did not know well, she ran into their arms and was sucked into the middle.

"You have brought my babies back to me," their dad gushed, releasing his hold. "For this, I owe you a great debt."

"Good sir." She curtsied within the circle. "I am nae wholly responsible for your daughters' freedom, for they are as responsible for mine." She glanced back and forth between them. "Together we escaped."

"Come," their father said, breaking the circle and gesturing to his hearth. "Take a seat by the fire and tell me more. I suspect elements of danger, daring, and deviousness were involved."

The girls chuckled, and they all followed him, Ursula taking up a stool next to the girls. When their father started to bow before he sat, Ursula waved him off with a tsk. She was considered a lady but was as comfortable sitting before a servant as she was before a king.

"Ursula, this is our father, Johnathan," Eliza said with a tinge of pride in her voice." Swiveling toward Ursula, she continued the introductions. "Father, this is Ursula, a healer and a—"

"Witch," Ursula finished for Eliza.

"Magician, was what I was going to say." Eliza gave Ursula a disgusted look, but her eyes were still smiling. Eliza was the younger of the two and the most demonstrative.

"Father," Eliza moaned, standing up before the hearth as if taking the stage, pretending she had a broom in her hands, "we were put to work by the scullery maid. Sweeping the kitchen floor, cleaning the tables, and rinsing out the iron kettles. We had to finish all these chores before we could sneak out the back of the buttery."

Her father's eyes glowed with pride as he listened to every detail. With animated movements, Eliza continued. "Ursula knew a way out of the castle grounds through the courtyard and a break in the seawall. The plan we concocted was executed flawlessly. As proof, here we are before you."

She giggled before she added, "You have nae even commented on how filthy and muddy we are."

Her father could not stop smiling. "The mud will wash off, a wee trifle to contend with. I am giddy with glee to see my girls before me whole and alive." He sniffed loudly. "The smell or the state of your dress does nae bother me," he said with a hint of sarcasm.

Erica raised a damp sleeve to her nose and almost gagged after taking a whiff of it.

Her father roared with laughter. "You all shall have a proper bath in the morn."

"Aye, to wash off the sea and the muck from wading to the shore. Ursula led us across, for we would ne'er had the courage to do it alone."

All eyes turned on her, and although everyone was smiling, Ursula sobered. Her journey did not end here like the others.

Eliza must have sensed her change of mood, for she gave her a wink and turned to her father. "Da, when we agreed to the plan to help Ursula and ourselves escape from the MacDonalds, we also made a promise for you."

His eyebrows rose at her words, but the smile stayed on his face. "I will hear you out. As I said when you walked in the door, I owe her a debt."

Ursula started to protest, but Eliza put a finger over her lips to silence her eager objections. "A promise is a promise," Eliza said sternly, then looked to her sister, who nodded her head profusely. "I have never broken a promise, and I'm not about to start now."

Ursula nodded, and Eliza removed her finger, then turned to her father. "Da, we promised you would take Ursula to the faerie pools at Glenbrittle."

The girl's father rocked back in his chair and stared off into the hearth. For a long moment he was silent. Finally, he turned to Ursula. "'Tis no secret on Skye Isle the faeries mean more harm than good."

Ursula wasn't surprised at the commentary. She was well versed in the harm faeries could cause. The ones who inhabited Skye Isle were the darkest, most mysterious, and the least understood of all the faeries in the Highlands.

Unless you were from these parts, you feared them like the plague. But she would defend them nevertheless. "Aye, sir, they have their malice, but they also have their good. Many encounter only the bad, but remember, they retreated from the mainland to the glens on Skye Isle because of us."

He was silent, and so were the girls. It had been a long time since she had walked the glen as a young girl with wonder and awe. The faeries needed defending. "There is always a price for power. It is the ignorant, the fool, who is enticed by the faeries' offerings. Even though gold is not precious to the Fae, they understand that gold is precious to mortals.

"Those who are promised eternal life should know that it comes at a cost. Enslavement to a faerie is the exchange for the magic of a life with no death."

"What you say bears merit, Ursula, but many of us have become fools under their spell. Perhaps you have special gifts that allow you to be immune to their mischief and magic." He paused and looked up. "My wife was nae so lucky."

Ursula's heart went out to him. "She was taken by the Fae, good sir?"

"Call me Johnathan," he insisted, his hands fidgeting in his lap. "The Fae took Eliza from her crib when she was barely a week old," he began, glancing over to his daughter with watery eyes. "I had ridden out with the MacKenzie clan to defend Eilean Donan from the advancing MacDonalds. It had been their obsession to rule over that castle as long as I can remember.

"My wife, Molly, had been left alone many times before and had always been able to defend herself, so I did nae think there would be any danger for her and the girls.

"But all I know is what Gladys could tell me." His attention drifted to the older girl, who immediately cast her gaze to the floor, her cheeks turning pink.

The silence was deafening for a few moments with the exception of the dry wood crackling in the hearth. Finally, in a timid voice, Gladys spoke up.

"I was only nine summers at the time Mama was taken by the faeries." She sniffled and stopped.

Her father stood and walked to her side. "If you do nae want to talk about the story, we'll end it here and now."

Ursula reached over to pat Gladys's hand. "Aye, the Fae have their pranks and mischief, but without warning, their actions can cause harm. You do nae need to recount the tale," Ursula insisted.

Gladys shook her head. "'Twill help me to recount the story to someone who understands their magic. Perhaps you can help us understand why they are so evil."

As much as she wanted to continue to defend the mysterious creatures of the glen, she needed to be respectful of the damage they'd done to this family. She could not reverse their deeds, but perhaps she could help these kind people understand the Fae ways.

"The faeries do not know what it is like to be human," Ursula began. "They look upon us with curiosity. They cannot help but want to interact with us. The heather pixies do not mean harm. When they feel threatened, they lash out."

"We didn't invite them to our home. They invaded it," Gladys defended, her eyes tearing up. "Four of them, with golden auras and translucent wings." She paused, staring off beyond Ursula into her memories. "I wanted to touch them. They appeared friendly when they came in through the open windows," Gladys told them with vacant eyes.

"They picked up the baby." Her gaze moved to her sister, Eliza. "At first, I thought they might be angels coming to bless her, but when they handed my sister out the window, I rushed to wake mother."

"The Fae love beauty and babies," Ursula said.

Gladys gave Ursula a steely stare before she went on. "In moments, mother and I were out the door, not taking time to cover our shoulders with a cape or put slippers on our feet. We raced after the band of wee folk as they floated across the glen." She blinked hard. "They were flying and taking my sister with them." She choked on the words and shook her head, clearly unable to go on.

"I shall finish the story," Johnathan said with a soft voice, stroking Gladys's hair while he talked. "My wife, with young Gladys in tow, followed the faeries as long as they could until they lost them in the clouds."

Gladys let out a whimper but raised her head. Eyes glazed over, she said, "Mama took me back to the cottage where we dressed properly for the weather. Although she wanted to leave me with the McCullums, I begged her to take me with her. Perhaps she knew all along what would happen," Gladys admitted, then she put her head in her hands and began to sob.

Ursula held up her hand. It tore at her insides to see her new friend distraught and clearly in pain. "I have heard enough," Ursula said, moving from her stool to kneel at Gladys's feet.

The girl took Ursula's hands and gazed into her eyes. "You must know the story. I must tell it," she said.

"Go on," Ursula urged from her spot at Gladys's feet, trusting the act of sharing would allow for deeper healing.

"Mother knew where they'd go. The faerie pools at Glenbrittle. I did nae know the place, but I fear it now," she admitted.

When Ursula squeezed Gladys's hands, the girl appeared to gain the strength and courage she offered her.

"Once we found ourselves at the faerie pools, mother called out Eliza's name. 'Twas mere moments afore a beautiful faerie materialized before us wearing long green robes of fern and a crown on her head made of golden vines."

Ursula was shocked. The Faery Queen rarely surfaced unless answering a special call. The heather pixies were more mischievous than most of the Fae and delighted tricking humans whenever possible. Perhaps another faerie had posed as the queen? But she would not dispute Gladys's account and nodded as the girl continued.

"My mother begged the queen for Eliza to be returned to her. Our family did nae have much in the way of land, but we had rare gold coins we'd inherited from the Viking side of our family. My mother offered them in exchange.

"But the faerie shook her head and said it was nae enough. Instead, the queen asked for an exchange, the baby for me.

"My mother had been desperate. Crying and pleading. She pushed me behind her skirts.

"Finally, my mother suggested another option, the gold and my mother's service in exchange for the baby to be returned home with me, and a guide for our journey back.

"The faerie accepted, and that was the last time I set eyes on my mother, Molly."

Chapter 38

Ethan was weary of walking. With no warhorse, he was forced to travel by foot. Yet that was no consequence at the moment, for a horse couldn't tread on this landscape. The faerie glen was a maze of rounded grassy mounds interspersed with oddly shaped ponds.

After surviving the fall from the seawall, there had been little left to accomplish on Skye, except for hunting down Moaning Molly's treasure.

With the MacDonalds' rule of Eilean Donan and Ursula in the dungeon beyond his reach, Ethan focused on the directions Molly had given him to find the gold she'd promised was here for the taking. He'd promised himself to salvage something from this peculiar journey.

But he was not all heartless. He did regret having to abandon Ursula at Eilean Donan. But with no weapons and no contingent, what was a Luttrell lord to do? What would his father, Nicholas, do? Focus on acquisition of land or money.

As much as the Eilean Donan castle was legendary in the Highlands, Ethan had no further interest in tending a lairdship this far removed from civilized life. It may have been a haven for his mother, but he'd be content to let the MacDonalds and the MacKenzies battle it out.

Ursula would no doubt land on her feet, like the black cat sorceress she was. He'd tired of her after all. The chase had only become interesting because the damaged Highlander had appeared to take an interest in her.

He'd not been himself until the swim to shore and his found freedom. Even if he had to steal food and coin, he was resourceful when he had to be. But finding the treasure would fatten his purse. It would not only provide him with a horse and guided protection, but a victory for his trouble.

The wind picked up unexpectedly, tossing him forward as if pushed. He spun around, half expecting to find someone behind him. The only thing that greeted him was a bit of the sun trying to burn a hole though the foggy morning.

Ethan turned back to the path that led toward the water. A low cloud hung just above the ridge, hiding the Cuillin Hills from view.

Rocks covered in green moss and peat, along with heather growing in between, lined the stream that he followed. Directly before him was a low, rocky ridge worthy of climbing, if it were not for the waterfalls and crystal-blue pool below.

The closer he came to the faerie pools, the louder the sound became, the blue liquid rushing down the slick rock walls.

But then a loud hissing sound had Ethan frantically turning from side to side seeking its source. Before he found it, a mist materialized out of nowhere, forming a wall, blocking him from his progress. He'd not come this far to be stopped, so he walked into it.

As he crossed through the foggy mist, Ethan had the sense of being pushed into another time and place. It was as if the pools in front of him were invisible to the outside world.

"Are you brave or ignorant?"

The voice jolted Ethan from his illusions. He drew his sword. "Show yourself," he demanded, turning in a half circle, ready for an attack.

"Brave and ignorant, I'd say," a female voice chimed in.

"Show yourself," Ethan said again, inching toward where the voices had come from.

"We are here in front of you," the female voice answered.

"But because you are ignorant, you cannae see us," said the other.

"Brave or ignorant does not matter for I am here to search for Molly's treasure."

The female voice let out a haughty laugh. "How do you proposed to find it if you are ignorant?"

Ethan had not expected his search to be impeded by spirts, or faeries, or whatever these aberrations were who chose to interrogate him. His goal was to find the treasure and leave this desolate place as soon as possible, so he would do his best to trick these spirits.

"How can I be ignorant if I know a treasure exits here? Otherwise, you would have told me there was no treasure."

"There is no treasure here," the male voice screeched.

"Leave me be, and I'll ascertain that for myself." He advanced with his sword battle ready, determined to get to the pool and begin the trek around to the hidden cavern Molly had told him about.

But before he made it to the water's edge, something shoved his shoulder. The force was strong, and it made him stumble forward, almost dropping his sword. Once he regained his footing, Ethan wheeled around with his sword leading his movement.

"He's ignorant if he thinks that sword will do him any good," the female voice said.

"We've already established that. Now we need to see if he's as stupid as he appears," the male voice added.

Ethan sheathed his sword. Even though he hated to admit it, slashing through the air at spirits he could not see wouldn't aid him.

Once his weapon was secured, Ethan started toward the water's edge again. Without mishap, he managed to reach it, then he walked around the perimeter toward the cave behind the falls.

Yes, the opening was there just the way Molly had described. The sound of the crashing water around him was deafening now. For a while, Ethan made his way uninterrupted. Placing his feet carefully with each step on the wet stones that circled the pool's perimeter, he hoped the spirits had flown off to bother someone more ignorant.

As he came closer to the cave opening, Ethan slowed his pace, for the rocks here were slick from the misting water all around him. Even the face of the rocks behind the falls showed signs of nature's abuse, as the water's path was marked by reddish-brown irregular stripes.

The pool itself was mesmerizing, the crystal clear surface more translucent than glass. The rocks under the surface looked like bright, oversized gems. Ethan stopped for a moment to gaze at them, wondering if they could be precious stones.

"What the—?" Before he could finish his question, he'd was shoved from behind. Breaking the clear surface he'd been staring at, Ethan panicked, fighting to get air. He thrashed about, trying to keep his head above the surface. His clothes, laden with water, dragged him down.

Chapter 39

The blood was worse than the wound, and once it was cleaned, Alasdair chuckled at the size of it. While he waited patiently for his injury to be bound with a clean linen wrap, the shock of Ian's words cut him deeper emotionally than the laird's sword had physically.

"Here, drink this," Kenneth insisted and shoved a full goblet under Alasdair's nose.

With his free hand, he took the goblet and drank some of the dark liquid. A welcome diversion, the comforting taste of a strong wine lingered on his lips.

"Crotach, I did nae think you'd make it through that skirmish. Ian MacDonald had you cornered," Kenneth reminded him.

"Without your help, I would be a dead man. First I had him cornered, but I must admit the moment when he knocked my sword away . . ." Alasdair closed his eyes. "If you hadn't tossed me yours." He shuddered. The images of the battlefield and the axe coming down on his shoulder flooded his memory. He took a deep breath and shook them off.

"I wasnae going to stab him in the back, but it was time for the MacDonald rule to end at the tip of my sword," Kenneth MacKenzie declared.

"We both had vindication. My hand and your weapon," Alasdair said, raising his chalice. "I'll drink to that." Then he guzzled down the rest of the strong wine.

"Now that Ian is in the dungeon with his clansmen, I can get this castle right again," the MacKenzie laird said with a stubborn resolve. "You are welcome to rest here until your wounds heal," Kenneth added.

Alasdair sighed inwardly. The rage was still inside him. *Ursula gone?* He could not believe it. Refused to believe it. Wouldn't his heart tell him if it were true?

Perhaps the only way to satisfy his uncertainty would be to search the lochs for her body. If she was pushed off the seawall as Ethan had been, that would be the natural place to look.

Although Alasdair had made it to land, he'd had plenty of experience in the waters around Dunvegan.

It was still light when Alasdair stood at the seawall and gazed out over the lochs. After some serious consideration that afternoon, he decided instead of looking for Ursula's body, he'd honor her instead. He would take up her quest to find the guelder rose for her friend Rosalyn.

Talking long strides back to the keep, Alasdair reviewed his plan. It would call for the services of only a few of his clansmen. He would deliver the flower to Fyvie for Rosalyn, then journey to Edinburgh to meet with King James and report on his recapture of Eilean Donan for the MacKenzies. After gaining the alliances of the key Highland clans, Alasdair was one step closer to becoming Lord of the Isles.

Once he'd reached the great hall, he joined Kenneth Mackenzie at the head table, ready to bid his farewell, stronger in his resolve to honor his lost love.

"*Sláinte mhaith*," Kenneth called out, raising his challis.

"To your good health as well, my friend," Alasdair concurred. He followed the salutation with a long guzzle of the sweat mead. Whilst he was tempted to accept the reinstated MacKenzie laird's hospitality, he was ready to honor Ursula and needed time for solace.

"The mead cannae be that terrible," his host said, breaking through Alasdair spiraling thoughts. Then he gestured to the filled trestle tables. “Any unmarried Highland lass can be yours, my friend.”

When Alasdair balked, Kenneth exploded in laughter. With a heaving chest and sputtering words, the laird claimed, “I’m not insisting on marriage, although a union between our clans would be mutually beneficial. I suggest only a distraction from your . . . well, em, concerns.”

Alasdair laughed like a man who hadn’t done so in a long while and rose from his seat. Grabbing his host’s forearm up to the elbow and giving it a tight squeeze, he replied, “Consider our alliance as strong as one bound by dutiful marriage. I thank you for your offer of female distractions without matrimony, but I have promises to keep and a sovereign who requests my presence.”

Kenneth eyed him like a knowing father. “Suit yourself, Crotach,” his host replied, completing the parting salutation, their arms clasped in farewell and friendship. “My good steward will see you to your horse in the morn when you are ready, and my loyalty will follow you to our king.”

After leaving the great hall and his host, Alasdair gathered his men, instructing half to return to Dunvegan and the rest to join him.

The next day, his group of loyal clansmen reached Glenbrittle at the foothill of the Cuillin Mountains by late morning. Alasdair knew Skye like a mother knew her children, but he’d not been to this place where the faeries dwelled. In a way, it was odd that he hadn’t, considering his family’s history. But he’d always felt the faeries would do his bidding when necessary.

The legends of the Faery Queen and his great-great-great-grandmother could be highly exaggerated, but he entered the glen with confidence, the family flag wrapped in a protective satchel and tucked in his sporran.

Although he trusted his clansmen, Alasdair chose to leave the group and venture into the falls alone.

Following the River Brittle, Alasdair stopped when he reached the first place where the water ran in large torrents down the low cliff walls into the aqua-colored water below. It was mesmerizing to watch the water cascade into the pool from the lofty ridge above. He marveled at the speed the water traveled until its thundering crash in the calm pond below.

"Are you brave or ignorant?"

Alasdair spun around, seeking the person belonging to the query, not surprised he was not alone.

"Brave," he answered confidently.

"We shall see," promised the squeaky male voice.

Alasdair did not budge but stood tall and ready for whatever came at him. From what he knew of faeries, they could take any shape and most would rather do harm than good.

He was prepared to fight for the guelder rose and slowly withdrew his sword from its scabbard. Assessing his surroundings, he waited, weapon in hand.

"Over here." The words were whispered in his left ear. But in addition to the roaring of the water, he could hear something breathing beside him.

He shifted his gaze to the left without moving his head. Nothing.

"Over here." Now the voice came from his right. Again, without moving his head, his eyes skirted across to the far side of his vision's range. Nothing.

Then out of nowhere an imposing wolf materialized before him, blocking his path. The animal's brown fur was a stark contrast to its glaring fangs. Alasdair took a measured step backward.

"I come for the guelder rose. Will you let me pass?" He'd been told by Ursula it grew in the cave behind the falls.

"That depends," answered a tiny female voice.

Alasdair waited what seemed an eternity to defend against an attack from the wolf or to hear an answer from the faerie.

"What do you have to barter?" she finally asked.

"As Laird of—"

"No, wait," the male voice called out "You will have only one offering. You must choose something near and dear to your heart."

"Or else?"

"Or else you shall be deemed ignorant after all and will have only your bravery to save you."

Alasdair wanted to laugh, but at the same time, he knew Faery magic to be an unpredictable and powerful thing. He didn't want to mock them, and although he was certain he'd never find a woman like Ursula again, he would rather honor her legacy with the quest for the guelder rose than die trying to fight a magical beast.

With his decision made, Alasdair sheathed his sword, then reached for the Faery Flag. Once the silk family heirloom was in his hands, he spoke.

"This is the Faery Flag of Dunvegan, given to my great-great-great-grandfather by his Faery Queen."

An audible gasp interrupted Alasdair.

"You are an imposter, sir. That cannot be," the tiny female voice accused.

"Nay, spirit, the flag is true. He laid it on the ground with the satchel underneath. "Examine it, but do not unfurl it completely, or you will release its magic."

A buzzing noise sounded in front of Alasdair. He imagined petite, gossamer wings beating frantically.

"Let him pass," the breathy female voice said clearly.

"Yes, my queen," was the response from the other spirit. Perhaps it was a wee bit of Faery magic, but in a blink of his eyes, the menacing wolf disappeared along with the flag. All that remained before Alasdair was the empty satchel.

"What are you waiting for?" said the male voice.

Alasdair blinked again and started around the pool. He was not sure how long he lingered after the flag disappeared, but he certainly did not want to remain long. He was ready to find the guelder rose and be on his way from the glen.

With quick strides, he made his way to the falls and behind them to the cavern. His sacrifice a worthy one, to honor his lost love.

Chapter 40

Johnathan had insisted she get a good night's sleep, then a large breakfast in the morn, before the two of them saddled the farm's only horses and took off for the faerie pools of Glenbrittle.

The teary goodbyes were bittersweet, with hugs and good wishes, as the two sisters sent them off with a satchel of worthy traveling food for their journey.

The road through the Highland heather had not changed since her last visit with her mother over ten summers ago. Ursula shivered with some trepidation as they approached the glen early that afternoon.

Following the river, it did not take long before they arrived at the faerie pools and the ridge of the falls covered in mist. As she stopped before the largest pool, filled by the perpetual waterfall, she was taken back to the moment when she'd come for the first time with her mother.

Standing before the roaring water, Ursula remembered her mother's warning. *Do nae be afraid, for the Fae can sniff out fear.* 'Twas advice she would put to use now that she was within range of her goal.

"The guelder rose is known to grow in the cave behind the falls," she said to Johnathan, pointing to where she could make out the shape of an entrance behind the curtain of water that shielded it from view. "If you did nae know it was there, it would be difficult to spot," she added.

Ursula turned toward the cave opening but screamed when her right shoulder was jerked back by such a force she was almost knocked to the ground. She spun around to accuse Johnathan, but he was nowhere to be seen.

Vanished into the mist?

Before she had a chance to call his name, a high-pitched male voice spoke to her, "Are you brave or ignorant?"

A trick question? She thought for a moment before she answered. "The ignorant believe they are brave, so they are both. For real bravery is not named, and real ignorance is not claimed."

"Then are you ignorantly brave?"

"I am Ursula of Clan Fraser, witch and lover of the Fae," she announced with a slight curtsy.

"What do you have to barter?"

"A broken heart," she said honestly.

"We accept souls, not hearts," the male voice snapped. "That you should know, witch."

"What I know and what I want to accept are not the same. Do you nae have pity for a broken heart?"

"We do not understand pity," a female voice piped in. "Human emotions are stupid. The Fae mate for life. When our mate dies, we die," the faerie said in a heartless tone.

Ursula was numb from the loss of Alasdair, but her purpose had been fulfilled by healing others before she'd met him. Now she needed to focus on bringing the guelder rose back to Fyvie for Rosalyn's sake, so Ursula would push through her sorrow.

"My broken heart will mend, and I will honor my mate, not die for him," she promised. She reached into her herbal bag. "I have frankincense. 'Tis said when mixed with myrrh, it will turn rocks into diamonds."

"Diamonds?" The faerie woman's voice rose on the end of the word.

Could she be the queen of the faeries? Ursula was encouraged. "Aye, the most precious gem to own. Only kings and queens have access to diamonds," she said, knowing diamonds were something the faeries couldn't produce. "You might make a crown for your queen," she suggested.

"I do not believe you," the female voice shouted. "You aim to trick us," she accused.

"If you do nae believe me, then I'll show you," Ursula said. This was a talent that had served her well. The alchemy skills she'd learned from her grandmother had been passed down for generations.

"In the arts I practice, the seed of an item is needed to manifest it," Ursula said. "All I do is speed up nature's process.

"Diamonds are mined and are buried deep in the ground, but they are only stones at their birth," Ursula added.

"When nature and the art of alchemy embrace each other, art is not denied what nature requires. The soul of a stone is germinated when rubbed with this root. Just watch."

Ursula selected a few stones from the path before her. She crouched low, and after unfolding a square of black silk cloth, she laid the stones in the middle. Taking the frankincense in her hand, she rubbed the surface of each of the stones vigorously.

Next, Ursula took the myrrh and sprinkled it over the stones. Then she sat back on her heels.

"In just a few moments you will witness diamonds growing from the seeds of themselves. But if the seed of a diamond were not in the rock, it would not be possible."

As she waited, she held her breath. This was a trick she'd learned as a girl and the reason her mother had been burned after being called a witch. She always carried the root with her, expecting a day when she might need its magic. As much as it frightened her to have this knowledge, now was the time to use it.

When shocked *oohs* and *aahs* came from the faerie voices, Ursula's focus sharpened. Yes, she still had it.

"You see, diamonds," she said, scooping up the glittering gems that had been gray stones moments ago.

"You have earned the guelder rose you seek. Go and pluck it from the cavern behind the falls," the female faerie told her.

Ursula wavered. "What of my friend, Johnathan? He must be returned to me."

"Is he not Molly's husband?" the faerie male voice asked.

"Aye he is, but he did nae come here to follow her fate, he came because he owed me a debt."

"He owes us a debt. We wanted his baby, and we settled for his wife."

"He does nae owe you if you settled for his wife. The baby Eliza is now a grown woman. Do you forget that babies grow to be adults?"

The Faery Queen revealed herself, perhaps because she wanted to or maybe because Ursula was not fearful.

"I know you, Ursula," the queen said, hovering before her. Dressed in a mossy green gown, a golden crown of vines atop her head, the petite faerie flew on gossamer wings.

"I know you, too," Ursula whispered.

"Make your home here with us. We cannot mend your broken heart, but once you join us, you shall forget your pain."

Tempting. But that was what the Fae were good at, tempting humans to join their beautiful world with promises of living forever.

"Please do nae think I'm not grateful for the invitation, but I've a noble reason for stopping here and gathering the flower. A friend of mine is in need."

"The guelder rose has been popular today, for a brave Highlander was here earlier wanting the same."

Ursula's heart skipped a beat. "What did you say?"

"Is there something wrong with your ears?" the Faery Queen asked, flying over to inspect one before Ursula retreated.

"Stop tickling me," Ursula protested, laughing against her will and serious about knowing more. "Tell me about the Highlander."

The Faery Queen zipped back in front of Ursula like a bee inspecting the heart of a flower. "What is the Highlander to you?"

"Must you ask questions before you answer them?" Faeries were difficult to converse with. They purposely loved to lie, play tricks, and misdirect humans. She needed some answers.

"Remember, I'm half-Fae," Ursula said. "Stop the shenanigans. Tell me about the Highlander."

The queen huffed. "You do nae have to be so bossy."

"Please," Ursula amended.

"All right. A tall but bent over Scottish laird came to the pool this morning with a broken heart, telling of a lost love and promised redemption."

Without warning, the Faery Queen flew off to Ursula's left, then snapped her fingers.

Ursula blinked and rubbed her eyes, surprised to find Johnathan standing next to her. He appeared a bit bewildered but smiled when he looked at Ursula.

"Thank you for returning Johnathan to me. But this is not the Highlander. What did you do with him?"

"Do you mean what did we do to him?"

"Either, or."

"Neither, nor."

"'Tis not a game."

"'Tis a game," the Faery Queen confessed.

Ursula blew out a frustrated breath.

"We sent him on his way with the flower," piped in the male faerie. "He was not ignorantly brave," he said, revealing himself. A handsome wisp of a man with golden hair and transparent amber-colored wings. He was flying by the queen's side.

"He was half-Fae like you, Ursula," the Faery Queen admitted. "Do you know him?"

"Perhaps." Ursula's answer was vague, but she wanted to shout to the heavens her gratitude. Alasdair was alive. At least it appeared to be so. As much as the faeries were tricksters, it appeared they didn't know her connection to him.

"My heart has been repaired. Perhaps you can mend broken hearts after all."

"Not on purpose," the Faery Queen mumbled. "But I must be kind to one who is bearing a child."

A child?

Ursula's gut lurched. *Could she be with child?* It had been almost two weeks since she and Alasdair had joined as one for that purpose. She sighed. If she could not have him, at least she could have his child. The thought of it made her heart sing.

After the exchanges were made, diamonds for flowers and a pretty piece of silk, Johnathan seemed more clearheaded than when he'd first reappeared. He and Ursula said their goodbyes and left the faerie glen.

Could Alasdair have taken on her quest? Ursula would always be wary of what the faeries claimed. Had it been Alasdair or Ethan who had come to the pools? A lost love and promise of redemption?

Now they needed to make haste and head for Fyvie to save Rosalyn. The flower could arrive in time, but what Alasdair did not understand was Ursula needed to be there, too.

Chapter 41

Lachlan paced in Rosalyn's bedchamber. It had been well over three weeks since Ethan and Ursula had left Fyvie Castle for Skye Isle. He'd quietly regretted his decision, knowing Ethan was only out for himself, and he worried something terrible may have happened to Ursula. He'd expected she'd have returned before now.

Rosalyn tossed and turned before him in the bed. As he sat by her, his frustration mounted, for there was little he could do to ease his wife's discomfort. He'd been at her side every waking moment, and most nights, she had slept very little.

Thea, the midwife Ursula had chosen to take her place, was at the ready, but she was not Ursula.

Where was Ursula? Every morning and every night, that was the question on Rosalyn's lips. Lachlan wondered if in some way Rosalyn's pure will was keeping the babes in the womb.

What disturbed Lachlan more was the unruliness of the outlaying clans. Lachlan didn't regret it, but had called in his Garter Knight family, James and Elena, from King Henry's court. Word that the gilded guards had arrived had settled some of the unrest.

A sharp rap on the chamber door shattered his musings. He rose to his feet and quickly answered it.

"What news have you?" Lachlan asked when he found his loyal castle steward at the door.

"A visitor from Skye Isle," Shawn announced. Lachlan's

heart sank with the news, but he refused to think the worst until he heard the words from the visitor himself.

"Take me to him," Lachlan requested, closing the door behind him, pleased Rosalyn had not been disturbed by Shawn's visit for it appeared she had finally fallen asleep.

Once in the great hall, Lachlan took ample strides to the head table. Giving the guest's hand a firm shake, he invited him to take a seat, while one of his servers poured strong wine into their goblets.

"Welcome back to Fyvie Castle, Laird MacLeod," Lachlan said with a wide sweeping gesture, trying to hide his surprise at finding the Highlander in his great hall. "My steward, Shawn, said you have just arrived from Skye Isle."

"Laird MacPherson, I am honored to be back here."

"Please, call me Lachlan."

"You may call me Crotach."

Lachlan laughed and was immediately at ease with the Highlander. They'd met weeks ago when the Highlander had delivered the king's missive. At the time though, Lachlan had been distracted by the potential threat of losing Fyvie. The unrest only exacerbated his already growing insecurities over his recent new role ruling over his wife's homeland.

The smile faded from his guest's face. "As much as I wish to bring you all good news, I cannot," Crotach told him. "I met Ursula on the boat to Inverness and traveled with her to Skye on her quest to help your wife."

Lachlan wanted to interrupt and ask about Ethan, but he was prepared to hear out the MacLeod laird. And as the Highlander explained what had happened over the last few weeks, he clarified what Lachlan had expected. A selfish and disruptive Ethan was missing, as was a courageous and selfless Ursula.

Even though Crotach did not say he thought them both dead, there was little evidence to support they weren't.

"Here it is, the guelder rose," Alasdair said proudly. The beautiful bloom, with its thick bark stem, appeared miniature in the Highlander's hand.

Lachlan plucked it from his guest and studied the fragile bloom more closely. "Thank you for carrying out Ursula's quest," Lachlan said.

"'Twas my honor to do so." He leaned in closer. "I didn't think the Fae were going to tell me how to use the flower, but I tricked them into showing me."

Lachlan chuckled, imagining this gruff and seasoned warrior conferring with faeries. Although Lachlan had spent some of his early years with his Scottish mother, most of his rearing had been at the hand of his English father and the royal courts.

Since that time, however, Lachlan had not heard much about faeries again until he moved to Fyvie Castle in Scotland.

The two men drank more strong wine, and the fragile flower made its way into a safe container. It was getting very late into the evening when Shawn burst into the great hall.

"My lord, your garrison captain sent me with-urgent report." His steward was out of breath. "The south wall-under attack."

Lachlan rousted himself to his feet. Too much wine sloshed around in his gut and clouded his thinking. Could the clans have chosen tonight to lash out against his rule?

Crotach was on his feet as well, sword drawn, looking as if he'd just awakened from a refreshing nap. "I'll take care of Rosalyn. Send me to her room, and I'll guard her with my life," the Highlander pledged.

Normally Lachlan would be suspect of such a promise, but he'd been fostered in British royal courts where snobbery was perfected. Crotach's sincerity appeared genuine. Lachlan had no reason not to trust him.

"Godspeed to us both," Lachlan told Alasdair as the two lairds parted at the arched entrance of the great hall, the Highlander to protect Rosalyn and Lachlan to defend his castle.

~ ~ ~

Once the guards had recognized her, and after seeing Johnathan off to a guest chamber, Ursula headed straight to Rosalyn's room. Slipping in quietly, she found her sister of the heart sleeping peacefully. Where was Lachlan? She'd expected he'd be by her side, but then she was reminded of the clan unrest. Perhaps the defense of the castle demanded his attention.

No matter. Ursula was home. Walking first to the table by the window, she picked up her favorite mortar and hugged it to her chest. After the boat, the castles, the wedding, the dungeon, the faerie pools, and the final ride to Fyvie, Ursula was thrilled to be with people she loved and a place she could call home.

What sustained her over the last four days as she crossed Scotland on horseback with Johnathan was her hope of catching up with Alasdair. As much as she should be suspicious of anything the Fae had said, she was certain the Faery Queen had told her the truth about her Highlander.

Ian MacDonald had done more than torture her physically, he had abused her mentally as well when he'd lied about Alasdair's death. No doubt he'd lied to Alasdair about hers.

Although she was elated he was alive, she feared he still thought her dead. He could have stopped by Fyvie to deliver the rose and left the same day.

Her musings over his whereabouts were interrupted by an ear-piercing yell. Ursula quickly set the mortar down. No doubt, she'd gotten here just in time. Glancing over her shoulder, she found Rosalyn wide-eyed and clutching her bulging belly.

"'Tis about time those babes came into this world," Ursula said with a chuckle.

Rosalyn squealed. It was a happy sound, and Ursula rushed to her friend's side.

Tears welled in Rosalyn's eyes. "You are alive? I cannae believe my eyes."

"'Tis so." Ursula nodded. "Just in time, for the babes, they must have known I'd arrived."

"You are alive?"

She didn't trust her ears, until she turned to find Alasdair standing in the chamber doorway.

"You're not the only one who cannae believe their eyes," Alasdair exclaimed, rushing forward. "I was told you were dead, but I did nae want to believe it. In my heart, you were still alive."

Ursula hastened her steps, anxious to meet her Highlander. When they finally embraced, Alasdair showered her with kisses, from the top of her head to her lips, but another rousing scream from Rosalyn had them both scrambling.

"I have the guelder rose," he said, producing a vial with the young bud inside. She didn't have the heart to tell him she had the same.

"You thought me dead?" she asked, gazing into his eyes and taking the flower from him.

He nodded solemnly. "But I wanted to honor your promise to Rosalyn."

She grinned until another screeching outburst from Rosalyn had Ursula jumping. She squeezed his hands. "Thank you for risking your life for me and Rosalyn. I will never be able to repay you."

Now it was Alasdair's turn to grin. "I will figure out a way to get payment." Then he turned toward the door to answer the brief but persistent knocking.

"We heard screams coming from the mistress's chamber," explained the one of the two knights who looked like the leader.

Alasdair chuckled nervously. "Your mistress is in labor. All is well here. How goes it on the parapets?"

"Not well, mi lord, many men are lost."

Ursula was at Alasdair elbow in moments.

"James," she cried. "Elena." She glanced over at Rosalyn. "Come, you two are not midwives, but I may need your help."

James raised a brow but entered the room as if he was commanding it. She and Elena followed him to Rosalyn's side.

Elena smiled at her sister-in-law and smoothed back Rosalyn's untamed red bangs. "Lachlan sent a messenger for us not long after you left for Skye Isle," she said, looking up at Ursula.

James turned away from the screeching Rosalyn. Although she was certain he'd never be squeamish on the battlefield, his tolerance for birthing seemed lacking. "I'm needed on the parapets. Rosalyn is in good hands with you both."

Ursula turned to Alasdair. As much as she wanted a reunion, now was not the time. "Go with James," she urged. Elena will stay with us. We have our own battle to fight. Lachlan needs you more." She quickly gathered up her skirt and loosened a satchel tied there, then pushed the bag into Alasdair's hands. "You left something behind on Skye. You may need it."

His face twisted into a confused expression, making her laugh through all the chaos. "A bit of Faery magic," she promised, "now go." Without any further encouragement, he was out of the chamber room with James on his heels before Rosalyn screamed again.

Ursula turned and exchanged grins with Elena over Rosalyn's riotous, bulging belly.

"The last time we were together like this, I was at your other end helping your son into the world."

Elena glowed.

"Motherhood suits you."

The next screech from Rosalyn was louder and longer than the last. A signal to Ursula the babes were on their way.

After telling Elena what to prepare, Ursula quickly walked to the worktable. There, she took the guelder rose and began plucking the thorns from its stem. When it was clean, she took her dirk and stripped the stem of its bark. Once she had ground the bark into a fine paste, she added the rose petals and mashed them with some water until she had created what she needed.

With a goblet full of the concoction, she made her way to Rosalyn's bedside. Tilting Rosalyn's head back, Ursula set the goblet to her lips and helped her friend down the amber liquid.

In just a few short moments, the yelling subsided and Rosalyn began breathing more deeply, allowing Ursula to attend to another visitor at the chamber door.

It was Thea, her distant cousin. "I received word from one of the guards the labor has begun."

She gave the midwife a hug. "Aye, I can use two sets of experienced hands, for two babes are twice the trouble," she said with a grin.

Thea joined Elena, and the three women prepared to guide two new souls into the world.

~ ~ ~

After Alasdair and James walked out on the castle's parapet, it did not take the Highlander long to assess the situation was grim. Bodies lay scattered about the narrow walkway, while a handful of soldiers continued to defend the castle with bows and arrows from where they stood.

After observing the defenses and assessing the ammunition, Alasdair solved the quandary. While Lachlan's clan fought with the traditional longbow, the attackers used a combination of catapult and flaming arrows. Similar tactics he had used himself when storming the MacDonald-occupied Eilean Donan Castle.

James had joined the soldiers, shooting arrows with his longbow in an attempt to stop the advancing clansmen, who were at the main gate with a battering ram.

When Lachlan noticed Alasdair, he met him at the parapet entrance. "This is not your battle."

"Any battle that involves family of the woman I love becomes my battle," Alasdair declared in earnest.

When Lachlan appeared confused, he offered an update. "She's alive." He slapped Fyvie's laird on the shoulder. "Ursula is alive."

Lachlan's heavy concern lifted for a moment, lightening his expression. "Aye, it's good news and more reason to fight to defend our women and the castle."

Alasdair waved the laird into the alcove away from the fighting. "Lachlan, you may not have the same experience in battle as I, but you'd have to be blind not to notice your main gate is about to be destroyed. It's no longer protected, and even with our efforts on the parapets, the garrison here cannot stop what's happening below. The women we love are at risk."

"Then we continue to fight," Lachlan vowed. "There is a secret tunnel. You can take the women to safety," Lachlan suggested, his eyes wild with concern.

Alasdair didn't want to break his spirit, but Rosalyn was in no condition to be moved. "You are about to become a father, Lachlan."

The Fyvie laird stumbled backward, but Alasdair grabbed his arm before he fell, lifting him back on his feet, anxious to share more good news. "Your midwife has returned not only to deliver your babes, but also to deliver this."

Lachlan appeared perplexed until Alasdair produced the secret of Skye Isle, the yellow silk flag from the satchel Ursula had handed him earlier.

Then his confusion lifted. "The Faery Flag?"

Alasdair nodded. "And Godspeed," he promised, unfurling the legacy of the MacLeod clan with pride.

Chapter 42

The great hall at Fyvie Castle had been cleared of the cursory royal courtesans, and those who remained were bound by blood or oath. Tossing a handful of gold coins in the middle of the rough trestle table reminded Ursula good luck was never random and the quest for power ever present.

Two days had passed since the clan uprising had ended with the unfurling of the Faery Flag. Rosalyn had been blessed by two healthy twins, and Ursula had reunited with her Highlander.

She counted those blessings as Alasdair counted his coins before tossing them in the center with her own. Ursula never liked to gamble, but once again, she'd found herself at the table rolling dice and playing thirty-one with three men.

"Ursula, you've been unusually lucky this evening. Let me examine those dice," Lachlan requested, grinning at her from across the table.

"It's just witchcraft," she answered with a wicked smile, handing the dice over anyway. "They are the same you rolled afore my turn."

James pushed her hand back. "Lachlan is a sore loser," he told her, counting the few coins he still had. They were dwindling.

Lachlan tugged on his dragon tail ring. "Let's up the ante for Ethan's sake," he challenged those at the table, setting his ring in the center.

Lachlan's half-brother James pushed away from the trestle table and turned to his wife, Elena, who'd been standing behind him. "My Garter knight wages are still not large enough to keep up with the likes of you," he said, standing and putting his arms around her.

"Elena and our new baby boy are my fortune," James said, kissing her atop of her head. "Those I will never gamble away."

"Is there an empty seat at the table?" The question came from across the great hall, and they all turned to gape at Ethan, especially Ursula.

As he sauntered across the expanse of the great hall in his usual way, Ethan kept his eyes planted on her. How could it be that things never changed with this one? She'd thought he was dead, and he deserved to be. Yet, here he stood at the table to prove her wrong.

"Missed me?" he asked, taking the seat across from her, the one James had vacated.

Alasdair rose to his feet, the chair he'd sat in bouncing to the floor. Before anyone could say a word, his hands were around Ethan's throat.

"I thought you said this seat wasn't taken," he choked out with little air, his eyes bulging.

"He's harmless," Ursula said, although she shouldn't have. She hated Ethan for so many reasons, but he'd always survived his misadventures like a cat with nine lives.

Alasdair gave her an apologetic shrug when he released Ethan and returned to his seat.

"What are we playing for?" Ethan asked, smoothing his embroidered collar back in place and eyeing Alasdair, who'd sat back at the table again.

Before anyone else spoke, Ethan spotted the dragon tail ring in the center of the table. "Is Fyvie Castle in play?"

Lachlan grunted, and James laughed. Ursula wanted out of the game. But Alasdair sat stoically at the table, no doubt unaware of the innuendo behind the question.

Ethan slipped off his matching ring and placed in on the table. "Eilean Donan Castle."

"You mean Dunster Castle," his twin brother corrected him.

Alasdair glared at Ethan across the table. If given another chance, he'd most likely tear Ethan's head off, but instead Alasdair loosen the sporran around his waist and placed it next to the dragon rings. "The Faery Flag of Skye Isle."

Everyone gasped except Alasdair.

Ursula reached under her skirt for her herb satchel. As she stirred the contents around with her fingers, all eyes were on her.

Finally, she found the item she needed and placed it in the center of the table. "My heart," she said directly to Alasdair, placing a petite heart-shaped locket next to his sporran.

"Are all bets in?" James asked the group, assuming his role of leader and referee.

Lachlan stood and chuckled. "The ring was a jest," he admitted, but then looked to his half-brother. "Now that the real jester has joined us, I withdraw my bid," Lachlan said with an edgy tone and slipped his dragon tail ring back on his finger.

Ursula sucked in a breath and waited to see what would happen next. It had been rewarding when the coins were piling up in her corner, but now there was much on the line.

Alasdair cleared his throat and directed his question at Ethan, "Is your bid Dunster Castle?"

Instead of answering, Ethan drew a large velvet pouch from his traveling cape and set it in the middle of the table, then withdrew his dragon ring. Slipping his family heirloom back on his finger, he said, "Moaning Molly's treasure."

Alasdair's and Ursula's eyes met, and their brows rose. Ursula shrugged her shoulders. Now she knew what had happened to Ethan. He'd sought out the treasure for himself and ignored the need for the flower or the flag, the items he'd been entrusted to collect.

"Is that enough?" James asked Ethan what they were all thinking.

In response, Ethan looked at Alasdair, and then to Ursula, before he dumped the contents of the velvet bag onto the middle of the table.

Ursula gasped when she spied a tiny golden crown made of thorns sitting amongst the gold coins.

"Aye, it's enough," Ethan said, his eyes trained on Ursula.

Would he still continue to pursue her after all that had happened?

Ursula turned to James. "'Tis enough," she said confidently. "Let the game begin."

James had each of them roll one die for the order of the game. As it turned out, Ursula would go first, followed by Alasdair, and Ethan last.

The game was simple and required no specific skill other than strong nerves, a steady hand, and a straight face.

But James was the obvious choice to serve as mediator, making sure there was no deviation from the rules or the dice in play. And the more matched the score, the more on edge she became.

Finally, the scores were close enough to thirty-one that each would have at least one more turn.

Alasdair went first, finishing with thirty.

Ursula went next, finishing at twenty-nine. She stole a look at her Highlander, and he grinned back.

Ethan was at twenty-five. He'd have to roll again. If he went over, Alasdair would take it all, the flag, the faerie crown with the gold, and Ursula's heart.

Ursula banked on Alasdair to win. She had no worldly possessions, and her heart was the only item of value she could offer. James had allowed it, she guessed, because he, too, assumed Alasdair would win. Or that her Highlander would simply crush Ethan if he won.

The image of Alasdair's hands around Ethan's neck made her crack a smile as she glanced down at her own hands. They were gripped so tightly her knuckles had turned white while she waited for the dice to roll.

The sound of the square ivory stones pinged across the wood, and then the dice stopped.

Alasdair roared.

Ursula squeezed her eyes tight. Was it in his favor or was he angry?

The next thing she knew, Ursula was hauled up into his arms and he was kissing her face.

Eyes popping open, Ursula sighed inwardly, happy to find Alasdair's face smiling into hers. She clapped her hands together as her gaze traveled to the table to find a set of fives on the dice and Ethan nowhere to be seen.

In the center of the table sat her locket, Alasdair's sporran, and the Faery Queen's crown. The gold was gone.

Her eyes sought out James. "I didn't have the heart to tell him no," the Garter knight said apologetically.

Ursula laughed along with Alasdair, Lachlan, and Elena. The mighty Garter knight was crestfallen, as if he'd lost a major battle.

"I won what my heart desires when Ethan lost," Alasdair said proudly, gazing into her eyes after the laughter had stopped. "I have no need for gold coins when I've won a heart of gold instead," he added.

Ursula's heart was bursting. If it wouldn't have been considered inappropriate, she would have smothered him with kisses.

There had been very little time for them to be alone, what with defending the march on Fyvie with the Faery Flag and guiding Rosalyn through a safe labor with the aid of the guelder rose.

Although they'd not talked about the future, Ursula needed to know if she had one with Alasdair. Many would find him intimidating, but not her. She'd discovered he was not the tyrannical clan laird who'd demanded an heir when they'd met, but instead, he was a gentle giant with a generous heart who'd traveled the breadth of Scotland for a noble cause.

Ursula gazed into his dark-hazel eyes. His rustic locks framed his charismatic smile, and she all but melted into his arms.

"Come love," he whispered to her. "We must celebrate our victory."

Setting Ursula down on her feet as if she was lighter than air, Alasdair took her locket and the Faery crown, then tucked them carefully in his sporran before he secured it around his waist.

After saying their goodnights to Lachlan, James, and Elena, they promised to check in on Rosalyn and the twins. Then Alasdair took her hand and led her across the great hall. When they passed under its grand arch, he swept her up in his arms again.

"You are my winnings," he said, grinning broadly and climbing up the stairs on the way to the solar.

"I've never been a prize to be won," she told him. "But I'm grateful you did not haul me over your shoulder like Lachlan used to do with Rosalyn."

Once they'd reached Rosalyn's room, he gazed down at her again, his lip twisting into a mischievous shape. "Well, if it's commonly done here, who am I to break tradition?" he said, flipping her over his good shoulder.

"Put me down, Alasdair MacLeod," she shouted as he crossed the threshold into Rosalyn's room. As Alasdair turned to shut the door, he spun her around to face her sister of the heart, who sat in her bed with a babe in each arm.

Rosalyn's eyes lit up. "I see Alasdair will fit into this family just fine." Her friend appeared to be deriving too much pleasure from Ursula's inconvenience.

"We wanted to say goodnight," Alasdair offered, twisting around halfway so they could both see Rosalyn.

"Say goodnight, Angelica and Andrew," her sister of the heart said, taking each of the newborn's hands and waving.

Alasdair chuckled at the gesture, the gleeful rumbling traveling through him, making Ursula vibrate, too. She cracked a smile. How could she be grumpy when the babes looked so cute and their mother so happy?

A short knock and a moment later, Thea bustled across the room with a nod of acknowledgment, intent on getting the babies settled for the night.

Ursula waved back at the twins from her perch on Alasdair's shoulder, and he carried her out, leaving Thea to her fussing.

Out in the corridor, Alasdair continued to carry Ursula like a sack of grain, passing by her chamber room next to Rosalyn's and continuing toward his own.

When she wiggled, he spanked her bottom. Not hard, but to show her who was in charge. For a moment, it brought back the frightful memories of Ian MacDonald swatting her arse to her utmost embarrassment.

"Put me down," she demanded. The ruse was up, and she'd had enough of his winner-take-all demonstration.

"All in good time, my lady," he said as he slowed before his chamber door. With a slight lean to reach the latch and release it, he passed through the door and dropped her face down in the middle of his bed before she could shout her refusal.

She sputtered, flipping over. Then she blew her hair out of her face with one big exasperating breath. When she could see again, it was to find Alasdair on one knee before the edge of the bed.

"Come here, my Faery Queen." He made the plea with such a husky voice and a burning desire in his eyes that all her petty frustrations melted away.

Taking her hand, he guided her to the edge where she could sit before him. Then Alasdair took a deep breath and held it for a moment, as if he had something important to say and was gathering the nerve to set the words free.

"Even before I met you, I knew you from a prophecy passed down from my great-great-great-grandfather. It foretold the MacLeods sons that followed would be destined to be lonely until the day they could find a worthy Faery Queen.

"Ursula, you have proven yourself worthy to any man in all of Scotland, but I ask you find the worth in me.

"When I thought you were dead, I died, too. I was tortured by the loss and unsure I could go on. Until I took up your quest to help Rosalyn.

"Before I met you, my goal was to become Lord of the Isles. With King James's blessing, I've gathered the support to earn the title.

"But what I've found is the only title I really want is husband. I ask you again what I did days ago, but before I knew what you truly meant to me."

"Will you bear me an heir?" she asked, not because she wasn't thrilled to hear what he meant to her, but to prove a point.

"Yes, will you bear me an heir, because I love you."

He loved her? The wall around Ursula's heart crumbled. She had given away her heart ceremoniously in the game, but now it was time to set aside her callousness and let Alasdair's love in.

"Yes, I am bearing you an heir." She waited until her words registered and his eyes went wide, then she finished her thought, "And I love you, too."

"You are?" He stammered. "You do?"

"Both," she said, laughing at his disbelief. "If what the faeries said is true, I am."

"You believe in faeries?"

"I believe in the Faery Flag and its magic."

"Well, its magic is spent. It's not much more than a family memento now." He stared at her. "How did you convince the faeries to return the flag to me?"

Ursula leaned forward and stroked Alasdair's hair. It wasn't often he was at her level like this, and she enjoyed it. But he still had a lot to learn about her.

"'Do nae doubt the flag has more magic.' That's what the Faery Queen said when she gave it to me." She paused and then cracked a smile. "I told them you'd stolen it from me." Ursula shrugged her shoulders. "Faeries deserve some of their own trickery. Although they did nae want to help mend my broken heart, they were willing to return the flag to whom they believed was its rightful owner," she said in a boastful tone, pointing at herself.

Alasdair's laugh was like a golden light. It bounced off the walls and lit up the room. "I won your heart, but you've won the bargain."

Apparently satisfied with Ursula's answer, her Highlander kissed her as if he'd love her for all eternity.

They were both of the Fae, so she believed he would.

Also from **Soul Mate Publishing** and **Maria Dillon**:

THE LADY OF THE GARTER

When Henry VII takes the throne, not all are loyal to the new king. Garter knight, Sir James, is charged with bringing dissenters to justice. Determined to fulfill his vows, he's unprepared for Lady Elena, a girl from his past.

Lady Elena defies her family and disguises herself as a squire to reunite with the man she's always loved. She might be able to wield a sword, but she still possesses a woman's heart.

Thrust into a world of danger and family rivalry, James and Elena face the ultimate test.

Can James avenge his father's death and find passion, or will his Garter oaths hold him to a life of service without love?

Available now on Amazon: **THE LADY OF THE GARTER**

THE GOLDEN ROSE OF SCOTLAND

When poisonings are an everyday occurrence, healer Rosalyn Macpherson must be ready with an antidote. Unless it's for the English Lord who means to claim her clan's Highland castle.

What's in a name? Everything, for Lord Lachlan de Leverton, a charismatic English aristocrat. He'll break the law to sever his ties to his notorious family. But first, he must secure the deed to Fyvie Castle before the feisty Scottish lass wins it.

Because of their conflicting claims, Rosalyn and Lachlan are ordered to appear in Edinburgh's royal court, and in an unusual twist of fate, they are assigned as guardians, rather than prisoners, to a caravan carrying the Golden Rose, a papal gift for the King of Scots.

When the royal decree becomes a forced union between the two, it's not the remedy Rosalyn had hoped for, but by now she doesn't hate this Englishman quite as much.

Before the knot is tied, the Rose is stolen and Lachlan's suspected of the crime. Rosalyn then faces the hardest decision yet. Must she sacrifice her precious Philosophers Stone or the land she loves, or both, to save him?

With a bachelor's degree in journalism, Marisa has spent many years writing for the television industry. As an award-winning producer/director/marketer, she has worked on commercial production, show creation, product branding and social media.

Marisa has always enjoyed reading romance novels and now fulfills a dream by writing romantic adventures not for the faint of heart. *The Secret of Skye Isle* is her third book in the Ladies of Lore series with Soul Mate Publishing.

You can visit Marisa at: www.marisadillon.com.
And you can connect with Marisa on
Twitter.com/marisadillon,
https://www.goodreads.com/author/show/10792736.Marisa_Dillon,
and https://www.bookbub.com/profile/marisa-dillon

CPSIA information can be obtained
at www.ICGtesting.com
Printed in the USA
FFHW010700301019
55863485-61738FF